IN SEARCH OF
TRUE
NORTH

Kathleen Neely

Candlelight Fiction is an imprint of LPC Books
a division of Iron Stream Media
100 Missionary Ridge, Birmingham, AL 35242
ShopLPC.com

Cover design by Elaina Lee

Library of Congress Control Number: 2021936147

ISBN-13: 978-1-64526-321-0
Ebook ISBN: 978-1-64526-322-7

Praise for *In Search of True North*

In Search of True North is a heartwarming and gripping story of love, loss, and learning to love again. You don't want to miss Mallory's journey. A story of forgiving others and forgiving yourself. Kathleen Neely crafts stories you won't forget and can't wait to read again.

~Barbara M. Britton
Award-winning author of the *Tribes of Israel* series

In Search of True North is a lovely story that shows how one decision can impact so many lives in various ways. Mrs. Neely does a wonderful job of ironing out the wrinkles of dysfunction of a family suffering from such a decision while God is behind the scenes working all things together for the good of everyone concerned.

~ Pamela S Thibodeaux
Award-Winning author of *My Heart Weeps*

ACKNOWLEDGMENTS

Despite a cover that carries only the author's name, many people contribute to creating a work of fiction. Early in the creation of this story, Cynthia Owens and Tim Suddeth provided valuable brainstorming and critiquing to help shape the plot. Their job was difficult because they saw the skeletal sketches of a developing work in its unpolished form. Thank you for bearing with me and believing that something good would surface.

A big shout of thanks goes to Marcia Hammerle and Sandra Johnson for reading the final draft and providing feedback. They were the first to experience the completed story and comment on its contextual fluidity. Every writer needs someone to cheer them on while providing constructive advice. Thank you to Kathy Gaul, who has become a cheerleader and positive voice in sharing my writing. Despite hundreds of miles that separate us, we enjoy a lifelong friendship.

Many thanks go to my agent, Linda Glaz, my managing editor, Jessica Nelson, and my general editor, Nancy J. Farrier for careful reading, editing, and refining. Your professional eyes make *In Search of True North* better. Thank you, Iron Stream Media for getting *In Search of True North* out there for readers to enjoy.

Above all, thanks be to God, my True North; the Author of my life story.

Dedication

Dedicated to Marcia, my sister and friend
There's not a moment in my life when you haven't been there,
Helping me, encouraging me, and loving me.

Chapter 1

Mallory Carter's phone vibrated for the third time in the last hour. She stole a glance at the low buzz from the shelf under the counter where it rested. Dad—again. It must be important, but she couldn't talk from work. She had no one to cover the register. Still, it was unusual to see a call from her dad's cell phone. Tightness gripped her chest. Should she answer it? A customer entered, settling the decision. Her dad would have to wait. Her shift ended soon.

The high humidity brought beads of sweat to Mallory's forehead as she called out the customary greeting. "Hello. Welcome to Cape Fear Emporium." She tucked the phone away. She'd call him from home.

A middle-aged lady, her cropped hair sticky with sweat and clinging to her face, breathed a satisfied response. "Ahh. Air." The relief would be short-lived. The air conditioner had difficulty cooling this space beyond seventy-six degrees.

She turned a friendly smile toward Mallory. "There's not a hint of a breeze out there. It's stifling. Is North Carolina always like this?"

Mallory could pick out the northerners every time. She cooled her face with an oriental folding fan as she answered. "May's usually nice. This is unseasonably hot. Feel free to look around. It's better than walking the boardwalk in this heat."

Dozens of colorful T-shirts hung from a circular rack. The shelves held coffee mugs depicting the Cape Fear River, Wrightsville Beach, and the boardwalk. Seashell jewelry dangled from a rotating display. The ice cream typically drew people in, strategically located

1

in the back of the store so they'd pass shelves filled with novelties that no one needed but most people bought.

Mallory worked the front register, giving her a view of the river. Today, not a ripple stirred that water. Three customers wandered the store, picking up items only to replace them a moment later. They'd find their trinket before leaving. Very few people left empty-handed. A brief swish signaled that a voicemail had followed that unanswered call. A chill prickled her skin. Her father rarely contacted her. Something *must* be wrong. Mallory glanced at the voicemail text. It simply said to call him. She preferred to do that from the privacy of home.

The chimes inside the door sounded their deep, metallic dong. Mallory looked up to see Chloe swing through the doorway, her caftan flowing, each movement rustling its bold shades of red and yellow. The silky frock with its wild geometric patterns didn't cling to her with sweat as Mallory's T-shirt did. Her armful of bangle bracelets shone with the sunrays that bounced from each silver and gold band. A straw sunhat and dark glasses embellished her flamboyant look.

She bounced toward the register. "Hey, girl. What's shaking? Business been good?"

"Slow and steady."

"Well, they say that wins the race." She laughed at her own quip. "You ready to sally on outta here?"

Mallory had worked for Chloe since moving to Wilmington ten years ago. She touched her cell phone to check the time. It automatically provided notifications of the missed calls and voicemails. She caught herself biting her bottom lip, a habit she worked hard to break. "I have ten more minutes, but we can balance the register."

Chloe took her key and pulled up the day's total receipts, flipped through the currency on hand, and checked the charge sales. She flicked the cash drawer closed in her flashy style. "And you are good to go. I'm headed to the Rococo Lounge when I close. Join me if you're free."

"Maybe." The locals met up for reggae music, Cajun food, and Bahama Mamas. Mallory's tight budget prevented her from frequenting the lounge as often as some of the others.

She left the emporium and turned toward Wilmington's Historic District to her apartment on Third Street. The antebellum house had fallen into disrepair when a greedy landlord got his hands on it. The outside was a masterpiece of architecture with Corinthian columns and Greek revival moldings, but he chopped the interior up, fitting it into tiny efficiency apartments. The price had been right when Mallory moved here ten years ago, but rent increased each year. If the trend continued, it would price her out of living downtown.

She had to return her dad's calls, but not in this suffocating heat. After climbing the three flights to her apartment, she kicked the AC into action, and downed a tall glass of ice water. Then she sat close to the vent that began to release cool air, and placed the call.

"Mallory Rose, I've been trying to reach you." His voice cracked with emotion.

She bit her lip as a wave of apprehension rippled through her. "I saw that, Dad. I was working. What's wrong? You sound upset."

"Sit down, Mallory Rose."

He continued to use her middle name. Her parents, in true southern style, chose six names for their three daughters—Jolene Rae, Savannah Joy, and Mallory Rose. She couldn't remember ever being just Mallory until she left home.

"I am sitting. What's wrong?"

"It's Jolene Rae and Mark. They were … were …" It took him three tries to get the words out. "There was an accident. A terrible accident."

Mallory waited through his silence, her pulse pounding stronger with each soundless moment. When the void of information became unbearable, she broke his reticence. "Dad?"

He choked out the last two words. "They're gone."

"No!" Mallory sprang to her feet with nauseating force. Jolene Rae, her oldest sister. She couldn't be gone. A vise squeezed Mallory's chest. She swallowed the lump that jammed her throat. "Samuel?" She whispered the panicked question.

"He wasn't in the car. He's here with us."

****

Mallory made the two-hour drive to Raleigh with her mind in a fog. This couldn't be happening. Jolene couldn't be dead. Every mile brought flashbacks of her childhood. Jolene—ten years older than Mallory and so gentle spirited, even as a teenager. Visions of Jolene, her hand wrapped around Mallory's four-year-old hand, holding firmly as they crossed a street. Her graduation, photos of her and Mark on prom night, at their wedding. Mallory's eyes misted remembering Jolene's face when she held Samuel. Pure love radiated from her, like the aura of an angel.

Mallory parked in front of Savannah's small, red brick ranch and climbed the three steps to the porch. Her sister's text message asked her to stop here before going to her parents. Savannah Joy held the door open, and they fulfilled a courtesy embrace. As always Savannah maintained her poise, but bloodshot eyes betrayed her.

"Please, come in. Thank you for coming here first. We need to talk before you see Mother."

Mallory looked around the house but saw no one else. "It's quiet. Where're your kids?"

"Richard took them out so we could talk in private. Please have a seat. What can I get you? Sweet tea? Water?" No circumstances stripped Savannah of southern hospitality.

"Just water, please." She lowered herself onto the well-worn sofa. Spotting the photo box on the coffee table, Mallory reached for a stack of pictures. They dated back to Jolene's teenage years; most of them showed the two older sisters, with Mallory noticeably absent. She should be offended, but she was ten years younger. The two oldest sisters had a natural bond.

One picture caught her attention. She shifted the stack to free it, enabling her to examine the details. The three sisters sat on the step of their Charlotte home—the house they sold when she was sixteen. A pang of homesickness stung Mallory, even after all these years. The photo showed Savannah and Jolene as teens, bookending her, their arms draped across her four-year-old back. In those days, they pampered her. So much had changed.

Savannah returned and set the water on a coaster far from the pictures. "I'm pulling some photos together for a display. We're still planning details for the funeral." She held out her hand to reclaim the photos that Mallory had picked up, then moved her chosen stack to another table. Others were returned to the box before she secured the lid and scooted it to the far end of the coffee table, out of Mallory's reach.

Savannah sat in a wingback chair and smoothed her skirt. Her attempt at mimicking their mother's perfectly bobbed hair fell short as the coffee-brown tips curled with humidity. "Mallory Rose, we need to talk about Samuel. You know that Mother's not doing well. I'm sure you haven't seen her, but when did you last have an update?"

Five minutes in the house and the darts were already hitting their mark, reminding her that she hadn't been a good daughter or they wouldn't need to give updates. She wouldn't be consulted on funeral plans or pictures. Everything had been safely moved from her reach.

Her eyes rose in challenge. "I talk to Mother each week."

Savannah crossed her arms. The condescending tilt of her head took Mallory back to the principal's office, seated across from his huge desk. "Talking to her and seeing her aren't the same thing."

Mallory clenched her jaw and took a deep breath. "I know she has Alzheimer's."

"Not just Alzheimer's. Hers is early onset. It's far more significant and progressing fast."

Mallory leaned forward, unable to hide her annoyance. "I don't need a medical lesson. I'm aware of the significance. Get to the point, Savannah."

Her sister sat up straight and spoke with finality. "You have to take Samuel."

Her next breath was exhaled in a rush of air. "I know you're kidding me here. Remember who you're talking to. I'm the irresponsible sister."

Savannah's words squeezed through the tight pursing of her lips. "I'm aware of that."

Spoken in sarcasm, yet Savannah offered no word to counter that claim. Instead, she continued with a decisive voice. "There's no one else. In another year, Mother won't know his name. Daddy has a full-time job taking care of her. We can't sanction a move that lacks permanence. Besides, with her condition, Social Services would never allow it."

Eight years had passed since Mallory last saw Samuel. He was no longer the delightful four-year-old who squeezed her heart until she couldn't breathe. She'd seen pictures that Jolene posted on social media. Samuel was twelve, rapidly growing into manhood. He needed so much more than she had to give. Mallory stood and paced the living room. "He barely knows me. I haven't seen him in years. You're the obvious choice. He knows you, and your kids would be here to help him."

"Look around, Mallory Rose. I have five kids living in 1,500 square feet, and Lillian's hearing-impaired. I take them to four different schools. It's impossible for me to take on a grieving pre-teen."

Mallory looked around the small space, the dated furniture, the miniscule yard. It was still more than she had to offer. She returned to her chair. "At least you know how to raise a kid. I know nothing about them, especially teenagers."

"Well, you're going to have to learn fast. You're the only option."

Mallory leaned her head back on the chair, closing her eyes. Both hands fingered through her long, dark hair. Samuel. He deserved so much more than she could give him. She'd get nowhere with Savannah by challenging her. She needed to make her understand.

"My lifestyle isn't conducive to raising a child. My hours are irregular. My income's in the day-to-day survival range. My apartment's an efficiency. I wouldn't even have a bedroom for him. It's not what Jolene would want."

Savannah's head volleyed back and forth. "No. No. You don't understand. You can't take him to the coast. We don't want him to change schools. We want you to move into Jolene Rae's house. Their will leaves all possessions to Samuel, in trust until he's of age. I'm executor of the will and checked with an attorney yesterday. We can keep the house until he's old enough to decide what he wants to do with it."

Mallory sat with her mouth gaping open. "You want me to move to Raleigh? Absolutely not. My life's in Wilmington. I have a job there."

Savannah began losing some of her practiced composure. "Let's get serious, Mallory Rose. You're twenty-eight years old and your life's on a fast track to nowhere. You have an on-and-off boyfriend and a hippie boss. It's time to grow up."

Mallory sprung to her feet. "Really? Hippie? What decade are you living in?"

Savannah flicked her hand, dismissing the criticism. "Hippie. Yuppie. Whatever you call them now."

Mallory's jaw tightened. "And why do we have to call her anything? I wouldn't be too snooty with seven people living in this shoebox of a house."

Both sisters were on their feet now, voices elevated.

"So, you'll just waltz back to the coast and let Samuel be fostered out to God only knows who?"

Mallory pointed an index finger at her sister. "Why don't *you* move into Jolene's house? Doesn't she have some big home with tons of bedrooms?"

"Four. It has four bedrooms. It's a different school district. I can't move my kids. Spencer's going into his junior year. Lillian's in a hearing-impaired classroom. It's not feasible to make that kind of change." Savannah leaned forward and lowered her voice. "He *is* your son."

Mallory stepped into her space, and met her whispered voice, laced with rage. "How dare you? We had a pact. That is never to be spoken."

"You and Jolene Rae had a pact. I sat by and watched the deceit. Only for her sake did I keep my mouth closed." She stabbed a finger in Mallory's direction. "You broke the law. Do you want that exposed?"

Heat climbed to Mallory's face. "Are you threatening me?"

"It's up to five years imprisonment and a ten thousand dollar fine for falsifying a birth certificate. I checked."

"You checked?" Mallory stepped back and shook her head in disbelief. "I was sixteen years old when that decision was made. Barely seventeen when I gave birth. I did what Mother asked me—practically told me—to do. Are you prepared to incriminate her?"

In the silence that followed, Mallory lowered herself to the chair. It had been so long ago, not that she ever forgot. Samuel's birth cost her dearly. She couldn't watch her sister raise him as her own. Couldn't watch him grow up calling her Aunt Mallory, or worse yet, Aunt Mallory Rose. Surely Jolene would have insisted on the full name, if only to please their mother. Because of Samuel's birth, she'd moved away and lost her family.

"Wait a minute." Mallory began thinking through Savannah's words. "I know Jolene and Mark. They wouldn't have drafted a last will taking care of their money and not their son. Who did they name as guardian?"

Savannah's eyes lowered and she gave no answer.

Mallory was back on her feet. "You?"

"That was twelve years ago. Life wasn't as complicated back then. Besides, no one expects it will ever really happen."

Mallory picked up her purse and stormed toward the door. "I'm going to see Mother."

Savannah hurried after her. "I need an answer."

"Well, we all have something we need." She yanked the door open. "And I need time to think."

Savannah followed her out to the porch. "Don't take too long. Social Services will move him if the family doesn't have a solution."

8

Chapter 2

Mallory drove at a snail's pace, pondering all her options. Never before today had she heard the family secret spoken aloud. Savannah acted like the whole family came together to protect her, but that wasn't the case. It had never been the family standing beside Mallory, loving and supporting her. It had always been about Jolene. Poor Jolene who miscarried three times. Poor Jolene whom the doctors advised against another pregnancy. Poor Jolene who wanted a baby so desperately.

Savannah acted like the family had sacrificed for Mallory because she'd been a foolish teenager. In truth, she was their sacrifice, laid on the altar for Jolene. At sixteen years old, keeping the baby had been unrealistic. Adoption had been a good option, but there was poor Jolene Rae. They thought of every detail—how to hide the pregnancy, how to time the move so no one would wonder how Mark and Jolene suddenly came up with a baby that she supposedly birthed, how to bring in a midwife at the eleventh hour, claiming that Mallory was Jolene Rae Donaldson. Yes, they thought of every detail that mattered—to Jolene.

Yet did anyone give a thought to Mallory, how she'd be impacted by handing her baby to her sister, watching her raise him? How she felt quitting school, trading a high school diploma for a GED. When Mallory turned eighteen and moved away from the family, hadn't everyone breathed a sigh of relief? After all, nothing really mattered except Jolene. Years of resentment. To what end? Had the bitterness served any purpose?

Mallory eased the car into a parking space on the street in front of her parents' home, her first visit in years. She wouldn't pull into the driveway where her exit could be blocked. Today, she'd see Samuel. All she knew of him came from social media and the family Christmas photo, the annual newsletter filled with sugar and spice, detailing a year in the life of a perfect family.

She'd saved pictures, creating an album from birth to his last birthday. Facebook made it easy to know him vicariously through pictures. On good days, Mallory would open the album, taking a picture walk through his life. On bad days, pain prevented her from opening the book.

Mallory sat in the car, staring at the ranch home. It was smaller than their old Charlotte house, the two-story home she'd grown up in. She had lived in Raleigh for less than two terrible years before moving to the coast, and she hated every day of it.

It was time. Beyond that front door, she'd see her son. She made the awkward gesture of knocking. She couldn't exactly march in like it was home since she hadn't been here in years. The door opened, and her father pulled her into his arms. "Mallory Rose." Then he cried in her embrace. The tears that eluded her since the phone call, now flooded her eyes as she held her father, feeling the grief in his quivering chest.

When he released her, she studied his face. She had seen him last year, the day after Christmas when her parents took a ride to Wilmington, but he looked like he'd aged ten years since then. Sagging shoulders brought a slight curve to his back. Glimpses of his age-spotted scalp could be seen through a mat of thinning gray hair.

Mallory stepped from the entry into a living room that never changed. The same hand-crocheted doilies sat on age-old tables. Dated pictures hung on two walls. New sags were visible on the worn sofa. She had moved into this house at seventeen, immediately after giving birth to Samuel, and moved out at eighteen. "Where's Mom? Where's Samuel?"

"Mom's in the kitchen, and Samuel's in his bedroom. He doesn't want to come out."

"I'll go see Mom first. How's she doing?"

Her dad shook his head. "Not good when she remembers what happened. The Alzheimer's is unpredictable. I never know what she'll remember and what she'll forget. This time her forgetfulness is a blessed relief. That is, until she comes back and realizes Jolene Rae's gone. It's like she hears it again for the first time. I told her you were coming." His head shook in despair. "I hope she remembers."

Mallory stepped into the kitchen, the brightest, sunlit spot in the house. Her mother finished drying a skillet, an apron tied around her slender waist, protecting her cotton dress. Always prim and proper, no matter the circumstances. Unlike Savannah, her mother's came with authenticity. A gentle spirit. Would the disease eventually strip that away? "Mom?"

Her mother turned perplexed eyes in Mallory's direction. She tilted her head, biting her bottom lip, the same bad habit that Mallory had developed. "Mallory Rose? Your father said you'd come."

Mallory exhaled a sigh of relief before embracing her mother. When her mother wriggled out of her arms, she asked, "Did your father tell you Samuel's staying here?" Her detached tone accompanied the return to her task of drying dishes.

"Yes, Dad said he's in the bedroom."

"And he's just fine, so you two go and have a nice time. And don't forget I'll be making Sunday dinner tomorrow."

Mallory's chest tightened, her pulse hammering. "I'm Mallory, Mom. Mallory Rose."

Her mother examined her, starting with her loose, dark hair down to her shorts and sandals. "Yes, of course." She turned away, resuming the task of tidying the kitchen, but not before Mallory saw the confusion etched on her face. "You go have a good time, too."

Mallory took the dishtowel from her mother and untied her apron, laying it over the back of a kitchen chair. "Come in and sit down, Mom. I'm staying here for a while."

She led her mother to a seat on the sofa and sat beside her. Mallory made casual conversation about the house, a tangible subject that wouldn't require memories. Something that wasn't likely to confuse her.

"Mallory Rose, it's time to get that long hair trimmed. Now I know what you're going to say, but college visits are coming up. First impressions are critical." Mallory stared at her mother, battling the decision to correct her or allow her the blessed oblivion of living in the past.

"And you'll need a ..." Her mother paused midsentence. Her eyes filled with confusion and her voice not much more than a whisper. "That's over, isn't it? College?"

Mallory didn't know how to respond. She just nodded.

A guttural choking sound escaped her mother's lips. Her hand flew to cover her mouth as she whispered Jolene Rae's name.

****

The small ranch house had three bedrooms. Four woodgrain doors, including the bathroom, lined the dim hallway. Only Mallory's old bedroom had a closed door. Her heightened awareness of that door distracted her. At some point, she'd go and meet Samuel. She wanted the initiative to be hers, not a random moment when he surfaced to pass through to the kitchen or bathroom.

She rose from the sofa. "Dad, I think it's time for me to see Samuel. I'm going to go say hello. Anything I should know?"

"Only that he's hurting." Each word was laced with sadness.

For the second time in an hour, Mallory stood outside a door and knocked with trembling hands. "Samuel?"

The door opened about four inches, enough space to take all the breath from Mallory's lungs. She pulled in a gasp of air. She was sixteen again, looking into the familiar face, the one that she had visualized every day, dreamt of every night. A young man stood before her, the picture of his father. She had seen the resemblance in photos, but looking at his blue eyes, the blond hair that belonged to no one in the Carter family, the square jawline. It catapulted her back in time.

12

"Samuel, I'm your Aunt Mallory." Did her voice sound as shaky as she felt? But then, Samuel didn't know her. He'd have no reference to normal where she was concerned.

"I know. Grandpa told me you were coming."

"May I come in for a few minutes?"

He opened the door wordlessly.

Mallory scanned the room that had once been hers. Her parents had moved from Charlotte a month before Samuel's birth. On her eighteenth birthday, one week after Samuel turned a year old, she had packed everything she owned and drove until she could drive no farther, to a spot that provided enough distance.

Samuel plopped on the side of the bed facing the desk. Mallory pulled out the chair and sat. "How are you doing, Samuel?" What a thoughtless question. What do you say to a twelve-year-old who just lost both parents?

He shrugged then reached for his baseball on the nightstand. He tossed it in the air and caught it repeatedly—a juggling act with one ball.

"Do you remember me? I think you were about four the last time I saw you."

"No, but my mom talked about you. You're her youngest sister." He cut his eyes in her direction before returning them to the baseball.

What else had his mother told him about her youngest sister? She never finished high school and had to get a GED. She had no education and no decent job. She left home for the coast and lived a carefree life without responsibilities. Negative examples are a great teaching tool. Don't grow up to be like your Aunt Mallory Rose.

"Tell me about yourself. Do you play baseball?"

He still did a toss and catch with the ball, each movement showing the developing bicep. "Yeah."

"Are you any good?"

"I guess."

"What position?"

"Usually first base." Brief answers and no eye contact.

She'd need questions that required more than a one-word answer. "What else do you like to do? Do you like school?"

He placed the ball back on the nightstand and laid back on his pillow. "I don't know."

Mallory sensed the dismissal. "Okay. I'll be here for a few days. We can talk another time."

Samuel closed his eyes and turned over, his back facing her. Mallory returned the chair to the desk, took one backward glance at his form stretching the length of the twin bed, and quietly left his room.

Her dad sat alone in front of the TV, watching the evening news. "You hungry? We had an early dinner, but there's lots in the fridge. Help yourself."

"Where's Mom?"

"Lying down. Oh, and Mallory Rose, we lock the front and back door with an inside key so your mother can't wander off. The key's up in that blue vase if you need it."

Locked, like a prison. A house with grief dripping from every corner.

Chapter 3

When Mallory woke, it took a moment to remember where she was. She shook off the sleepy fog and sat up on the unfamiliar bed. A jumble of thoughts collided in her head. Samuel, Jolene, her mother's Alzheimer's. Today they'd face a double funeral.

In her hurried departure from Wilmington, Mallory had tossed clothing into an overnight bag without giving thought to the funeral. She tossed the yellow sundress aside. That left only the blue one. Savannah would frown at the sleeveless frock and the scoop neckline, but that couldn't be helped. She smoothed the dress out and hung it up. A slight knock sounded at her door.

"Come on in."

She expected to see her dad, but Samuel entered instead. He closed the door behind him with a quiet click. His sky-blue eyes carried the weight of fatigue and unanswered questions.

A lump filled her throat. "Hey, Samuel. You doing okay this morning?"

He shrugged and sat on the bed. Fine facial hair had begun to peek through his fair skin. The definition of muscles formed on his biceps, evidence of hormones that surged through his young body. A little boy trying to break through the barrier of manhood. He was exactly four years younger than she and Elliott Moore had been.

"Grandpa told me that you're going to move in with me."

It took all of her effort not to show her surprise. How dare he tell this boy something that hadn't been decided? Did anyone in this family ever once think about her? Drawing in a deep breath, she took a seat beside him.

Mallory longed to pull him into her arms and comfort him. She had imagined it so many times over the years. But in her imaginings, he was always younger, a little tow-headed boy. She refrained from touching him. He was no longer that four-year-old, and he didn't know her.

"What do you want, Samuel? I realize that you don't really know me."

He shrugged again. Was this a new habit since his world had imploded? "I guess it's okay. At least I'd get to stay at home. I wanted Uncle Brady to do it, but he can't."

Brady Donaldson, Mark's younger brother. The last time she saw him was at Jolene's wedding. Mallory had been thirteen years old so Brady must have been around fifteen. He had been two years ahead of Mallory in high school. All she remembered from those years was thick eyeglasses on a lanky, acned teen. The last she heard, he still lived in Charlotte. "Why? Did someone ask him?"

"I did. He said he wanted to, but he travels too much for his job. Besides, he can't move here. I'd have to go there."

She calculated Brady to be around thirty years old now. "Is he married? Is there a wife at home?" Surely there was someone better than her who could provide a good home for this boy. Someone with stability and an income. A home with a family. Mallory swallowed the painful regret of missed opportunities. Her life had veered far from all that defined normal.

"No, just him."

"Are you close with your uncle?"

"Yeah. He likes to fool around. You know, play ball and take me to games when he can."

That was the most Samuel had spoken since Mallory arrived yesterday. His voice was that of a boy, but she caught the times when it deepened, trying to change. "Were you hoping to go with your Aunt Savannah? I know you've been close."

He gave a mock shudder. "No. That's a crazy house."

Mallory laughed. "I guess it is with five kids." She reached a tentative hand and patted his shoulder. "We're going to work this out for you, Samuel. We'll make sure that you're taken care of by people who love you."

He stood and when Mallory rose up to join him, she realized that they were the same height. Soon he would tower over her. "This will be a hard day for everyone. We'll talk more about this tomorrow."

Before opening the door, he looked back one more time. "Thank you, Aunt Mallory Rose."

She cringed. "Samuel," Mallory leaned in close. "It's just Aunt Mallory. Unless Grandma's around."

He gave her the slightest hint of a smile.

****

Only moments remained before they had to leave. Samuel opened his bedroom door and stepped into the living room wearing a dark suit and light blue tie. His black shoes were polished into reflective mirrors.

Mother's tears had already soaked the embroidered handkerchief she held tightly in her fingers. "Oh, Samuel, you look so handsome. Your parents would be proud." At least she remembered they were headed to a funeral.

Mallory stood like a stone statue, dreading the day on so many fronts. She hadn't seen Jolene in years, but today she would look at her lifeless form. The lost time could never be recaptured. She had no recent memories. What had she gained from the years of bitterness?

Could she bear to watch Samuel grieving the loss of the only parents he'd known? She wished for a tiny piece of that love. What would it have been like to be his mother? To nurse the infant and rock him to sleep? To hold waiting arms while he took that first shaky step? To cry on his first day of school? Those were moments that Jolene had lived.

Moments denied to Mallory.

But were they denied? Jolene welcomed her to be part of their lives. Part of Samuel's life. Bitterness had driven her away. She fled to avoid hearing her son call someone else *Mother.* Mallory denied herself the chance to share those moments. She couldn't rewind life.

Mark and Jolene would be buried after the joint funeral with all of the Donaldson family attending. Friends from Charlotte would make the drive. Old high school friends. Old neighbors. Former church members. Mallory took a deep breath and readied herself for anyone she might have to face.

****

The Donaldson family arrived minutes after the Carters. Mark's parents, his brother Brady, his sister Elise, and his grandmother were ushered to the room where the Carters waited. If they hadn't been expected, Mallory wouldn't have recognized any of them. Time had rendered its change. The years aged Mr. and Mrs. Donaldson, while Elise, the middle child, had grown into a lovely woman. Brady, without the glasses and acne, showed no likeness to the teen she met years ago. Samuel, who had been somber all morning, sprang to his feet, hugging his uncle Brady first, then his grandparents, and his aunt Elise. When they were seated, Samuel settled at Brady's side. Mallory saw the first of his tears. With Brady Donaldson, Samuel felt safe enough to cry.

They were taken into the viewing room of the double funeral before visiting hours for guests. Mallory stood back, watching as each one cried. She wished for tears but they refused to come. Instead, she felt numb. She splintered her family circle years ago when she left, but somewhere deep inside, she always expected to right that wrong. A day of reuniting. Now that hope shattered. Lost opportunities never to be reclaimed.

When the service ended, flocks of people gathered in the church's multi-purpose room where a lunch had been provided. Mallory's dad ushered her mom to a seat in the back, as far from the foot

18

traffic as possible. Her dad feared that the crowd may confuse her, causing her to lapse in and out of forgetfulness.

As Savannah mingled with guests, Mallory stood before a table with flower arrangements. Condolences from people she could barely remember. She touched a velvet rose petal, flattened now from being moved around. She had no ability to return its vibrancy, not since it had been cut from its life-giving vine. Her introspection was short-lived. Mallory heard her name spoken from a voice distantly familiar.

"Mallory Rose Carter."

She turned to see her old high school friend. "Lauren Winters?" They had been best friends from elementary school until Mallory moved away in her junior year.

"Oh, my. It hasn't been Winters for a long time. Lauren Edwards."

Mallory raised a questioning eyebrow. "Edwards, as in Jeremy Edwards?"

"Yep. He was a grade ahead of us, but we reconnected at Clemson." Lauren wrapped her in an embrace. "I think of you so often. Why did you lose contact with everyone? We have so much to catch up on."

Mallory had disappeared without a word. Lies require more lies until you're tangled in them, so she had chosen to leave her best friend with no good-bye. No explanation. Friends were on the list of things taken from her when she was forced to move. Shouldn't she welcome this chance to reconnect? But it carried questions she had no intention of answering.

Mallory's head tilted with her question. "What brought you here? I didn't think you knew Jolene or Mark that well."

Lauren repositioned her thick hair, pulling it forward over one shoulder. The honey gold color always glowed with warmth. "My mother is friends with Mark's mother. She didn't want to make the drive alone. You know that my dad died last year?"

Of course, she didn't know. Her family had distanced themselves from as much of their former life as possible. "No, I'm so sorry to hear that. I'm afraid I lost touch with everyone since I moved."

"Long, hard battle with cancer."

"I'm sorry." Mallory didn't know what else to say.

"So, married? Children?"

Mallory shook her head. "No and no. How about you?"

"Yes and yes. We have a three-year-old son, Brandon." Lauren zipped her phone from the front pocket of her purse and pulled up his picture.

"He's adorable." Mallory looked away quickly. The familiar stab burned in her chest when she saw old friends and their families.

Lauren dropped her phone back into her handbag. "Are you still living in Raleigh?"

"No, Wilmington. Just a couple hours away."

Lauren tapped a finger to her chin. Her eyes held a look of mischief. "Let me guess … marine biology."

Mallory shot her a confused look.

"You were the science geek. I figured you'd go into some occupation in science. Wilmington's coastal so I'm guessing marine biology."

Mallory attempted to laugh. "Nope. Marketing." Not a lie—just a protective half-truth. She had no desire to tell her she worked as a souvenir shop clerk.

"Marketing? I wouldn't have predicted that. What company?"

"A small, local one. I'm sure you've never heard of it." Time to shift the focus. "How about you? Working mother or stay-at-home?"

"I taught school after college, but quit when Brandon was born. Jeremy's a reporter for the *Charlotte Post*, so we couldn't count on regular hours for him. It's easier having me home. I'll go back to teaching someday, but I'm happy to just be a mom for now."

Savannah's face came into view, providing the excuse Mallory needed. "I think my family's looking for me. I better go."

"Is that Jolene and Mark's son?"

Mallory's eyes traveled to the table with her parents and Samuel. "Yes, that's Samuel sitting with my parents."

"Poor boy. How terrible to lose both parents!" Lauren squinted for a closer look. "Where in the world did he get the blond hair? Are those eyes blue?"

Heat climbed Mallory's face as she scrambled to answer. "Mark's hair wasn't too dark. It may have been lighter as a child."

"Not *that* light." Lauren's brows arched a little higher as she stared at Samuel.

Her snarky tone grated on Mallory. "Recessive genes, Lauren. We learned it in tenth grade."

A laugh pressed through her lips. "You seriously think I remember that stuff? You're the science geek. I taught elementary students." Lauren lifted her phone and snapped a picture in Samuel's direction.

"What are you doing?" Mallory stepped between her and the view of Samuel.

"Just in case my mother didn't have a chance to meet him. I told you she's great friends with his grandmother."

And his grandmother would have pictures. Mallory had an irrational urge to grab the phone and erase Samuel's image.

Lauren tucked her phone away before giving Samuel a long once over. "We have to stay in touch." One more glance in his direction. "I'll catch you up on the old gang, who married who, what they're doing, and all that. Are you on Facebook?"

"I'm not. I don't do social media." Another half-truth. Her username had been designed so she couldn't be found. She only used it to keep up with Jolene's postings of Samuel.

Lauren's head shot up. "Marketing, and you don't do social media?"

Mallory froze. Stupid, stupid blunder. "Not personal sites."

Lauren reached in her purse and again retrieved her phone. "What's your number?"

"Oh, I imagine you're busy with your little one and taking care of your mother. Neither of us have much free time."

Lauren pulled an odd expression. "Are you planning to disappear again? Do you know what it's like for your best friend to leave without a word? I cried for days when you left."

Mallory had cried too. Cried for weeks. Months. Pregnant and hidden away like it was the dark ages. Ripped away from everything familiar—her home, her school, her friends, and Elliott Moore. "I'm sorry, Lauren. It was a hard time for me."

"Did you ever even think of me? I couldn't believe you left without telling me, your best friend since first grade."

Mallory's cheeks warmed from the reminder. She hadn't given much thought to the feelings of those she'd left behind. "I'm sorry." She dug her fingernails into her palm. "Moving before my senior year was difficult for me."

"And for me." Lauren held her phone up. "I'd still like your number." She wore a staged smile that gave Mallory chills.

There was no tactful way to refuse. Mallory recited her phone number while Lauren entered it in her contacts. Then Lauren pulled out a pen and scribbled something on a scrap of paper. Her eyes darted in Samuel's direction again, lingering a moment too long. She handed the card to Mallory. "Here. Call me."

Mallory tucked the paper in her shoulder bag and made her way back to the table where Samuel sat between her parents. She joined them, filled with a new sense of protectiveness. But there was no need to worry. It was only a picture.

From this vantage point, she saw many old acquaintances, people her parents knew and with whom they'd lost touch. "Dad, why don't you walk around and mingle. I'll stay with Mom and Samuel."

"No, Mallory Rose. I'll stay with your mother. She does better when I'm here."

They had all stood in a receiving line, shaking hands and hearing condolences. So many folks from the past had pummeled Mallory with questions. She excused herself and stepped outside for a moment of quiet. She strolled toward the cemetery where the undertakers were finishing their thankless task.

Granite headstones of gray and russet peppered the landscape, each representing a life, lived and gone. Numbers etched the years. Most would exceed Jolene's brief span. Another site, some distance away from Jolene's and Mark's, had freshly turned dirt. The air carried the scent of the disturbed soil and cut grass.

Brady Donaldson stood close to the grave site, hands in his pockets, watching the men at work. The lanky teenager had grown into an attractive adult with a clean-cut look. Contacts must have replaced the glasses. He had spent hours greeting people as well. He probably came seeking a few moments of solitude. She turned away.

As she started back toward the church, she heard him call out, his long stride moving him in her direction. "Mallory Rose, can we talk?"

She retraced her steps to meet him.

He had shed his suit jacket and loosened his tie. Mallory looked into eyes so much like Mark's. They shared the same caramel brown hair and deep dark eyes. Today, Brady's eyes carried a heavy weight. Mark was his only brother.

An ache formed in Mallory's throat. "I didn't want to disturb you. I figured you needed a little quiet."

"Probably the same reason you came out here. It's been a tough day."

She nodded. "Yes, it has." Understatement of the century.

"Savannah Joy told me you're considering taking guardianship of Samuel."

She focused her eyes on some obscure blade of grass near her shoes. "I'm thinking about it." Mallory looked up and met his gaze with a challenge. "He'd like it to be you."

Brady shifted, adding space between them. "I know. He told me. This is what he doesn't get. I'm the fun uncle because I can be. I see him every few weeks and we have a blast. Mark's the one who had to teach him responsibility, hold his feet to the fire, so to speak. If I took that role, he'd lose his fun uncle."

"What's the greater need? A fun uncle or a guardian that he loves? Samuel doesn't even know me."

"A temporary dilemma. He just needs time with you. I'm the wrong choice. I can't move from Charlotte. It's my home base for work. I'm an architect and have to spend time on building sites, sometimes gone the whole week. I'd take him if I could. He's a great kid."

Mallory shifted her focus back to the ground. "I don't know if I'd be good for him. I haven't made the best life choices, as you've probably heard."

Brady drew his brows together, puzzled. "No, I haven't heard that. I know you moved to Wilmington. I figured you had landed some pretty good job there."

She let out a cynical laugh. "Not exactly a high-end position." Could it possibly be true that she hadn't been the topic of whispered conversation?

Brady relaxed the puzzled look. "Here's what I do know. Even though I was two grades ahead of you, I knew you were one of the smartest kids in high school. Jolene said you would have been in line to be valedictorian or salutatorian if you hadn't moved. Why did you decide not to do college?"

Mallory caught herself biting her bottom lip. "Book smart doesn't always transfer to life smart. I'm a little short on that end."

"I don't believe that." His soothing tone almost convinced her.

"Believe what you want. I just don't want Samuel to become my experiment." She curved her fingers forming a set of quotations. *"Let's see if Mallory Rose can do something right for once."*

Brady's face softened into a look of compassion. Was it for her or his nephew? He ventured a smile, so welcomed amidst the solemnity. "I know Samuel. I think you're the perfect person to see him through this. I'll help you any way I can." Brady's confidence contrasted her uncertainty.

"I don't know, Brady. I just don't know."

Three hours away and traveling all week? How could he help?

Chapter 4

The family gathered in the Carter living room. Mallory's mother sat on the sofa, her petite frame lost in the deep cushions. With her blouse buttoned and tucked into dress slacks, she still looked refined. Genteel laced with tenderness. The only sign of her dementia was the biting of her bottom lip, eyes darting from person to person. "Where's Samuel? Will he be joining us?"

At least she hadn't asked about Jolene. Mallory sat beside her, inhaling the clean scent of the freshly laundered quilt across the back of the sofa. "No, Mom. He's with Brady today. They went out to eat so we can make some plans."

She nodded, but resumed biting her lip.

Savannah and Richard sat across from Mallory. He draped his arm behind his wife though she needed no support. Savannah sat ramrod straight, a failed attempt to mimic their mother's grace. Her rigid posture lacked the softness.

Her father wore the heaviness of burying his firstborn. He moved without energy as he lowered himself into the only remaining chair. The drop of his shoulders broke Mallory's heart. He turned dull, expressionless eyes toward her. "Mallory Rose?"

They all looked her way, waiting for an answer. She took a deep breath. "How do I begin proceedings to become Samuel's legal guardian?"

Savannah's eyes rose in challenge. "And you *are* moving to Raleigh? You don't plan to take him to the coast?"

Mallory stared her down before turning toward her father. "How do I begin, Dad?"

"We petition the court to grant you guardianship. Savannah Joy has been named in the will, so they'll probably want her signature of release from that responsibility. I'll help you get started tomorrow."

Mallory turned back to her sister. "Yes, I'm moving to Raleigh. I'm not a complete idiot."

"And you're moving alone? The surfer boyfriend won't be coming?"

The clock ticked away the seconds, matching her silent count to ten. "Savannah, I …"

"Savannah Joy," her mother corrected.

"Savannah Joy, Liam is not, and never has been, my boyfriend. He's a friend." Her sister had met Liam once, on her only trip to Wilmington. She drew her own conclusions about their friendship.

Savannah lifted her pointy chin and crossed her arms. "He's a middle-aged beach bum with no home and no ambition. We can't have him bringing that influence to Samuel."

Mallory drew in a deep breath, gathering enough self-control to swallow the harsh reply that begged to come. She had to keep this conversation civil, if only for her mother's sake. "Liam's a minimalist. He rents a room and lives simply. He's entitled to his life choices. And to answer your question, I have no expectation that any of my Wilmington friends will be visiting me here in Raleigh. If they do, I'll gladly welcome them into my home."

"You mean, into Samuel's home."

Was that the issue? Was Savannah jealous that Mallory would be living in Jolene's home while her own family crammed into a doll house? She made her choice. Why take it out on Mallory?

Her father's sharp reply startled them all. "Savannah Joy, that's enough."

Mallory glanced around the room. Savannah's mouth tightened into a taut cord. Richard remained silent, stroking his wife's hand. Her mother had a dazed look and Mallory wondered if she had any understanding of the conversation.

"Dad, I want to do this, but I need help. I'll have no job when I move. I have very little savings and not a lot of occupational skills. I know that Samuel's in private school. Does Jolene Rae's estate provide for that to continue?"

Her dad turned a questioning eye toward Savannah.

She answered in clipped words. "Yes, and for his college."

Mallory directed her questions to Savannah. She was the one with the financial details. "Is there provision for his support—food, home, healthcare?"

"Yes, if we use the money carefully. It will see him through until he leaves for college."

The implication was clear. Six years. At that point, Mallory would again be on her own.

Her mother reached for her hand and patted it. "Mallory Rose, I'm glad we're speaking of college. We need to start college visits. The biochemistry program at Vanderbilt is excellent. I suggest you consider it."

Mallory forced a smile through the knot in her throat. Ignoring everyone else in the room, she rubbed her mother's arm. "Good idea, Mom."

****

The sign on the door of Cape Fear Emporium said *Open*. Chloe rang up a sale as Mallory stepped through the door. They were ten miles from the beach, yet somehow the shop had the smell of the sea. Mallory inhaled the salty, briny scent, mingled with ginger and coconut from the open infusers.

"Hey, girl. Welcome back." One long braid in an unnatural shade of red swayed as Chloe turned her head. She took great care packing whatever trinket lay hidden in that brown wrapping paper, her long fingernails painted with nail art. Then she handed it over with a smile. As the customer left, Chloe came from behind the counter. Layers of Native American beads fashioned from turquoise and feathers jangled from around her neck. "You doing okay?"

Mallory dreaded telling Chloe she was leaving. She had rehearsed it in her car, but there was no easy way. "It's been a tough week, Chloe. Brace yourself. I've got some news for you."

One eyebrow arched. "Uh-oh. Good or bad news?"

Tilting her head, Mallory gave a puzzled look. "That's a hard question to answer. Bottom line is this—I'm needed at home, so I'm moving back to Raleigh."

"Girl, that's not a hard question. That's bad news any way you look at it. You're the best help I've had here since I opened these doors fifteen years ago."

Chloe's words lifted her spirits. *Someone* in this world didn't think she was a complete loser. "Thanks. Every little bit of encouragement helps right now. I'm feeling a little inadequate."

Chloe's hands found her hips. "Why's that?"

Inhaling a deep breath, Mallory said the words that still sounded surreal. "I'm going to take guardianship of my sister's son. Moving to Raleigh will allow him to stay in his school."

Chloe's smile filled her face. "Well now, there's the good news part. You're an incredible aunt. That's one lucky little boy."

Savannah had called Chloe a hippie or yuppie. Her life may be different from the Carter's, but Chloe was the only one who saw good in Mallory. Her chest tightened at the thought of leaving.

"How old is this little guy?"

"Twelve. It's scary to take on a pre-teen."

"You got that right. But you'll be fine. When do you have to be back?"

She spoke words crammed with guilt. "In a few days. I'm so sorry. I'm just back to pack up my things."

"No worries. I've got scads of people wanting to work. You just go take care of that boy of yours."

That boy of mine. The words caressed her soul. And they scared the daylights out of her.

****

Paying off her lease exhausted the balance of Mallory's savings. Savannah and Richard convinced her to ditch the few pieces of furniture that belonged to her. Nothing she owned justified the cost of moving it. Boxes were piled high in her backseat, mostly memorabilia that she'd saved and a growing collection of books.

She carefully laid her homemade telescope in a box, cushioned with bubble wrap. The eleventh-grade science fair project was one of the few things that she took pride in. Mallory had spent many evenings on the beach identifying constellations and was able to catch a few meteor showers over the years. It didn't have the strength of commercial-grade scopes, but served its purpose.

She enjoyed the role of amateur astronomer, showing Liam the wonders of the skies, explaining the order of the canopy above them. He had stared with awe. "I looked at this all of my life, but never saw it until now." Would Samuel share that wonder? Teens weren't easily impressed today. Would he understand her passion?

Three days after returning to Wilmington, Mallory closed the door to her Third Street efficiency apartment. She drove the short distance to Wrightsville Beach. Leaving her shoes in the car, she slid into flip flops and started down the sandy path toward the water. The sound of splashing waves and squawking seagulls had become so familiar. Sand crabs scurried sideways to move from her path. She stopped at the beginning of the wet sand and held her breath, waiting for a wave to roll in. A quick scan of the water showed no sign of Liam, no trace of his wheat-colored hair and bright yellow surfboard.

Savannah was wrong. He'd never been her boyfriend. He had been the first person to befriend her when she arrived in Cape Fear at the age of eighteen, alone and disappointed in herself. Liam convinced her that life didn't have to be an experience in ladder climbing. It could simply be lived—day to day, dollar to dollar, without the stress that today's culture placed on achievement. Had that been good advice or bad? The words sounded so freeing at the time.

Mallory had been raised with high expectations. She could still hear her dad's voice. "What's your plan, Mallory Rose? A goal without a plan is just a daydream."

But then there was Liam. His goal was simple—be happy and enjoy each day. But did that free her? Did taking the easy road only serve to create a hard one?

Mallory stood in front of the water, inhaling the salty air, allowing the breeze to blow her hair back from her face. A wave came in, splashing her legs and drawing the sand from beneath her feet as it receded.

Was this her goal? To meander the beach alone, to stargaze at night, pondering the mysteries of the sky? No, it had to be more than that. At one time, Elliott Moore had been her goal—until he married Andrea. Then her dream shattered like a broken mirror. Samuel. She couldn't hit rewind, but she could move forward. Life handed her an opportunity to finish raising her son. But as her dad said, a goal without a plan was just a daydream. She had a two-hour drive ahead to work out a plan. With one final breath of ocean air, she returned to the sandy path that would take her to the parking lot.

Back at the car, Mallory found the beach towel that she kept in the trunk, dried her legs and wiped the sand from her feet. Someday she'd bring Samuel here. She'd show him her favorite beach spots, walk the historic district and marvel at the architecture. They'd stroll down the boardwalk along the Cape Fear River, ending up at the Emporium for ice cream. Someday they would sit on the open beach at night and gaze at the constellations from her telescope. Mallory would adapt to his life, but one of these days, she'd share a little piece of hers.

What would Samuel think of the simplicity that life offered in this small coastal town? Would he understand the attraction, or would he judge her decision like the rest of her family?

Chapter 5

Mallory squeezed Samuel's overnight bag into the backseat among her boxes and bins. Clothes, still on hangers, that didn't fit in her one suitcase had been strewn over the top of the boxes. "Sorry for the clutter."

Samuel offered no response as he slid into the passenger seat of Mallory's old car.

The overcast day matched the mood. Dark threatening clouds were ready to shed their tears on the occasion. Her mother stood by the front door staring at some obscure speck in the distance. Her dad walked with Mallory to the driver's side. "Call me if you need anything." It broke her heart to hear the sadness in his voice mingled with the look of desperate isolation. She pecked his cheek with a kiss before sliding into the car and driving to her new home.

Samuel wore a bright blue T-shirt with the name Royals and the number twelve. Mallory snatched onto that as a springboard for conversation.

"Twelve—is that your number?"

"Yeah." Samuel gave the visor of his baseball cap a tug, pulling it lower on his forehead. He shifted his body closer to the door and stared out the window. He obviously wanted to be left alone, a feeling she understood completely.

Mallory drove, allowing Samuel his solitude. Any kid in his shoes would be sullen. A difficult task awaited them; returning home without his parents. Entering the house with their fingerprints everywhere. Memories waiting in every room. There would be time enough for chatter once that ordeal was behind them. They'd settle into a new routine.

Many of his teachers had attended the funeral. She'd have to stop by the school with copies of her guardianship papers. Things would be better when he went back to baseball and started seeing his friends.

When the GPS directed her to the left, Mallory clicked her signal and slowed down. As she began the turn, Samuel frowned in her direction.

"This isn't the way we go."

The car had been committed to the bend and she couldn't safely redirect. "This is what my GPS said. Will this get us to your house?"

"Yeah, but we don't come this way because of the traffic."

She glanced around at the near empty street. "Looks like traffic's light today. I'll keep going, but you'll have to show me your route the next time."

He shifted in his seat, pivoting toward the window again. When the GPS directed them to enter a subdivision, Mallory asked before turning, "Is this your street?"

"Yeah. It would have been closer to go in the other entrance but you passed it."

She'd failed him already. This might take some time. As the road snaked through the subdivision, the clouds opened up, spilling huge drops of moisture on the windshield. The heavens cried as they arrived at her sister's home.

"Is this it?" Mallory hesitated before turning into the driveway of a beautiful red brick two-story colonial with white columns in front.

"Yeah. You should park there." He pointed to a space just beyond the two-car garage. Mallory pulled the car forward.

When they stepped out of the car, Mallory picked up a box from the back seat. Samuel hoisted his own overnight bag, and they hurried to the garage. Samuel punched a series of numbers into the keypad and the door made a smooth ascent revealing the inside of the garage, clean and organized. Wall shelves and hooks held all assortment of lawn tools and labeled boxes. One side of the garage was empty while a Silver Volvo SUV filled the other. The Volvo must belong to Jolene. It put Mallory's little dated Civic to shame.

The empty space threatened tears. Mallory struggled to hold them in, wondering if Samuel had the same thought. A glimpse in his direction showed a firm jaw with eyes fixed on the door, avoiding any lingering glances at the empty parking spot. Mark's vehicle had been totaled in the accident, never to return to this garage. The first of many sights waiting to remind them when they walked through the door.

As they reached the door, Mallory realized she had no keys to the house. Samuel pulled his from a pocket and unlocked the door. They entered a mudroom with built-in cubbies along one wall. The first held Samuel's baseball mitt, cap, and sweatshirt. Another housed a silky pink jacket and white fluffy slippers. Jolene's. Mark's golf clubs took up the entire bottom space in another.

Mallory set her box down and returned to the car. She'd make one more trip and leave the rest for later. When she stepped back into the mudroom, Samuel waited. He had removed some sports gear from a fourth cubby.

"You can use this one." He steered her clear of the spaces belonging to Jolene and Mark.

"Thanks. I'll get the rest of my things a little at a time when the rain stops." Would Jolene remind him to take his hat off in the house? Probably, but Mallory wouldn't start that way. "Would you like to show me around?"

He shrugged his shoulders. "I guess." He opened the adjacent door and stated the obvious. "This is the kitchen."

Mallory gazed into a state-of-the-art kitchen with gleaming black granite over white cabinets. Every stainless-steel appliance had been shined to a polished glow. A counter had four stools with an oblong light fixture over it. A fine blanket of dust covered the wood surface of the table in front of a large bay window adorned with a vase of wilted hydrangeas in the center. Fallen petals, tipped with brown, surrounded the base. It struck Mallory that ten days ago, the flowers and Jolene were both very much alive.

Samuel pointed out the dining room, family room, and formal living room, a trip through the pages of a decorating magazine, despite the musty air. The house had been closed up for ten days. She'd need to open some windows in the morning when it was cool outside.

The family room alone showed signs of life. Cozy pillows and throws, a basket of magazines, bookshelves filled with novels and photos. A large screen TV rested on the shelf of an armoire. Mallory spotted a familiar family picture. She remembered sitting for it, cushioned between her teenage sisters with her parents standing behind them. Her smile revealed shiny metal braces. She'd been in the fourth grade.

"Bedrooms are upstairs." Samuel approached the staircase.

"Wait one minute and let me grab a box of my things."

Mallory hurried to the mudroom and picked up a box. Samuel waited at the top of the stairs while she climbed each step, the box resting on her hip. A balcony overlooked the foyer before leading to a hallway of doors. Mallory stopped at the first doorway on the right and peered at a king-sized poster bed, high and filled with plumped pillows.

Samuel reached past her and pulled the door closed.

She looked away, embarrassed. She never had any intention of taking his parents' room.

The next room on the left had a desk, chair, and TV—the only room with some level of disarray. "This is my room. This one and the next one. My mom set it up so I'd have a place to do homework."

Jolene had used two bedrooms with a Jack and Jill bath to set up Samuel's own little suite. Another bathroom accessed from the hallway on the right. The last door beyond it showed signs of being a guestroom.

Samuel pointed. "That can be your room."

"Great. This will be fine." Smaller than the others, it still had more space than her efficiency had offered.

****

Samuel squirreled away upstairs in his two-room suite. Mallory stood in the kitchen and took a deep breath. The journey had begun. She opened the large, double-door refrigerator and took inventory. The bottom freezer had been loaded to capacity.

Mallory had no idea what Samuel liked. She should have asked what he wanted for dinner, but he'd been defensive. He was protecting the life his parents had built, and it would take a while before he let go. He needed time and space to grieve.

Shuffling through the frozen foods, Mallory pulled out a package of ground meat. She wasn't much of a cook, but could manage a passable meatloaf. An hour later, she realized her mistake. It would never thaw in time for dinner. Going back to the freezer, she found a casserole that Jolene had stored. She peered inside, trying to discern the contents. Finally deciding it held a chicken and rice dish, she put it in the oven on a slow bake. Mallory set the timer for forty-five minutes before making another trip to her car.

After unloading two boxes, she checked the casserole, then pulled vegetables from the refrigerator. Mallory eyed them, discarding some that hadn't survived, but found enough salvageable greens to make a salad. Surely Jolene would have set an attractive table. Mallory discarded the dying hydrangeas, moved a decorative candle to the table for a centerpiece, and scrounged the drawers until she located placemats. She set them with the earthenware plates and water glasses filled with crushed ice.

"Samuel, dinner's ready." Mallory hoped her voice carried up the stairs so she wouldn't have to trudge back up.

Minutes later, she heard his door. Samuel came down and took one look at the table before removing the candle. He placed it back on the shelf where it had been located. "I'll just have a sandwich. I don't eat that casserole." He headed toward the refrigerator and pulled out deli meat, cheese, and condiments.

"Samuel, wait. That meat's been around too long. I'll need to clean out the fridge."

He looked closely at the package before tossing it in the trash. Without another word, he reached for a jar of peanut butter and made his sandwich.

Another failure. Mallory attempted a casual chuckle. "Well, we'll have to talk about what you do like. After dinner, let's sit down and I'll make a list."

She saw the familiar shrug as he fixed his sandwich. He reached in a high cupboard and found a bag of potato chips. "Okay if I take this upstairs?" Without waiting for an answer, he was gone. Mallory gave a half-hearted nod to his retreating back, then sat down to eat in silence.

****

Mallory had seen Elliott's co-hosted show a few times since the cable news hired him. Mitch Bouchard, an older and seasoned broadcaster, had the lead, but at twenty-eight years old, it had been a golden opportunity for Elliott. Certainly, his attractive face and blond hair hadn't hurt. Viewers liked to see pretty people, even if the show's purpose was to debate political issues.

Elliott's face waited as close as the remote control. His show aired daily at seven p.m. She could never watch it in Samuel's presence. One look and he would see the resemblance.

Elliott was part of her past. The star football player running for a touchdown as the crowd went crazy. The ace student with defined career goals and a life that included Andrea, the rail-thin debutante who came nowhere close to Elliott's intellect. Yet he remained devoted to her—except for that one evening. That one fight. The night that Mallory longed for, when an angry Andrea left and Elliott finally looked her way.

How foolish she'd been to think it might last. A shattered goal. Don't go there. Instead, she focused on her plan—become the best mother for Samuel despite the circumstances. Elliott Moore would not fill their family room each night at seven. She couldn't allow that distraction.

But Samuel remained upstairs. Mallory sat alone on her sister's sofa, looking at a silent TV. It had been a hard day, following a hard week. Perhaps just one brief peek. She picked up the remote and clicked to the cable news where Elliott Moore appeared.

She didn't care about the political issues they were batting around. She examined his handsome face, more rugged and mature than it had been back then. She gazed at him and recognized the face of her son. So many viewers watched this show. Had anyone else questioned the resemblance?

Chapter 6

The ringing startled Mallory. It was unusual to hear a land-line phone. She'd only had a cell phone since leaving home years ago. She reached for the family room extension, but the tolling sound stopped. Samuel's voice sounded from the kitchen. Mallory lowered the volume of the TV, expecting Samuel to call her at any moment. But as he continued talking, she realized the call must be for him. She heard his clipped responses.

"It's going okay."

"She's been home every day."

"Yeah, but not always what I like. A casserole one day. Meatloaf another."

"No, it hasn't been out of the garage. She only asked for house keys."

Mallory's pulse quickened as adrenaline rushed through her body. Savannah. Her sister was the only one meddlesome enough to question her actions. She stood and stomped to the kitchen, making no attempt at quiet. She wouldn't put Samuel in the middle by confronting him. This wasn't his fault. But she would invade the privacy of Savannah's interrogation. She filled the teakettle and lit the stove before slowly examining the assortment of tea.

Samuel looked from her to the phone. "Uh, do you want to talk to Aunt Mallory? She's here now."

Mallory raised a questioning eyebrow, feigning ignorance about who was on the other end of the call.

"Okay. I'll tell her."

He said good-bye and hung up, but not before Mallory caught the slight rolling of his eyes. It only infuriated her more. Samuel should not be put in this position.

His cheeks wore an embarrassed flush. "Aunt Savannah said to say hi. She said to call her if you need anything."

Mallory pasted a smile on her face. "Thanks, Samuel. Did she have anything else to tell you?"

He hung his head. "No. She was just checking to see if we needed anything."

The teakettle let out a shrill whistle. Mallory poured steaming water over the tea bag, releasing spicy ginger steam.

She bounced her tea bag to hurry the flavor. "Hey, can you sit for a minute? I'd like to talk."

"I guess." Samuel turned and hopped on the high stool.

Mallory pushed her mug to the space beside him. "Can I get you anything?"

"No, thanks."

She stepped from the opposite side of the counter and sat beside him. Samuel stared at the recipe card that she had left sitting out. He picked it up and ran his finger over the list of ingredients, then reached to swipe the corner of his eye where a tear had gathered.

A lump formed in Mallory's throat. "Your mom had beautiful handwriting."

He nodded, still holding the recipe card. "She always put a note in my lunch—every day. When I was little, I pulled it out and showed everyone, or I'd let it sit on the table where kids could see it. When I got older, I was embarrassed. I didn't want kids to think I was a sissy, so I'd hide it. But deep down, it still made me happy. I'd tuck it in my pocket and read it when no one was around."

Samuel set the recipe card down and Mallory examined it. "When I was a kid, I envied your mom's handwriting. All those frilly curls and curves, perfectly sitting on the lined paper. I tried to mimic it, but left-handers have a disadvantage. Mine was always tiny and had a back slant."

A sigh escaped. "When I was in elementary school, your mom tried to teach me cursive—her stylish cursive. I never managed to master it." With a flicker of sadness, Mallory pulled the recipe box closer to refile the card. "I promise you this. I'll protect these recipes. You'll always have them, written in her beautiful script. Someday you can give them to your wife."

They sat in silence for a few moments. Mallory swiveled her stool to face him. "You had a really good mom."

"I know. She's the best." He spoke in the present tense, like speaking past tense would be too painful a reminder that she'd never be back.

"Samuel, I know this has been a hard week. I promise you it's going to get easier. I want you to know I'm doing my best."

He stared at the counter in solemn stillness. "I know."

"There are some things that will help us both while we get adjusted, but we need to work together. Can we do that?"

He shifted his position to catch a glimpse of her. "Like what kind of things?"

She took a deep breath and said a quick prayer. "I'd like to spend a little more time with you, like maybe watching a movie, playing a game, or going out to eat. Anything that would help us to get to know each other better. I know you're almost a teenager, and teens like their space. But maybe just once or twice a week we could set a time for something special."

He absently focused on some unseen speck on the counter, brushing it away. "I guess."

Talking with a twelve-year-old required resilience. It was up to her to lead every conversation. She longed for the day he'd open up with excitement and chatter endlessly.

"And I think it's time for you to get back to your baseball team. I'm sure they can use your help, and it would be good for you to see your friends."

"Yeah, coach called me yesterday."

"Oh, you didn't tell me."

"He said he didn't want to hurry me, but I should let him know when I'm ready."

He spoke a full sentence and even looked at her when he talked. "So, do you think you're ready?"

Samuel fidgeted with the recipe box, his long fingers testing the hinges. "I guess."

"Would you like to call him, or would you like me to call him? Do you know when the next game is?"

"I'll call. The game's on Saturday, but we'll have practice the next two days."

"Great. I'll take you to your practice, and I'll be at your game."

"You don't have to. I can get a ride."

Mallory mocked an upset look. "Please, you've got to give me an excuse to get out of the house."

A tiny grin surfaced. "Okay."

****

A second phone call came a few hours later. Samuel answered again, this time from the family room phone while Mallory unloaded the dishwasher. She braced herself. She didn't want to develop a pattern of eavesdropping on him, but neither could she allow Savannah to poison their budding relationship. Mallory stepped closer to the family room to hear.

Samuel jabbered non-stop about the Atlanta Braves, a game he must have watched from his upstairs TV because he described specific plays and new player stats.

Definitely not Savannah. Mallory's tense shoulders relaxed and she moved back to the dishwasher.

Within a few moments, Samuel called into the kitchen. "Aunt Mallory, can you pick up the phone? Uncle Brady wants to talk to you."

She dried her hands and reached for the phone. "Hello, Brady."

"Hi, Mallory. Samuel sounds good. I just wanted to see how you're doing."

42

"We're making headway. It's going to be a process. Grief can't be rushed." She heard the sigh and remembered that Brady grieved as well. Like her, he was the youngest of three. They both lost their oldest sibling. "How about you, Brady? Are you doing okay? And how are your parents?"

"You said it well. Grief can't be rushed. We all have our moments when it hits us like a crashing boulder. We're holding on to God's promises and doing the best we can do."

Mallory envied that faith. The Carter family went to church but faith never went deep. Church was something you did. A cultural mandate. Her grief was so different from Brady's. Jolene hadn't been part of her life for ten years. She didn't miss her day-to-day presence the same way that everyone else did. Instead, she grieved the lost opportunities.

"I have a project in Raleigh, so I'll be there for a few days later this week. I'd like to stop in to see Samuel, if that's okay."

"Of course. It's always okay." Mallory said the right words, but furrowed her forehead. Samuel had wanted Brady for his guardian. Would Brady's presence compromise her growing relationship with Samuel?

****

When Samuel arrived at his baseball practice, his teammates surrounded him with hugs and high fives. He had lived through every kid's nightmare, losing both of his parents. Mallory stood at the fence to watch. Samuel made a quick dash back to her.

"You don't have to wait. Parents don't stay for practice."

She looked around and saw no adults except the coaches. "Okay. I'll be back at four."

"Oh, and you don't get out of the car. Most moms just pull in and wait."

Mallory gave him a thumbs up. "Got it. Be as invisible as possible." She grinned and watched him sprint back to the field, his Royals T-shirt a contrast to the blond hair. *Most moms just pull in and wait.* She knew it was a generality. He may never think of her that way. Yet her hands clamped to her chest. She couldn't think beyond the word *Mom.*

Mallory used the time to stop at the grocery store. She returned to the field at 3:50, but stayed in the car. Sure enough, other cars pulled in and waited. She'd learn all of the rules, little by little.

A sea of blue shirts bounded toward the parking lot, each finding their car. Samuel opened the passenger door waving a sheet of paper. "We made the playoffs. We'll be traveling to compete with other leagues. They found out last week."

"Traveling?"

"Yeah, but not far. Coach said our farthest game will be in Greensboro."

"That's great." It was the first time that Mallory saw any enthusiasm. This would be good for Samuel. "What's that?" She pointed toward the paper as she began to merge into the exit line.

"A permission slip. You'll have to sign it. Oh, and I'll need to take a copy of my birth certificate."

She gasped, then drew in a breath to cover her reaction. Hearing the words *birth certificate* brought images rushing to her head. Her body still weak and painful from childbirth, the midwife holding the clipboard. Terror gripped her. She didn't know she'd have to sign anything. The midwife explained. "During a hospital birth, the attending physician signs the certificate. For home births, we need signatures of those present."

Mark reached for it, and she watched as he signed it first. He then handed her the pen and clipboard. Her expression must have revealed the terror she felt, because Mark turned pleading eyes her way. The midwife waited. Mallory gripped the pen and held it to the signature line. She would be signing her baby away. But what else could she do? As they stood watching, she willed the pen to move and wrote *Jolene Rae Donaldson* on the form.

Samuel waited for her response. Mallory tried to bring some sense of normalcy to her voice. "I guess they need proof of age. I'll have to look through your mom's files."

"It's in my dad's office. He made a bunch of copies because I always need one when I sign up for a sport."

They rode home in silence. Mallory heard the ding of an incoming text message. She'd be inclined to steal a peek if Samuel weren't in the car, but she had to be a good example.

When she parked the car at home, they entered through the kitchen door off of the deck. Samuel set the form on the counter and went to the cupboard. He pulled out a bag of chips, then went to the refrigerator for a Coke. Mallory fought the urge to correct his choice. Surely Jolene would have limited those snacks. She bit her words back. It had been a good day. She wouldn't ruin it.

Samuel took his snacks upstairs and Mallory remembered the text message. She retrieved her phone and saw Lauren's name.

My mother told me that you moved back to Raleigh to take care of Samuel. Hope you're both adjusting well. Will you be looking for another marketing job? Stay in touch. I still can't get over that gorgeous blond hair.

Chapter 7

The following day, Samuel's team had another practice. After dropping him off, Mallory returned to the house, going directly to Mark's office. A heavy oak lateral file matched the desk. A tug on the drawer told her it was locked. Mark's uncreative hiding place under the pencil tray in the desk drawer made the key easy to locate. Rolling the desk chair close to the file cabinet, she set out to sort through some documents. Mark worked as an accountant for a manufacturing company. His files were meticulous—neat, labeled, and thorough. Everything she'd need regarding Samuel had been filed in one drawer.

A peek in the next drawer showed financial information—banking statements, an IRA, 401K, and annuities. The finances were Savannah's job, but the files remained here. Mallory had wondered more than once how he had amassed enough savings to supply all of Samuel's needs through adulthood. She couldn't resist a quick peek. The IRA and 401K showed minimal balances. The annuities were a different story. Her swift mental math added to a total beyond eighteen million.

Mallory's mouth gaped open. Eighteen million? How was that possible? She leafed through the remaining files, finding her answer. His grandfather bequeathed a sizeable estate to his three grandchildren, Mark, Brady, and Elise. Each received an equal share. The Donaldsons lived in an average middle-class neighborhood in a comfortable home, so much like the Carter's old home. Nothing flashy or extravagant. No one would ever guess they had this level of wealth.

Savannah had control of a small fortune. She had provided Mallory with a spreadsheet delineating every household expense and an allowance for each. Savannah would receive all bills such as utilities, insurance, and Samuel's tuition. Mallory had a food allowance and gas allowance. She also had a fund to use for Samuel's clothing, books, fees, and any other typical needs of a pre-teen. For those items, Mallory was required to provide receipts.

She allotted them with a warning. "Be careful, Mallory Rose. We have to make Samuel's money last."

Mallory slammed the drawer closed a little too forcibly. Savannah handled eighteen million dollars, receiving a percentage for the executor's fee, while Mallory had to clip coupons to make the grocery dollars work. She had no money of her own for clothing or health insurance. When she needed a new pair of shoes, she'd be in trouble.

She'd do it all for Samuel, for the chance to raise him in this second part of childhood. Yet the unfairness rankled her. This wasn't the plan for her life. All because of one night. One party. Elliott and Andrea had always been an item. But when he drank too much, they argued and Andrea left in a temper. Mallory sought her opportunity. She'd been obsessed with Elliott since the ninth grade. She'd console him. Make him forget about Andrea. One night. One stupid mistake.

No, that wasn't right. She could never think of Samuel as a mistake.

Returning to the drawer with Samuel's information, Mallory pulled out the one labeled "Documents – Samuel." Leafing through the file, she found his baptism certificate, social security card, and admission/acceptance documents for the private school. The birth certificate was near the back. With it, Mallory saw three sealed envelopes with Samuel's name. She picked one up but it gave no clue as to the contents. She wanted to open it, but then she might have to explain herself to Savannah. Holding it up to the light showed only a folded piece of paper. She dropped the envelope back in the file and pulled out the birth certificate.

Samuel had been wrong. Multiple copies had not been made. She took it to Mark's printer and chose the copy option. Might as well make a few. She set the number for five copies, then hit print. As the printer sent each copy through, Mallory looked at Jolene's name. The document lacked the feminine flowing script. Instead, each sloppy letter had a backward slant and carried a reminder of the painful moment when she had signed it.

****

Brady said he'd be in town on Tuesday and planned to stop after visiting his job site. Samuel announced his arrival by bounding down the steps and toward the back door. "Uncle Brady's here." Mallory watched Brady coming around from the driveway toward the deck off of the kitchen. He caught Samuel in some wrestling hold and the two of them tugged playfully. His athletic frame contrasted to Samuel's gangly build. Brady released his hold and ruffled Samuel's hair.

Mallory watched, enjoying the momentary happiness on Samuel's face, fighting the stab of jealousy that Brady could make it happen.

"Mallory, how are you?" A scruffy look replaced his clean-cut image from the funeral. Jeans, a tattered T-shirt, and sandals.

Awkwardness hung heavy, like some physical greeting should happen, but a hug wouldn't be appropriate and a handshake was too formal. Brady must not have felt the same hesitation. He closed the distance between them and gave a brief hug. Then stepped away waiting for her answer.

"We're doing well." She looked at Samuel for confirmation. But his eyes were scanning the floor.

"Where's your suitcase?"

"Back at my hotel. I'll be staying there while I'm in town."

"Why?"

"Well," Brady shuffled, looking at Mallory. "The jobsite I'm working on is downtown. I need to be close to my work."

Samuel looked back and forth between Mallory and Brady. "You always stay here. You can be in town in ten minutes from here."

Brady laughed. "Only if I speed."

Samuel turned toward Mallory, his voice louder. "Tell him it's okay to stay here."

Mallory hesitated, not wanting to put Brady on the spot, and not wanting to anger Samuel. "Um, Brady, we can ..."

He held out a hand to stop her, then addressed Samuel. "It's different now, Samuel. Your dad and I were brothers. That made it right for me to stay. I promise I'll visit you any free time I have."

Angry red splotches filled Samuel's cheeks. He fisted his hands, turning his anger toward Mallory. "Tell him he can stay."

She scrambled to ease the tension. "Brady, we have an extra room, and you're more than welcome to stay." Even as she said it, she knew that the only extra room was the master bedroom. Mark and Jolene's room.

"Thank you. The hotel will work better for me this time."

Anxious to change the subject, Mallory hoped to satisfy Samuel's need to hold on to routines. "How about dinner? Will you stay to eat?"

"I'll say yes to that one."

Samuel sulked and went into the family room, plunking heavily onto the sofa. Brady's eyebrows lifted and he turned toward Mallory. "Sorry. I didn't anticipate that."

"His life has changed so much. He's just trying to hold on to old patterns. I think he wants to feel some control to keep things normal."

Brady looked back and forth between Mallory and the back of Samuel's head on the sofa. "I don't like the way he spoke to you. I never heard that level of disrespect from him."

Mallory could see his jutted chin. A furrowed brow. The wheels of decision were turning. But this wasn't Brady's problem to fix. "He's never had so many major changes before. We're working through it."

Brady's look of agitation softened. "You may have more patience for that than I would. See, I told you you'd be good for Samuel." A soft smile formed and his eyes held hers.

His gaze felt far too personal. Mallory looked away. "Why don't you go in and spend some time with him while I run to the grocery store."

****

Mallory's cooking improved daily. She enjoyed fixing meals instead of fretting about her inadequacies. Brady and Samuel played a video game while she tossed a salad to go with the rice and salmon. Playful outbursts came through the doorway. Mallory drank in the delight of the sound. Samuel was healing. It had been three weeks and she could see progress.

"Ten-minute warning, boys. Dinner's almost ready."

Only Brady glanced at her. "Got it." He quickly turned back to the joystick in his hand.

The game wrapped up and they came in, hyped and out of breath. "You two look like you've been out jogging, not just exercising your thumbs."

"It gets the adrenaline going. I almost beat him." Brady's shoulder bumped Samuel.

"Almost? Not even close."

Samuel plopped into a chair at the table, but Brady came over to help. "What can I do?"

"You can pour whatever you'd like to drink."

He eyed the salad. "Samuel, will you pour the drinks? I'll get this."

Brady carried the salad to the table before going to the refrigerator for the salad dressings. When he set them down, he came back and lifted the platter from Mallory's hands. "Let me get that."

When they were seated, Brady held his hands, palms up, to each side of him. Samuel's eyes darted back and forth before joining his hand with his uncle. Mallory watched, then placed her hand in Brady's, holding the other for Samuel.

"You or me, buddy?"

Samuel kept his eyes down. "You."

Brady gave thanks for the food. Shame surged through Mallory as she realized how she had neglected prayer. She'd grown up in a family with roots in church, prayers at meals and bedtime, Sunday school and church each week. She'd been baptized at the age of twelve and said the right things, but had she ever really owned that faith? Most of her prayers had been spoken in desperation. Please help the paycheck to stretch. Please let the A/C work. Please stop the noise that the car is making. Her prayers had been short on the *giving thanks* end. This had been part of Samuel's life, another area where she had failed him. She hadn't been back to church since the funeral.

"Mallory, have you been using the Volvo?"

Her head sprung around defensively. "Of course not. I have my own car."

Brady buttered his roll while he spoke. "I hope you'll use it occasionally. It's not good for cars to sit idle."

Mallory glanced at Samuel. Tightness filled his jaw, giving it a square profile so like his father's. "I'll keep that in mind. I'm not sure what plans Savannah has for the car."

"This salmon is delicious." He finished his bite and sat back. "The way I see it, this shouldn't be Savannah's decision. As Samuel's guardian, you should have access to the car. Yours is older and switching may be in his best interest."

"No." The one word escaped Samuel's mouth with force. "She can't drive that car."

Tension filled the room like a thundercloud ready to burst. Brady set his fork down and turned toward Samuel.

Mallory placed her hand on Brady's arm. "Let's shelve this conversation and enjoy dinner."

He looked back and forth between Samuel and Mallory for a prolonged moment, then picked up his fork and returned to his dinner. The conversation ended, but all possibilities of enjoyment were over. Tension hung heavy while they ate in silence.

When they finished, Samuel headed for the family room. Brady's words stopped him. "Your Aunt Mallory's not the maid. Let's help clean up."

"I've got this, Brady. You two can play another game or something."

He ignored her and began handing dishes to Samuel. They loaded the dishwasher, wiped the table and counter, and put leftovers away quickly. Brady placed both hands on Samuel's shoulders and ushered him back to the table. "Mallory, will you join us?"

By now, Mallory was seething. He had ruined a perfectly good day. Samuel adored his uncle and if she argued with him openly, it would be yet another mark against her. She sat silently as Brady took charge.

"Samuel, I'm disappointed by what I'm hearing. Your aunt has given up a lot to come here and take care of you. Your disrespect is unacceptable."

Samuel stared at the table where his hands rested. Brady tapped the surface in front of him. "Eye contact, please."

Samuel looked up, and Mallory expected to see defiance in his eyes. Instead, she saw embarrassment. He chewed on his lip and a flush covered those ivory cheeks.

"Give me a good reason why your aunt shouldn't drive that car."

Samuel began to lower his head until Brady tapped the table again.

"'Cause it's my mother's car."

Mallory's heart broke at the sadness in his voice.

Brady's may have as well because his tone softened. "I know that, buddy, but your mom doesn't need that car now. Don't you think she'd want your aunt to use it since she's taking care of you?"

"Aunt Savannah said not to give her the car keys."

Brady jerked backwards. "What?" He stretched the word into two syllables, more indignation than question.

"She said Aunt Mallory shouldn't use my mother's car."

Mallory had heard enough. "Samuel, I have no plans to use the car. Would you like me to have your Aunt Savannah take it away from here?"

Brady sat slack-jawed, his mouth open in disbelief. Samuel looked ready to cry.

"I don't know."

Brady leaned back in his chair and ran a hand through his hair. Then he gave his head a shake and sat upright. "Samuel, let the adults work through the decision about what happens to the car. I'll talk with your Aunt Savannah. In the meantime, I'm trusting that you'll treat your Aunt Mallory with respect. Don't let me hear otherwise."

"Yes, sir."

"Now, if you'll excuse us, I'd like to talk with your aunt privately."

"Yes, sir." With that, Samuel went upstairs to his sanctuary.

Mallory watched him climb each step and waited until he was out of earshot. Then she turned toward Brady. "How dare you!"

Her words sent him reeling backward. "Excuse me? I was going to bat for you."

Mallory placed both hands on the table and leaned forward. "I don't need you to go to bat for me. That boy," she pointed toward the steps, "has been through more than you or I can imagine. I've been making progress and you just set us back to square one."

"You think that's progress? Letting him walk all over you, do and say as he pleases? In what world does a twelve-year-old get to make decisions about a $50,000 automobile?"

"The car wasn't an issue until you brought it up."

"Mallory, you said that you're trying to keep routines. Do you seriously think he had no discipline? His parents would never have tolerated the tone of voice he used with you. I hate to be the bearer of bad news, but it's going to get worse before it gets better. That's the nature of a teenager. If you don't rein it in now, you're setting yourself up for trouble."

"So now you're an expert on parenting?" Even as she said it, Mallory recognized some truth in his words. Hadn't she questioned herself about when to correct him? Her anger kept her from admitting it.

"I might not be a parent, but I've been a teenage boy."

"Samuel asked *you* to take guardianship and *you* declined." Her finger jabbed the air toward him with each *you* she spoke. "You had your opportunity. I'll thank you to let me make the decisions. Right or wrong, I'm the one who stepped up to the plate."

Brady leaned back in his chair, his expression impossible to read. The silence stretched between them. Mallory expected anger, but slowly a slight grin formed. "You're a spunky lady. I'll try to keep my big mouth shut."

Her anger softened. She had been quick to attack but he had only been trying to help. Mallory wanted him to understand.

"When I was younger, I went through a difficult time—nothing as painful as Samuel's going through, but a tough time. Everyone made decisions for me. I felt so out of control. I wanted someone to understand, someone to love me through it, to let me work through my mistakes. But they just wanted to fix it. I won't do that to Samuel. He needs some control. He needs to work through his anger and fear."

Brady tilted a puzzled head, but Mallory had no intention of sharing her history. No intention of telling him about her pregnancy—how her mother panicked with the news, afraid of breaking the perfect façade she'd created. Her plan solved everything. No one had to know that her youngest daughter brought her disgrace.

"All right, Mallory. But don't let yourself become his punching bag."

"I can handle a few blows. He'll learn to trust my love. Then this punching bag may become a soft place to land."

He stared at her, unconvinced. "Okay. Truce. But call me if you'd like any advice on teenage boys." Brady stood up to go. "Am I still welcome to see my nephew?"

No. I don't need your take-charge attitude. Mallory bit back her thoughts. "Of course, Brady. I'd never do that to him or to you."

"Thank you." He stepped back, his eyes holding hers.

Chapter 8

Mallory had missed years of Sunday dinners at her parents' home. They'd gathered each week without her. Now that she was here, her mother wasn't. At least not mentally. She phased in and out of reality. The family gatherings may be a comfort for her or another source of stress. Savannah decided that twice a month would be better, and she and Mallory would bring the food. Her father needed the support.

Her dad's arm caught her as she walked through the living room. He pointed toward the back deck. Mallory stepped outside with him, leaving Savannah and her mother in the kitchen.

"Samuel looks like he's coping. How are you doing, Mallory Rose?"

Her dad looked stronger today. The brutal journey of grief brought healing, sometimes at a snail's pace, but each day saw progress. "I'm okay, Dad. Samuel and I are getting to know each other. We're both finding a new normal."

"Good. I want you to think about something. Samuel will be starting back to school and you'll have time on your hands. Have you considered going back to school yourself? Getting that degree you passed up long ago?"

Mallory stared at him. Had he lost his mind? "First of all, I have a GED. I have no SAT scores or entrance criteria. Second, I have no money. I need to think about earning money, not spending it."

"You have your college fund. We never touched it. In fact, it's grown over the years. You could start at the community college. Once you complete that first year, you won't need SATs."

Her college fund? "You mean all these years I've had money and didn't know it? There were many times I could have used a little help."

Her dad pushed his shoulders back, standing straighter. "No, Mallory Rose, *you* don't have money. *I* do. That fund is earmarked for your education. If you never use it for that purpose, it will roll into my retirement fund."

He had paid for Jolene and Savannah to attend college. It felt unfair that she'd get nothing. But she knew her dad well enough not to argue. Could she return to lectures, textbooks, and exams? Would she obsess like she did back in high school? Samuel had to come first. Failing him wasn't an option. But her dad was right. She'd have plenty of free time.

"So, you'd really pay for my college, even now, after all these years?"

"Absolutely. That's one thing your mother insisted on when you girls were born. We set up your college accounts when you were less than a year old. It broke her heart when you didn't go."

Mallory stiffened. It had been her mother pushing the plan. She hid her away like it was the Elizabethan period. Anything to preserve the face of this family. Mallory didn't want to be angry, especially now that her mother had so few memories. But her mother's decision a decade ago shaped the path of her life. She didn't have the college experience, a loss she'd never reclaim. The old familiar resentment rose to the surface. "Well, she didn't exactly make it easy."

Her dad shook his head slowly. "No, Mallory Rose. You changed the course of action, not your mother. When it was all said and done, you could have gone to college. Now you have a second chance. The decision's yours."

He pivoted and went into the house. Mallory watched as he closed the door. She had grown so accustomed to shifting the blame. She didn't like having it turned back on her. Yet his words held truth. They had many conversations about school after Samuel's birth. By that time, a new obsession gripped her—getting away. Was this her year of second chances?

They finished cleaning and packing the leftovers. Mallory and Samuel said good-bye. When they started for home, Samuel turned toward her. "Grandma's getting worse, isn't she?"

Yet another loss for him. "Yes, Samuel. She is. She goes in and out of reality."

"She looked confused like she was trying to remember who I was. Then she said, 'You're Mallory Rose's boy, aren't you?' It was like she forgot about my mom."

Tightness gripped her chest. Was her mother forgetting or remembering? "I'm sorry, Samuel. She still remembers your mom now. She talked about her a little. The sad truth is that Grandma's going to forget all of us eventually. That's what Alzheimer's does. It's the worst kind of thief."

"I used to like going over there. It's really hard now."

"You've got that right. But even when she doesn't remember, we need to do it for Grandpa."

Mallory turned the car following the route that Jolene had always taken. She had fallen into that habit. As they pulled into the driveway, Samuel reminded her. "Did you fill out my permission form? I'll need it when I go to practice."

"Yep. All signed and ready."

"And don't forget my birth certificate."

****

School would begin in three weeks. Samuel would be gone every day from 7:30 until 3:30, and later than that on days he had practice. Mallory needed something to fill those hours. Could she enroll in classes this late? The answer was no for a traditional university, but what about the community college? With one quick phone call she had her answer. She could enroll, but many classes were filled. Samuel still had to come first and school suddenly felt overwhelming. She asked about entering in the second semester. That would give them the adjustment time they needed, and she'd have a plan in place.

Mallory made a compromise. She would ease into it. She'd take two classes starting in January. At the end of that semester, she'd know if she could handle full time. This would be a marathon, not a sprint. She'd spend time at the community college before needing to transfer. The NC State campus was a few miles away. An easy commute.

A goal without a plan was just a daydream. Her dad's words sprang to her mind unbidden. But she had no idea where she wanted the journey to take her. She had always loved the sciences, but could she make that a career? And what branch of science. Chemistry? Biology? Geology? She went to her bedroom and pulled out a box stored in the back of her closet. It held the object of her search. She carefully lifted her neglected telescope. Or astronomy?

Mallory set the telescope aside until after dinner. Samuel was upstairs when she headed outside. She nested the scope on the holder and set it on the deck railing. Dusk had settled over the city with still enough light to make viewing difficult. Nonetheless, Mallory focused the lens and scanned the heavens. She located the ascending moon, but the light sky prohibited viewing surface details. She would have to come back out when a black night sky brought the heavens to life.

Mallory kept watch for the fullness of night. When the sky looked dark enough, she tried again. A low bench allowed her to look up through the PVC pipes that nested together to form the body of the telescope. With her eye pressed against the subjective lens, she slid the nesting pipes slowly, pulling the moon into focus. Divots covered the surface. Some were tiny like a golf ball, while others looked like deep valleys. Black spots marred the gray hue like bruises of a black eye.

Turning the scope away from the moon view, Mallory located Polaris, in the northern sky, and followed the lines of Ursa Major and Ursa Minor. From there, she easily scanned to see Orion.

"What's that?"

The voice startled her and she spun around. Now was as good a time as any to see if he had any enthusiasm for stargazing. "Samuel, come here and take a look."

He sidled over and examined the device. "Is that some kind of telescope?"

"You might say that. I made it myself. Would you like to look?"

He hesitated before pressing his eye to the lens. "What am I looking at?"

"It moved so you may have to readjust. Slide the focus tube." She placed his free hand on the correct spot. "That will provide more clarity. I like to start with Polaris, the North Star. It's true north, so from there, I can easily identify other stars. Move the pipe in small bits until you focus."

She watched his long fingers gently focus the telescope. "Cool. Those are the big and little dippers, aren't they?"

"They are. What else do you want to see?"

"Can you see other planets?"

"Sometimes I can pick up Venus and Mars. This isn't a strong scope, but you can see more details than the naked eye." Mallory scanned the sky looking for the planet Mars. When she found it, she carefully backed away and motioned Samuel to look.

His hand reached for the tube, but Mallory caught it and stopped the motion. "Careful not to bump the scope. That's Mars."

He placed an eye against the viewer and squinted with the other. "Wow. It really is red. You can see lines like continents or something."

"Red dust covers the surface, and since Mars has wind, the dust blows around. You may think those masses are changing shape but you're seeing moving particles. Want to look at the surface of our moon?"

"Yeah." He moved back to allow Mallory to pull the moon into view.

"Cities have what astronomers call light pollution. The man-made lights from cars, streetlights, and buildings inhibits viewing. When I lived at the coast, I would take this to the beach and lay flat on a blanket. Everything's more brilliant there. I called it the ebony sky."

"This is really cool."

Mallory took a big, grateful breath. Finally, there was something they both liked. Something they did together that created a memory. "Do you think you'd like to take a ride to Wrightsville Beach before school starts? You'll see a big difference."

He moved his eye away from the viewer, his face reflecting excitement with her for the first time since she'd brought him home. "Yeah, that'd be cool."

****

A ten- by twelve-inch envelope held Samuel's permission slip and birth certificate so he could play on the traveling team. Mallory reminded him to take it when they were ready to leave for practice.

They buckled seat belts and she started the car. She hadn't noticed Samuel opening the clasp until he spoke.

"I never saw this. My mom always had it sealed in a small envelope." He pulled the birth certificate halfway to scan it without taking the entire permission slip out of the envelope. As he began to close the clasp, something caught his eye and instead, he pulled the document free. "Hey, this isn't my mom's handwriting. I always recognize hers."

The blood rushed from Mallory's head and she realized her foot had let off the accelerator. She took a deep breath and corrected her driving speed before forcing a short laugh from her lips. "She had just given birth. She was probably drugged and lying in bed."

He slid it back in the envelope. "Yeah, you're right."

The sealed envelopes in the file cabinet. She should have known. Still shaken from the close encounter, Mallory dropped Samuel off and returned to the house. She logged onto the internet and priced hotels at Wrightsville Beach. It was a splurge and Savannah might squawk but she had no intention of asking permission. She would put the cost on the charge, record the expense, and turn in her receipt. By the time Savannah found out, they'd be back from the trip.

She booked the room, entering her credit card number just as a text message sounded on her phone. With a rebellious sense of satisfaction, she hit submit and paid for the room before reaching for the phone.

For the second time in an hour, the blood drained from her face. Her heart raced and clammy palms dropped the phone.

Lauren's words were typed at the top of the pictures.

Isn't the resemblance amazing? Two photos appeared: Samuel and Elliott Moore.

Chapter 9

Mallory paced for an hour after receiving Lauren's text message, her mind whirling with the implications. The picture of Elliot had been a current shot from his broadcast, probably lifted from a news article on the internet. His high school picture would have been more incriminating.

Mallory drafted her response three times before she felt satisfied with her words. Keep it short and light. Give no indication that the photos rattled her.

Is that Elliott Moore? I heard he had some news job but I rarely watch cable. Yes, the blond hair is so similar. Hope you and Brandon are doing well.

What accusation did that text message carry? Jolene had been ten years older than Elliott and married. Surely that wasn't Lauren's speculation. Were her thoughts anywhere near the truth?

A knock at the back door startled her. She quickly deleted the text messages, watching the pictures disappear. Brady stood on the other side of the door.

"Brady, come in."

"Hope you don't mind. I didn't expect to be in Raleigh, but they had a glitch at the jobsite and needed me at the last minute." Today he looked less like an architect and more like a construction worker. Jeans, a T-shirt, work boots, and a five-o'clock shadow. His shoulders were broader than his brother's had been, but she saw Mark in his facial features—the prominent brow and aquiline nose. Mallory hadn't felt self-conscious with Brady when Samuel was around. Today, the draw of his eyes made her look away.

She glanced at the clock so her eyes had somewhere to focus other than the scrubby growth that gave him an appealing look. She didn't want to think of Brady that way. "I'm glad you stopped by. Samuel will be happy to see you. I have about ten minutes before I need to go pick him up from practice. I'm not sure what I'm pulling together for dinner, but you're welcome to stay."

"Why don't I pick Samuel up and bring pizza back? I've picked him up before, so I know where to go." He stood akimbo—wide stance and hands on hips.

That suited Mallory very well. She'd had two hours filled with anxiety, first explaining the signature on the birth certificate and then the horrific text message. "Great. Thank you."

"So, tell me how he's doing. How you're both doing together. Are things better?"

There had been enough emotional trauma for one day. She kept her response generic.

"He's doing well. Sometimes I see the sadness wash over him, but overall, he's returning to activities, talking with friends, and we're planning at day at the beach before school starts back."

"And he's being respectful?"

Mallory bristled. She didn't need Brady questioning her decisions. "Yes, he is. I told you I can handle that."

Brady stepped back, his hands lifted, palms out in front of him. "Just checking. You deserve to be treated well. You've done more for him than anyone else was willing to do."

Mallory glanced at the clock, hoping to end this conversation. "I think it's time to get the boy."

Forty-five minutes later, they came in through the mudroom. The aroma of hot pizza reached the kitchen before Samuel and Brady.

Brady put the pizza on the table, and Samuel reached for plates. Mallory stopped him. "You might like to try some soap and water before getting those. I shudder to think of what you pick up at the ballfield." He laughed easily and turned on the hot water. Samuel was a different kid with Brady around. They'd come a long way, but

Mallory held on to the hope that one day he'd be that comfortable with her.

"Have you taught your aunt to play Ticket to Ride yet?"

Mallory's head sprung up. "What's Ticket to Ride?"

"It's a game Uncle Brady likes."

"Uncle Brady and Samuel," he corrected.

"Yeah, my dad liked it, too." Samuel spoke the words casually, without the heaviness of grief.

Mallory had seen a stack of games on a shelf in the family room. "Well, I'm game for a game, but you'll have to teach me."

An hour later, they were adding up points and destinations and found Mallory to be the victor.

Samuel bagged his trains. "Beginner's luck."

Mallory defended her win. "I'd call it strategic planning."

Brady folded the now empty board. "I could have been harder on you."

Mallory tossed a coaster at him. "Don't even think of telling me you let me win."

Is this what families looked like? She had few memories of laughter in her parents' home and certainly the last ten years of her life looked nothing like this. She envisioned Jolene and Mark living as family. Laughing, loving, making memories, and Mallory knew she'd made the right decision. She'd given Samuel into a home filled with love. It had cost her dearly, but it was right.

"I hear you're headed to the beach?"

Samuel's face lit up. "Yeah, you should see what Aunt Mallory has. It's a telescope she made herself." Samuel's enthusiastic response brought Mallory a smile.

Brady's eyes widened. "No kidding?"

"An amateur prototype. A science project I made years ago. I'm a wannabe astronomer."

"I'm impressed."

"Don't be. It's just two nesting PVC pipes, lenses, and a magnifying glass. The trick is to get the right diameter concave-convex lens and correct focal length."

He laughed. "There. You've already lost me."

"Can we show him?" Samuel's enthusiasm warmed Mallory's heart. Brady wasn't the only one who could bring joy to Samuel's face.

"Sure, but it's not dark enough to see anything. Let me go get it."

When she returned to the kitchen with her telescope, Samuel was telling Brady that Mars had wind and sand and really did look red. She set the telescope on the kitchen table.

"See, it's pretty unprofessional but does the job. You can make one with mailing tubes instead of PVC. I've even seen them made with a Pringles can, although they provide less focal length."

Brady examined the telescope. "If you ever need mailing tubes, I can get you plenty."

"Oh, I guess you could, Mr. Architect."

He placed his eye on the eyepiece, testing it, although he'd see nothing inside the room. "Unfortunately, I can't stay until dark. I'm driving back to Charlotte tonight. I have an early morning meeting."

Samuel looked back and forth between their faces. "Can Uncle Brady come to the beach with us?" He turned toward Brady. "That's why we're going, to look at the sky without light pollution."

"Light pollution?" Brady gave an amused smile. "I see you've learned a lot."

"Can you come?"

Brady turned toward her. "Mallory?"

Was he really asking to join them? Mallory wanted that time with Samuel. When Brady was around, she became a third wheel. Yet if she gave any indication that she didn't want him, the whole trip would be ruined. Samuel wouldn't forgive her.

"Of course. But we have to stay over so we can stargaze late at night."

"No problem. I'll get my own room."

"Can I stay in the room with Uncle Brady?"

Mallory saw her get-away falling apart before her eyes. "Well, I've booked a two-room suite so you'd have some privacy."

Brady took one final look at the telescope. "Why don't you change that? It'll save you some money. I'll get a room with two beds for Samuel and me."

He had all the answers. Mallory smiled a plastic smile. "Great."

****

Sunday dinner at her parents would be burgers and sides. Savannah and Richard planned to grill and Mallory prepared a salad and dessert.

She had to prevent Samuel from mentioning their beach trip to his Aunt Savannah. She hated the thought of asking him to keep quiet like it was some forbidden fruit. And she certainly didn't want to teach him to lie.

Her answer came from Samuel himself.

"Do I have to go? It's hard to visit with Grandma, and Aunt Savannah sometimes lets her kids miss Sunday dinner."

Mallory saw her solution but hesitated. "I'm not comfortable leaving you alone for that long."

"I can go across the street to Jake's. I talked with him earlier and he said we could hang out. His folks are home."

"Tell you what, Samuel. I don't want you always missing. It's too important to Grandpa. But I suppose I could let you miss every once in a while. Promise me you won't ask each time we have a dinner planned."

"I won't. I'll go to the next one."

"Okay. You're sure it's good with Jake's folks?"

"Yeah, you want to call them?"

"No, but I'll walk over with you. I'm going to take them some of these brownies."

"Thanks, Aunt Mallory." He stood there awkwardly for a moment, then put his lanky arms around her shoulders and gave her a hug.

****

When Mallory took the brownies to Jake's house, she got tied up talking for a little too long. She arrived at her parents about twenty minutes late. As she entered the kitchen, Savannah gave a deliberate glance at the clock. Mallory ignored her. She wouldn't defend herself to her sister. Instead, she walked to the table where her mother sat and gave her a hug.

"Hey, Mom. How are you doing today?"

"Mallory Rose, you're thin as a twig. I hope to see you eating well today."

Was her mother fully coherent, or was she seeing her as a teenager? At least she knew who Mallory was. "I will, Mom. Promise."

Savannah sliced tomatoes onto a paper plate. "Where's Samuel?"

"He had some plans with a friend today."

Her eyebrows shot up. "What friend? You know Dad likes to see him."

Mallory stiffened. Questioned at every turn. What did she ever do to Savannah to incur her constant wrath? Well, she could dish it out too.

"Where's Spencer today? Doesn't Dad like to see him? And what about Hannah? I haven't seen her here the last two dinners."

Savannah stopped slicing and turned toward Mallory, one hand on her hip, the other still wielding a serrated knife. "Maybe not, but they've been here the past ten years while you were lounging on the beach."

They stared each other down, waiting to see who would blink first. Mallory swung around and exited the kitchen.

Her father and Richard were outside near the grill, the scent of burgers sizzling above the charcoal. Zeke and Colin played in the backyard. Mallory stood alone for a few minutes, feeling once again like an outsider in her own family.

She straightened her shoulders and stepped through the sliding patio door. "Hi Dad. Richard. Smells good. Is there anything I can do?"

"They might need help in the kitchen."

"I checked. They're good. Are we eating out here? I can gather a few more chairs."

Within moments, the burgers filled a platter and Savannah carried the condiments to the picnic table. Mallory returned to the kitchen for her salad and found her mother trying to turn the knob on the back door.

"Where are you going, Mom? We're going to go this way. To the picnic table."

Her eyes darted back and forth while her hand still fidgeted with the doorknob. She fingered the lock like it perplexed her. Mallory set the salad down and went to her mother.

"Come with me, Mom. I'll take you out." She draped her arm across her mother's shoulders and led her outside. She seated her at the table and reached for a bottle of water, opening it and placing it before her. "You sit here for just a minute and we'll get food on the table."

Mallory hurried back for the salad and brownies. She turned to find Savannah directly behind her. "She's in la la land. I told Dad it's time to think about a memory care facility, but he won't budge. He'll listen if you tell him."

Mallory's eyebrows rose. "Why do you think he'd listen to me?"

She released an exasperated sigh. "Oh, come on, Mallory Rose. He'll do anything you ask."

Where had that come from? "First of all, that's not true. Secondly, I'm not convinced it's time. She still has lucid moments."

"Less and less of them all the time. Have you even noticed how weary he is? Do you want him to have a heart attack?"

Mallory stepped back, her mouth dropping open. "Savannah, that was a terrible thing to say. We're all trying our best to get through this."

She pursed her lips tightly and cast an accusatory look toward Mallory. "Do you even know what stress can do to a person?"

No use entering a sparring battle of words. Especially since she had no idea what Savannah's issues were. Mallory again turned and left her sister in the kitchen.

Everyone talked during dinner except her mother and sister. The kids jabbered playfully. Her dad and Richard talked sports and politics. Mallory shared her news that she had spoken to admissions and planned to enroll for the spring semester. Her dad patted her arm. "Good girl." Savannah sat silent and rigid, her lips pressed into a tight line.

When the kitchen was cleaned and everyone had left, Mallory walked down the hall and stepped into her old bedroom, the same room that Samuel had briefly used.

She had stayed with Jolene and Mark for the final four months of her pregnancy. Her parents moved to this house weeks before Samuel was born. A week after giving birth, Mallory left Jolene's and moved in with her parents, leaving her baby behind. This had been her room for the worst time of her life. Standing here, all of the memories flooded back. By then, she had turned seventeen. She had no friends in Raleigh. No school. No future.

And she had no baby.

He was nestled into the designer nursery at her sister's home.

Her mother had been so enamored with Jolene's baby that, at times, she appeared to have forgotten whose child he really was. Dinners were spent talking about Spencer, Hannah, and Samuel. Samuel's first step. Spencer's first day at school. The pretty dress she found for Hannah. They were a big, happy family, and Mallory was the piece to the jigsaw puzzle that kept the image from being perfect. The big flaw right in the center that didn't seem to fit.

She stepped further into the room and looked at the bookshelf where her old books remained. Books she had loved as a teen. Ones she could lose herself in when she wanted to disappear. *Anne of Green Gables. Summer of My German Soldier. Jacob Have I Loved. A Wrinkle in Time. The Chronicles of Narnia.*

Mallory caressed the familiar spines. Stacked on the bottom shelf were taller books, picture books from her childhood. There among them were her high school yearbooks, grades 9–11. The glaring absence was a senior yearbook. She reached for her eleventh-grade yearbook. Even twelve years later, Mallory did what she'd always done—opened to Elliott's picture. They tried to maintain some semblance of friendship after their one night together. She closed her eyes as the memories rushed back.

He had waited for her in the hallway Monday morning. When Mallory saw him, her pulse sped up. Would he steal another kiss? Ask her out? But he wore no smile, no gleam in his eyes. Instead, he came filled with regret. "I need to apologize for Saturday night. I had too much to drink. I never meant for … for things to happen. Andrea and I made up. It was a stupid fight."

Humiliation washed over her as she attempted to act nonchalant, like he hadn't just delivered a punch to her gut. "Oh, that. Yeah, I guess we let things get outta hand."

He wasn't quite as remorseful three months later when she told him she was pregnant. "You're going to get rid of it, aren't you? I'll get the money."

When her parents devised their plan, she told Elliott she took care of the problem. Let him think whatever he wished. Two months after that, she disappeared without a word to anyone. She'd been shuffled off to Raleigh to live with Jolene.

Footsteps thumped behind her and she turned to see her dad.

He stepped across the threshold into her old room. "Those are yours. You can take them if you like."

She fanned through the pages one last time before closing the book. "Sometimes looking back is too hard."

"They're not all bad memories, Mallory Rose. Those pages will hold lots of good reminiscing, if you let them."

She replaced it on the shelf. "Like reading a good book only to find it ends a few chapters short."

Her childhood was incomplete. A song without a coda, music ending unexpectedly, leaving the listener unfulfilled.

They stood in silence for a moment. With a heavy sigh, he shook his head. "You can't change the past, but you can decide what you want to focus on. There are lots of memories in those books."

When her father left, Mallory closed the door and picked up a yearbook. Tenth grade. Her first year as a cheerleader. She found the page and scanned pictures, recalling the excitement generated by high school boys and a pigskin ball. The cheering crowd, the band, the announcers—they all worked together to create an emotion. An aura of triumph or defeat.

She cheered for her school, but mostly for Elliott, the star running back. Everyone expected him to earn a football scholarship to a division one school, but Elliott had goals more far-reaching than sports. He chose Syracuse for their broadcast journalism program. There had been little question about acceptance. He and Mallory competed with a half dozen students in line for valedictorian.

Her tenth-grade year meant this was Brady's senior year. She turned to the senior pictures and found him. His facial features had matured since they'd attended Jolene and Mark's wedding. She saw the emergence of the man she knew today, yet adolescent qualities remained. He wore no glasses for the picture. It was fair to say he'd grown up well, more handsome as an adult than a teen. The teenager looking at her from the pages of a yearbook had suddenly become a major player in her life story. Samuel connected them all—Mallory, Elliott, and Brady.

Mallory scanned his bio, landing on the senior superlative attributed him by his classmates. *Most likely to become your boss.* That brought a snicker, remembering Brady's ease in taking over with Samuel. It also held insight regarding hard work and responsibility. Another paragraph told of Brady's role in co-founding the STEM club. It had become the new buzzword in education. The interdisciplinary approach of science, technology, engineering, and mathematics. Mallory intended to register for STEM in her senior year—the year that never happened.

She slammed the book closed. Three high achievers. Elliott and Brady went on to accomplish something with their lives. How did Mallory fall so far off-track?

Chapter 10

Brady called to tell her that he wasn't able to get free until late afternoon. He suggested Mallory and Samuel head to the coast in the morning as planned. He would be there in time to meet them for dinner. His phone call rekindled Mallory's hope that the time away would help her relationship with Samuel. The hug he gave her on Sunday remained imprinted on her heart. She enjoyed time with Brady but longed for any opportunity for Samuel to draw closer to her. This would be the best of both worlds—time alone with Samuel followed by a fun evening with the three of them.

While Samuel finished a bowl of cereal and fresh strawberries, Mallory loaded the car. They didn't pack much for the overnight, but she fixed a cooler with water, sodas, and snacks. Her telescope had been carefully boxed and padded with bubble wrap so it wouldn't bounce around.

"Anytime you're ready. Everything's in the car."

"Okay. Five minutes." With that, he sprinted upstairs and sounds of him brushing his teeth drifted down. He bounded down the steps, hopping over the bottom two and landing with a thud, the most excited she had seen him.

They locked the house and went to her little Civic. When she turned the key, nothing happened, not even a grind. Mallory tried again with the same result.

"Good grief, I think my battery's dead. I'll have to call Triple A and have it changed before we can leave. Sorry."

His shoulders dropped visibly. "How long will that take?"

"Hopefully we should get out of here before noon."

He hesitated, looking back toward the house. "I guess we could take my mom's car."

Mallory gave him a long, hard look. "I thought you didn't want anyone driving it."

He shrugged. "It's okay. She wouldn't care."

"We can do that, but only if you're sure."

"Yeah." With that, he hopped out and began moving their bags to the Volvo.

Mallory put a hand on his shoulder. "Let me try it first. It hasn't been started in a while." That's when she remembered she had no key. In fact, she had never seen a key to this car anywhere in the house. When she stopped in her steps, Samuel seemed to read her mind.

"I'll get the keys. They're in my mom's jewelry box." He ran into the house and came back a few minutes later jiggling them. "You don't use the key to start it but you have to have them with you. It's a push button start."

"Okay. Let me see if it turns over." Mallory stepped on the brake and pushed the ignition button. The engine immediately sprang to life, then purred like a kitten, glad to finally be awakened. "Sounds good. Let's pack it up."

Within minutes, they were on their way, bright sunshine glinting off of the silver hood of the Volvo. "Before your Uncle Brady comes, I'll take you into Wilmington and show you where I lived and worked. You'll like the boardwalk along the Cape Fear River."

"That's a weird name. Why do they call it Cape Fear?"

"Yeah. Sounds like somewhere people wouldn't want to go. But it is beautiful. The name goes back to the sixteenth century when an explorer's ship became embayed—that's a sailing term for getting stuck in a recess of a bay. The crew feared they would wreck trying to free the boat so they named it Cape Fear."

"Cool. Will we get to see where they got stuck?"

"Not this visit. After we see Historic Wilmington, we'll head to Wrightsville Beach."

"I was there once with my parents. Usually we went to Myrtle, but one time we tried Wrightsville."

A lump rose, lodging in Mallory's ribcage, making it hard to breathe. They had been vacationing fifteen minutes away and never thought to call her. She spent hours on that beach. How awkward would that have been if she had run into them? Even as she nursed her disappointment, she realized the truth. It had been her choice to remove herself. Jolene didn't call her because she had honored Mallory's decision.

She chased away her self-pity. "Did you get into Wilmington when you were there?"

"I don't think so. It's been a few years."

"There's a really neat model train museum. If you're interested, we can find some time."

"Maybe tomorrow when Uncle Brady's with us."

"Sounds like a plan."

When they arrived in Wilmington, Mallory turned up a narrow side street, pointing out some of the historic homes. Sidewalks were thick with tourists going in and out of shops. She made the turn onto Third Street and slowed as she approached the antebellum home that housed her former apartment.

"That's where I lived. I had an attic apartment on the third floor. No elevator. It wasn't bad unless I was carrying groceries." With little traffic, she slowed to a crawl and cut her eyes upward to her former window.

"Cool."

"Maybe, but it's a shame what they did to that beautiful home. It was done before the Historic Preservation Committee set strict guidelines. Maybe someday it will be restored."

A car vacated a parking space just as they neared it. Mallory took advantage of the opportunity and eased the car to the curb, marveling at how smooth the Volvo handled. "It's an easy walk from here."

They went into a couple stores before reaching the Cape Fear Emporium. When they stepped in the door, a three-deep line of customers waited at the register where Chloe chatted easily with a smile that seemed permanently etched on her face. At the sound of the wind chimes, she looked up to call out a welcome, and her eyes widened. "Well, hello there, my friend. Look around and I'll be with you in a moment."

She motioned to a teenager with a nametag. "Kristen, work the register for a few." She turned the task over and hurried to where they waited, catching Mallory in a big hug. "And you must be Samuel." She held out a hand to shake his, her forearm layered with bangle bracelets. "Your Aunt Mallory is the best helper I've ever had. I bet she's taking good care of you."

"Yes, ma'am."

"It's your lucky day because we have free ice cream. Go back and pick whatever you want and tell them Chloe sent you."

"Thank you, ma'am." He looked hesitant and Mallory realized they hadn't had lunch. "Go ahead if you want some. It's an ice cream for lunch kind of day."

They watched as he strode to the back of the store, his long legs producing distance quickly. Chloe shook her head, her face fixed with a big smile. "Umm hmm. He's one handsome young man. And so polite. How you been, girl?"

"I'm doing okay. Samuel's such a joy. It's been hard watching him miss his parents, but he's healing slowly."

"Well, you'd be good medicine for anyone. Keep up the fine work."

They chatted for a few minutes before Samuel appeared with his ice cream. "Looks like the store's booming. I better let you get back to your customers."

"You bring that boy around here anytime."

Chloe went back to the register and Mallory motioned Samuel to the door. They sat on a bench in front of the store.

"She's nice." Samuel spoke while licking the melting drips of chocolate.

"Yes, she is. Very nice. When you're done, we can head to the beach. There's a place to buy a sandwich if you're still hungry."

They arrived at the beach around noon. The hot summertime typically saw crowds in the morning. Many tourists would spend the hottest afternoon hours basking in air conditioning or their hotel pools. Samuel and Mallory toted their beach umbrella and chairs down the narrow path that led to the ocean. Mallory knew the pattern of tides and set up far enough that the water wouldn't reach them.

Samuel had worn swim trunks under his clothes. He kicked off his shoes, then shed his shirt and pants. Mallory wore her suit under her clothing, but didn't plan to swim. She was satisfied to sit in her shorts and tank top, watching Samuel have fun.

"Sunscreen." She held up the spray. "Your fair skin will burn red as a ripe tomato." She sprayed his back and he took the spray, covering his torso, arms and legs. Then he sprayed some into his hand and rubbed it on his face, avoiding his eyes.

He handed the bottle back. "I'm experienced with sunscreen. My mom made sure of that."

Mallory applied a quick spray to her arms and legs, then pulled her sunhat on to protect her face. "Samuel, how good of a swimmer are you?"

"I do okay."

"The ocean's different than a swimming pool. I'd like you to stay close to shore."

"I know. My dad told me you have to respect the ocean's power."

A male voice sounded from behind her. "Good words of advice."

She spun around at the familiar tone. "Liam." She stood from her chair and he reached to hug her shoulder. "This is my nephew, Samuel. I guess you heard I moved."

"Yeah, Chloe told me."

"Sorry I didn't say good-bye. It all happened so quickly."

Samuel had been eyeing the bright yellow board that Liam held at his side. Liam didn't miss the eagerness any more than she did. "Do you surf? I've got another board."

A fleeting panic hit Mallory. "I don't think that's a good idea."

Samuel's eyes turned defiant. "Why not? I told you I can swim."

"Yes, but I told you I want you close to the shore."

Liam shook his head of honey-toned hair. It had grown past the nape of his neck, almost long enough to tie in a ponytail. "He'll be fine. I'll be out there with him."

Please," Samuel pleaded.

Mallory turned toward Liam. "Beginner waves, Liam. I mean it. Don't take him out any farther." She turned toward Samuel. "You stay on the closest waves and don't go far from Liam. Do you know what to do when you wipe out? Because you *will* wipe out. When you do, it's easy to get confused about what direction you're going."

"Mallory, chill. Let the boy have some fun. I'll teach him whatever he needs to know." He grinned. "Just like I taught you."

Her eyes softened at the memory. But this was Samuel. She shot Liam her sternest look. "You watch my boy. Every minute."

Sitting down was no longer an option. Mallory stood at the water's edge while Liam brought his extra board. "Mine's acrylic. You take the soft top. They're better for beginners. Take a few minutes to practice on dry ground. It'll help you get the feel for balancing."

Samuel stood on the board with his hands extended wide. He moved with the wobbles, staying on each time. Liam smiled, nodding his approval. "Let's roll, Sam."

Mallory started to correct him, but they were already paddling out. She cupped her hands and hollered. "Far enough."

They either didn't hear or chose not to.

Samuel rode his first wave sitting on the board. By the second wave, he managed to rise to his feet before it came and carried him in. He spilled from the board before reaching shore. Mallory lurched forward, about to run in when Samuel came up laughing. Liam had grabbed the loose board and returned it to Samuel. They high-fived and paddled out for the next one. Mallory's tension began to wane as she watched Samuel's fun. Liam had taught her to surf ten years ago. She remembered the exhilaration and suddenly wanted to strip to her bathing suit and join them. If she'd had a board, she might have done so.

Samuel rode a wave that carried him directly to where she stood, standing as it grazed the sand. He jumped from the board and wrapped wet arms around her. Her dry clothes were splotched with saltwater from his hug. "Thank you, Aunt Mallory. You're the best."

At four o'clock, they checked into her hotel room and got cleaned up. They waited for Brady's call to meet for dinner. Exhausted from the water and heat, Samuel dozed on her bed. Mallory sat on the desk chair and watched him sleep, her heart filled with wonder.

Grateful tears formed as she watched the rise and fall of his chest. Her son. She was finally part of his life. All the years of following her sister's Facebook, of watching him grow in pictures. Years of regret now melted into gratitude. Her heart swelled with love. As she watched him sleep, her eyelids grew heavy. They drifted closed with her head leaning against the hard wall. A musical tone from her phone startled her awake. Brady's name appeared.

"I'm almost there. The GPS says fifteen minutes. Did you pick a place for dinner?"

Mallory gave him the name and address. Samuel woke up when the phone rang. His hair had dried to a tangled haystack. Within five minutes, they were ready. They slid into their sandals and left to get a table.

Despite the sunscreen, a pinkish hue covered Samuel's face and arms. Mallory had fared better with her wide-brimmed sunhat. The plank ceiling of the open-air dining protected them from further exposure. Large fans kept the air circulating, masking the heat.

Brady arrived, navigating around the close tables. He stepped behind Samuel, putting him in a playful choke hold and rubbed knuckles through his hair. "Looks like you took on the sun and lost."

Samuel wriggled out of the hold, anxious to blurt out his news. "I surfed today. It was the coolest thing. Aunt Mallory's friend had an extra board and taught me how to use it."

Brady's head jerked back as he sent an incredulous look her way.

"Oh, don't worry. Aunt Mallory was a pit bull. She stood at the water and never took her eyes off me. I didn't dare go out too far.

She'd have called the Coast Guard." Samuel's eyes sparkled in a teasing way she hadn't seen before.

Mallory remained silent, not sure if Brady, like Savannah, questioned her judgment. Then she watched a grin form. "No kidding. Wish I could have been there. Did you get some video?"

Mallory relaxed a little. "No, that would have meant taking my eyes off him to grab my phone. Seriously, he only rode the closest waves."

Brady reached and squeezed her hand. "You don't have to defend yourself. I know you'll always take care of Samuel." He removed his hand and picked up his menu, keeping his eyes on the selections while he spoke. "So, who's your friend?"

Samuel answered for her. "Liam. He's really cool. He has this bright yellow board with zig-zag designs like lightning. I didn't use it. He gave me the soft top." He leaned in like a conspirator. "That's a surfing term for a beginner's board."

Brady glanced from the menu. "I didn't know you had plans or I wouldn't have horned-in on your trip."

"No, I had no plans except stargazing tonight. We just ran into Liam. He's an old friend."

"You're sure I'm not in the way?"

What was he suggesting? If Samuel hadn't been sitting there, Mallory would have quizzed him. "Of course not. I told you I had no other plans."

After eating dinner, they headed back to the hotel so Brady could check in and change from his work clothes. Samuel wanted to ride with his uncle, which suited Mallory. She could use a few quiet minutes. As they approached the car, Brady's brows rose when he saw the Volvo. He grinned and gave her an approving nod.

A few hours later, darkness covered the area. They walked the path that led to a deserted beach. Mallory smoothed out the sand where she would spread the blanket, her lantern illuminating the spot.

Pointing to the light, Samuel questioned her. "I thought we didn't want light?"

"Ha. Once I came without a lantern and couldn't find my way off the beach. I was terrified. You don't make that mistake twice. We'll turn it off when we're ready."

Brady sat on the blanket with his knees bent in front of him. "I'm psyched. I've never done this. What am I looking for?"

"We should be able to see the Perseids, a meteor shower that occurs every August. I checked the dates and we're within the range of possibility. I can usually focus in to view the Milky Way. It will look like an arch of lights. Then we can try to locate some of the planets. And of course, we'll see constellations."

They settled on the blanket and Mallory turned off the lantern, throwing them into an inky black expanse. The only sound came from the lapping waves as they peaked and hit the shore. Mallory focused the telescope and slowly spanned the universe. "There it is." Handing it off to Samuel, she directed his gaze. "You should be able to see the meteor shower. It looks like a mass of fireballs that form like ribbons in the sky."

"Wow. There's a million of them."

Mallory laughed, wishing she could see his expression. "Actually, there should be between fifty and one hundred."

Brady stared in the same direction. "I can see them with a naked eye."

"Yes, but you can catch far more detail with the scope. Samuel, pass it to your uncle."

He handed it over. Brady peered through the eyepiece and gasped. "I can actually see pieces of rock. It almost looks like the rock is on fire."

They passed the telescope back to Mallory. Once again, she spanned the vastness.

"Here's a double-double star."

"What's that?" Samuel asked it as he reached for the telescope. Mallory turned his head slightly so he could view the sight.

"This one's called Epsilon Lyrae. A double star is when there are two stars together. It looks kind of like one that has split in half. But a double-double is four stars where it looks like two that have each split. They're called star systems. Alpha Centauri is a well-known triple. Three stars in one cluster."

"Cool." Samuel again passed the device to Brady.

He searched but couldn't find the split star. Mallory crawled around Samuel to help Brady locate Epsilon Lyrae. She reached for the scope and her hand met his in the darkness. She was about to pull back when his hand covered hers, moving it to the focus tube. "You lead. I'll follow." His hand rested ever so slightly on hers, sending shivers that had nothing to do with the coolness of evening. Had anyone been on this deserted beach, they appeared to be a family of three. What would that be like? Would she ever know that level of belonging?

She willed her mind to stay on task. After a few turns of the focus tube, the double-double appeared.

They spent the next hour looking at planets and constellations. Excitement bubbled up in Mallory. Up until now, Liam had been the only one who had shown interest. Samuel and Brady were awed by the wonders of the sky, just as Mallory had always been.

The heavens declare the glory of God. The verse sprang to her mind. She hadn't thought of it in years. The wide expanse of the universe had always made her feel small and alone. But tonight, she felt like the double star, like she somehow belonged.

Chapter 11

A shopping bag filled with clothes that no longer fit Samuel's rapidly growing body had been placed in the mudroom for Savannah to pick up. She had informed Mallory that Jolene had always sent her the clothing that Samuel had outgrown before school started. Mallory noticed that she carefully avoided the word hand-me-downs. She expected Savannah any minute.

The family room clock sounded nine chimes. Mallory heard Samuel moving around upstairs. He'd need to shift his sleep patterns since school started in a week. She'd try to ease him into a seven a.m. start to his day.

Mallory sat at the kitchen table, making a list. She planned to take Samuel to shop for his school supplies. A slamming car door announced Savannah's arrival. Mallory watched from the back door as Zeke and Colin raced to the house. Savannah's youngest boys were always bursting with energy. Mallory knew they frazzled their mother while she made every attempt to maintain a poised front.

Zeke had been born two years after Samuel. Mallory never made the trip to Charlotte to see him as an infant. It was too painful to watch a mother holding her newborn. When Savannah announced her fifth pregnancy, they sold their Charlotte home and moved to Raleigh. Colin was born weeks after they moved into their little ranch. By then, Mallory had relocated to Wilmington. Before the accident, she'd only seen her nephews twice.

Mallory opened the back door and they rushed inside while Savannah attempted to keep up. "Wipe your shoes on the mat, boys."

Her call was futile. They were in the kitchen eyeing the muffins on the counter like they hadn't eaten in a week.

Mallory laughed. "Wait for your mother. If she says okay, we'll have muffins and milk."

Instead of waiting, they rushed to the back door, almost knocking Savannah off her feet. "Can we have muffins? Aunt Mallory Rose said we could."

Savannah shot Mallory a cold look. "Well, how can I say no if she already told you yes?"

"I didn't say yes. I said to ask your mother."

Savannah pointed them to the table. "Sit like gentlemen. Mind your manners."

"Yes, ma'am." They spoke in unison.

Their attempt at manners lasted about three seconds before they were kicking each other under the table and snatching each other's napkins.

Mallory poured milk and set a blueberry muffin on each plate before going to the mudroom to retrieve the shopping bag. Savannah followed her, glancing around the mudroom. Her gaze stopped on the cubbies that still held Jolene's fluffy slippers and pink jacket. Her eyes instantly moistened.

"It's a wonder she wasn't wearing this." Her hand brushed the silky fabric. "She almost always had it on. I guess we need to clean their things out."

Mallory resisted the urge to hug her. Savannah and Jolene had been so close. It was easy to forget that Savannah grieved. "I'm not sure Samuel's ready for that. He seems to want to hold on to things. To keep things the way they were as much as possible."

Her sister sighed deeply. "I'm not sure any of us are ready for that."

Savannah looked through the window of the door leading to the garage. Mallory saw her stiffen as she examined the car. Somehow, she knew it had been moved. Had she memorized the exact position?

The nostalgia of moments ago fled, clipped words replacing the melancholy. "Who's been driving Jolene Rae's car?" Her arms crossed over her chest.

"My battery died and I used it briefly." Why did she feel like a teenager talking her way out of a punishment?

"I see. Does Samuel know?"

"Samuel suggested it." Mallory immediately regretted her words. She didn't want Savannah badgering him. "Listen, Savannah. I'm Samuel's legal guardian and the car belongs to him. This has nothing to do with you."

"Technically, it does. Samuel's estate is in trust and I'm the executor. I'll have the car moved into storage." With that, she pivoted and began to leave.

"No."

Savannah swung around to face her sister. "What do you mean— no? It's not your decision."

"You're not taking the car away. Samuel likes to keep things the way they were. At least as much as he's able." She sighed. "I don't want to argue with you. My own car has been repaired, and I don't plan on taking the Volvo for my own, but I'm Samuel's guardian. I have to have a voice in these decisions."

Silence hung between their locked eyes. Savannah gave no response, just marched back to the kitchen. "Let's go, boys. Thank your aunt for the muffins."

"But I'm not ..."

"I said, let's go. Now."

Colin stuffed the rest of the muffin in his mouth, leaving a trail of crumbs. His shoe hit a fallen blueberry, creating a path of blue stains leading to the back door.

Mallory watched as the boys climbed into the backseat. Savannah closed the car door more forcibly than necessary. Why would Jolene's car upset her that much? From what she saw in the file cabinet, there would be no problem buying Samuel a car in four years.

Mallory stood at the window and watched them turn onto the road. *What's the real issue here, Savannah?*

"Are they gone?"

Samuel's voice shook her out of her contemplation. He stood behind her. "Hey, good morning, sleepyhead. Yes, they're gone. Were you hiding out?"

"Yeah. The last time they were here, they came upstairs and trashed my room."

"They're just energetic little boys."

"Yeah, that's what my mom always said. She was always pretty nice to them, like you were."

Had he been listening from the top of the stairs? "They'll grow up. Hopefully they'll put that energy to good use."

"Aunt Savannah gets mad but always tries not to show it."

Mallory raised one eyebrow. "You're very astute."

Samuel took a bowl from the cupboard and reached for a box of cereal. "I hope astute means something good."

"Of course, it does. Would I say something about you that wasn't good?"

A crooked smile formed. "Probably not."

Mallory motioned toward the plate on the counter. "I made muffins."

"I heard. Did they leave any or did they gobble the whole plate?"

"Be nice, Samuel. They're your cousins."

He found the tray of muffins and moved one to his plate. "You sound like my mom."

Mallory stared at him. He'd just compared her to the person he loved more than anyone. "Thank you, Samuel. That's a high compliment."

He so easily talked about his mother today. Not like the times when any mention of her fed his grief.

"Yeah, but you won't like what my dad said."

"What was that?"

"He whispered it when Mom couldn't hear. He said," Samuel leaned in conspiratorially and whispered. "She should have stopped after three."

Mallory laughed before covering her ears. "I'll pretend I didn't hear that." She reached for a wad of paper towels and a spray cleaner to erase the blueberry trail.

****

Samuel was across the street with Jake while Mallory filled out forms for his first day back to school. She didn't recognize the number of the caller when her cell phone rang.

"Hello?"

"Mallory, it's Lauren. I'm in Raleigh, and I'm hoping we can have lunch?"

Mallory grimaced. How could she graciously get out of it? "What brings you to Raleigh?"

"A teachers' conference. Keeping up with CEUs for my certificate. I'm not teaching, but if I don't do the continuing ed credits, I'll lose my cert."

"I'd love to have lunch, but unfortunately, my day is filled. Perhaps the next time you're in town."

"It's a three-day conference. Any day is fine. If lunch doesn't work, we can meet for coffee, or better yet, I can stop in and visit. See where you're living and meet Samuel."

A ripple of fear came with that last suggestion. Lunch was sounding better. She did a mental check of Samuel's schedule. He'd be gone tomorrow on an outing with his team.

"How about tomorrow? I'll meet you downtown. Do you know where Donovan's Deli is?"

"I'll find it. Noon?"

"Sure. See you then."

****

Donovan's Deli was packed by noon. Mallory walked from the parking lot, noting the people waiting to be seated. She prepared to join the throng but caught a movement from a nearby booth. Lauren waved her over.

As Mallory reached the booth, Lauren stood and hugged her. "I was afraid it would be crowded, so I came early."

They sat and picked up the menus that the server left with Lauren. "I haven't eaten here, but I heard it's good."

"It must be to draw this crowd." Lauren laid her menu down. "I've had plenty of time to look."

Mallory made a quick choice and laid hers down as well. "Shouldn't you be at the conference? How did you have time to get here early?"

"Ha. I could care less about the conference. I only care about the CEUs. They don't know who's there and who's not. I'll get credit because I registered and signed in."

Some things never changed. That was the big difference between them in high school. Mallory cared about learning. Lauren cared about grades so she wouldn't get in trouble with her dad. If she could skip a class and copy notes, she never hesitated.

They ordered and ate their salads while Lauren filled the conversation by updating Mallory on everyone from school. Where they went to college. Where they were working. Who they married. "Looks like Elliott Moore hit it big. "

Mallory stabbed a tomato and lifted it to her mouth, making every attempt to feign disinterest. "I heard. I don't watch much TV."

"You know he married Andrea?"

"I figured. They were always an item. So, tell me about Brandon. How old did you say he is?"

Lauren leaned back, a knowing look in her eyes. Mallory chastised herself. The subject change was too abrupt and came at the wrong time.

"He's three. He'll turn four right before Christmas." She leaned forward, elbows on the table with her chin resting on her cupped hands. "Jeremy and I have been married five years in September. We want a short get-away, nothing fancy or expensive. Have you been to Wrightsville Beach? I know it's in the Wilmington area."

Finally, a safe subject. "Sure. Many times. It would make a nice weekend trip."

"Good. I looked online and saw some hotels. Is there a bed and breakfast you would recommend? Those are so much nicer."

"Yes, and there's a nice lodge with rustic rooms or private cabins. It's not on the beach, but an easy drive. It's called Lindell's Lodge."

"Ohh, that sounds sweet." She dug in her handbag and pulled out a small tablet and pen. "Here." Lauren passed them across the table. "Write that down for me. I'll never remember. And maybe you could jot down any must-see attractions."

"Sure." Mallory wrote the name of the lodge as well as Airlie Gardens and Bellamy Mansion. "Here are two places I like, but check out their tourism site. There are tons of things to see."

Lauren tucked the tablet in a pocket of her handbag. "Thanks. I guess I better get back to the conference, just to show my face." She motioned to the waitress for the check.

They left Donovan's Deli, passing diners waiting to be seated. Lauren hugged Mallory. "Call me sometime. Let's stay in touch."

"Sure. Enjoy your trip to Wilmington." Mallory watched Lauren saunter down the street, her arms swinging in rhythm with the traffic. Something felt off about this whole lunch meeting. Lauren had barely touched her salad. Why the abrupt ending? And what mother didn't want to talk about her three-year-old?

Chapter 12

Jolene had taken a picture of Samuel on the first day of school each year since kindergarten. Mallory downloaded them from Facebook and kept them in her picture album. That tradition wouldn't die with Jolene. Her sister probably had a high-end camera, but Mallory's cell phone would have to do.

She snapped a picture of Samuel with his backpack and another as he entered the school bus. He paused to say something to the driver. Then with a brief wave of his hand, he disappeared from sight. Mallory scanned the seats for one more glimpse. The blinking lights of the school bus stopped as it started in motion, leaving a scent of diesel behind.

What would Elliott think of their son? Would his heart swell with love as Mallory's did? Would he agree that she had made the right decision? A cold chill sent shivers down her arms. What if she had done as he'd asked? That thought was too horrific to entertain.

****

Samuel had been in school for a week, long enough for Mallory to realize she needed something to fill those hours. Why not research career options so she could plot out a schedule for her coursework before the spring semester? But today, she'd tackle the laundry. She went upstairs to gather Samuel's clothes.

As she came down with a laundry basket perched on her hip, the doorbell sounded. The front door got very little use. She peeked out the window to see a man carrying a portfolio. A salesman? Soliciting was prohibited in this neighborhood. Mallory eased the door open a few inches. "Can I help you?"

"Yes, are you Mallory Rose Carter?"

"Yes, I am." He looked vaguely familiar but she couldn't place him.

"Legal guardian of Samuel Donaldson?"

"Yes." This must be someone from Social Services. She opened the door wider. "How can I help you?"

"Is there somewhere we can talk?"

He seemed perfectly safe, but Mallory hesitated inviting him in. She was ready to ask for ID when he motioned toward the porch chairs.

"This would be fine."

She stepped out and closed the door behind her. "I didn't catch your name."

"Jeremy. Jeremy Edwards. I believe you know my wife, Lauren."

All defenses went on high alert. Mallory fought the urge to run back inside and lock the door between them. She sat straight up in her chair. "Yes, I know Lauren."

He slowly unzipped the portfolio and removed a burgundy file folder. Then he pulled out a digital recorder from its Velcro holder. "May I record?"

Mallory stood up. "No, you may not. What's the purpose of your visit?"

"Please have a seat. I'm working on a story and would like to give you an opportunity to confirm or refute the information that I've uncovered." He turned a copy of Samuel's birth certificate so she could see it.

A pounding drum beat in her ears. Her knees weakened and she eased herself into the chair.

He shuffled through the other pages. "It seems that the signature on this birth certificate has been forged." He turned two copies of Jolene's signature for her to see. A marriage certificate and a high school term paper.

Mallory gave him the same response she had given to Samuel. "She had just given birth. Of course, her signature would be sloppier."

Wordlessly, he turned a photocopy of the information that she had given Lauren at lunch, the bed and breakfast, Airlie Gardens, and Bellamy Mansion. Jeremy held them side by side along with a copy of Mallory's GED application.

"Where did you get these documents?"

"Journalists always have sources. Everything you say is on the record. This report is from a forensic handwriting expert." He retrieved a document with columns of data. "You can read over his findings, but this ..."—he pointed toward the closing paragraph—"... shows his summation. The confidence level is 99.04% that this was signed by the same person who signed your GED application."

Rage built up inside of Mallory. With one quick movement, she swiped the folder from his hands.

His lips turned up in a smirk. "You can keep those. They're your copies."

"You're making inferences that you know nothing about. Even if they had any merit, which they don't, there's no story here. No one would care enough for a newspaper to print it."

He reached into his portfolio and retrieved another paper. As he turned it over, the faces of Samuel and Elliott sat side by side. "I think they'll care."

Mallory felt the blood rush from her head, certain that it left her pallor white. "The *Charlotte Post* would never print that."

"Oh, you're correct on that. I have a source in Washington that will print it."

Washington? Not the *Washington Post*. Suddenly it came to her. "A scandal magazine." She spit the words out through tight lips.

"Well, that's not a very complimentary term. Let's say, a magazine that prints what people love to read."

Mallory stood. "This meeting's over."

"Can you confirm that you falsified the birth certificate of a son you had with Elliott Moore?"

She turned toward the door. "No comment."

Mallory reached for the doorknob, but stopped short at his next words. "Thank you. I'll see Elliott Moore tomorrow. We'll see if he has a comment."

She would plead and beg, if it would help. But a man who could do this would have no compassion. Her shaking hand barely managed to turn the doorknob. She opened it and stepped inside without looking back. Once the door closed, she locked the deadbolt, then leaned against the wall for support. Mallory took deep breaths trying to regain her composure.

Elliott. She had imagined the scene so many times. Imagined looking into his face and telling him they had a son. In her fairy-tale imagination, he'd pull her into his arms and thank her for not listening to him. He'd profess his love and they'd ride off into some happily-ever-after world.

She never imagined he'd find out from a low-life reporter looking to make a name and a few bucks by spreading gossip. She couldn't let that happen. She had to tell him.

Mallory paced in circles trying to form a plan. She could call him, but this kind of news needed a face-to-face encounter. She couldn't take Samuel, but where could she leave him? Certainly not with Savannah. Was it feasible to drive to Washington and back in a day? And how in the world would she arrange a meeting?

Twelve years ago, her dad pressed her to tell him the father's name. Mallory had remained silent, determined not to tell anyone it was Elliott. Now her parents would find out. They'd never read that type of magazine, but if the story gained momentum, if it hit the news, Dad would know. All that secrecy twelve years ago and now it had the potential to become nationwide news. Would Alzheimer's protect her mother from understanding?

Brady. Perhaps he would come and stay overnight. She couldn't tell him why. But then, if it became news, he'd find out. Everyone would. Mallory lowered herself to the sofa in the family room and cried.

When she calmed her panic, Mallory took a moment to look at the documents. A professional letterhead had the company name of the handwriting expert. With great detail, the report analyzed size, spacing, slant, and pressure. Columns of letters were graphed to compare the letters that were connected and disconnected, wide and narrow loops, and pointed tops. It was irrefutable.

She lifted the photocopy of her scribbled information about Wilmington attractions. Lauren. Her best friend for years. Did she harbor that much bitterness over Mallory's departure? Enough to ruin three lives? The lunch had been a set-up. An intentional ruse to get her handwriting. Mallory and Elliott may deserve that, but Samuel didn't. He was the victim of Lauren's revenge. She surely knew the havoc that she'd set in motion.

Her hands shook as she picked up the receiver of the landline. "Brady, it's Mallory."

"Hi, Mallory. Something wrong? You sound upset."

Mallory attempted to laugh it off. "No, just trying to make some plans. Hey, I have a favor to ask."

"Sure. What do you need?"

"I need someone to stay with Samuel, hopefully tonight. I have to make a short trip and don't want to ask my parents."

"Actually, I'm on the road right now headed in your direction. I have to meet with the project manager. I'll be happy to stay there tonight."

"Thanks, Brady. I can have Samuel go to the neighbor's until you're finished."

"No need. My meeting's tomorrow. I'm headed in today to check things out before the meeting. I had planned to call you later."

"I'm leaving in about an hour. I'll leave the door unlocked from the garage. Do you have the garage keycode?"

"Yep. I'm all set."

Mallory sat down to write a note to Samuel explaining that she needed to see a friend about something important.

I'm so sorry I couldn't wait until after school. I'm sure you won't be too disappointed to find your Uncle Brady here.

She left the note with his name on it, written in her sloppy left-handed back slant. She hated her handwriting more each day.

****

Mallory hastily threw an overnight bag in her car and set her GPS with the address she found on the internet. She didn't know where else to go except the cable station's headquarters. She'd start there.

Heading east to reach I-95, Mallory rehearsed her words, trying to anticipate Elliott's reaction. She wasn't naïve enough to expect her fairy tale would become a reality. Unless something drastically changed in twelve years, two things were always of utmost importance to Elliott—career and Andrea. This news could damage both. Besides, years ago she gave up those destructive thoughts.

They probably lived in a beautiful home in suburban DC with two perfect children. Elliott would have planned his life down to the letter, leaving nothing to chance.

If Samuel found out, he'd want to meet his father. Elliott could say no and break his heart. Samuel didn't need another heartache.

Or worse, what if Elliott wanted custody? Mallory would have to fight him on that. But would she win? He could offer a two-parent home, a livable income. She had no job and no skills. And, if it got that far, she'd be a criminal. She could get jail time. The courts just might grant Elliott custody and Andrea would become his stepmother.

The thought almost convinced Mallory to turn her car around, but then Jeremy Edwards would be the bearer of that news. Fresh tears clouded her vision. She swiped them away as she took the on-ramp to I-95 heading north to the nation's capital.

Chapter 13

Cars on the Capital Beltway moved bumper to bumper while continually weaving in and out of lanes. Every muscle in Mallory's body tensed as she gripped the steering wheel, keeping up with traffic. Time was of the essence. Her car clock glowed a bright 3:10 and her GPS told her she was ten minutes from her destination.

As she moved into the right lane and eased off at the ramp, Mallory exhaled, releasing some of the tension of the trip. Her mind transitioned to the task at hand. That carried a different kind of stress, the same kind that she had twelve years ago as she sat on the bleachers waiting for Elliott. She had asked him to meet her and to come alone. She'd never forget his response when she said she was pregnant.

"And you think it's mine?" The question stung like a slap on the cheek.

"Of course, it's yours. There's been no one else."

Today she faced the same type of questions. How would he receive the news that he had a son? Of course, he'd be angry. She knew exactly what he had assumed twelve years ago when she told him she'd handled it.

Obeying the GPS, Mallory turned left and the brick-and-glass architecture of the cable news offices appeared. The curved building was fronted by a courtyard where tall fountain grass and fall mums adorned the benched areas. She pulled into the parking garage across the street and snaked her way up to the fourth level before an open parking space appeared.

At 3:55 she came to the heavy glass double doors at the visitor's entrance. Mallory squared her shoulders and pulled the door open with a confidence she didn't feel. Act like she belonged here, confident and collected. She had to get past the receptionist.

"Hello. I'm here to see Elliott Moore."

One arched brow rose above a heavily mascaraed eye. "Do you have an appointment?" Her garnet lipstick was fresh and moist, reminding Mallory that she wore none.

"No, but I'm sure he'll see me if you just tell him my name."

The receptionist reached to a shelf beside her desk and retrieved a trifold pamphlet. She handed it across the desk with a practiced smile. "There are a number of ways that you can reach any of our journalists. This lists their social media sites and e-mail specific for their listeners. If you contact him through one of these avenues, you should hear back within forty-eight hours."

Mallory held the pamphlet. "No, you don't understand. I'm a personal friend of Elliott's. He'll want to see me."

The smile disappeared. "Well, if you're a friend, I suggest you call or e-mail him personally." Her hand crept close to the telephone on her desk.

The last thing Mallory wanted was for her to call security. She took a step back from the desk. "I'll do that. I'm not sure where I put my contact information. I don't imagine you can help me with that?"

"No, ma'am. Just with the numbers in the pamphlet."

Mallory needed a new plan. She gripped the trifold. "Thank you." Turning around, she took in the sight of the atrium. She had walked right through it, but missed it in her haste to reach the receptionist. Visitors wandered around the marble floor, looking at the displays. Pictures lined the walls showing reporters with world leaders, famous athletes, sites of natural disasters. All stories they had covered. Gold trophies and award plaques were displayed behind glass. Mallory meandered around, giving herself time to think. She saw the narrow hallway to the restrooms and visited the ladies' room.

Leaving the restroom, she found herself alone in the hall. Mallory didn't clearly think out her plan. It was more of an impulsive action.

A glance in both directions showed no one in sight and no cameras in the hallway. She reached and pulled the red handle on the wall, setting off the fire alarm.

****

Within moments, sirens from the approaching fire trucks joined the screaming alarm from inside the building. Their horns blared an accusation. She had committed another crime. The sidewalk filled with frenzied people as everyone evacuated. Mallory wandered through the crowds, glancing behind her to see if anyone hunted her down. The left side of the building appeared to be less tourists and more professional staff.

As she continued to weave her way through the crowd, Mallory saw Mitch Bouchard's face. He spoke with a small circle of people, and someone facing away from her had Elliott's light blond hair, a shade she never forgot despite the twelve years since she'd last seen him. With deliberate steps, she hurried toward them, wanting to see the face.

Before she reached the circle, they dispersed and he turned toward her. She was another in the mass of people until she touched his shoulder. "Elliott?"

It took a moment before recognition hit him. His mouth gaped open, then formed a smile. "Mallory! Mallory Rose Carter. What brings you to this neck of the woods?"

They moved through the crowd to a spot where they wouldn't be jostled. "Actually, I'm here to see you. I need to talk with you about something." A shiver ran up her spine. "Something important."

She watched his expression, but he gave no sign of alarm or concern.

"Looks like you caught us at a bad time. We aren't typically huddled in front of the building with firetrucks everywhere. Let's get coffee. There's a bistro about a block from here."

Freed from the crowd, they walked down the sidewalk, his easy stride a contrast to her rigid limbs. It was too late to second guess her decision.

Elliott's voice shifted to compassion. "I heard about your sister. My mother called me when it happened. I'm so sorry. That had to be a tough one."

She kept pace, not looking at him as they walked. "It was. Still is."

"So, I hear your family is in Raleigh. Is that where you're living, too?"

Mallory answered his small talk, dread filling her as they entered the coffee shop.

Elliott held the door for her. "Why don't you find us a table? I'll get the coffee. What would you like?"

"A vanilla latte would be nice." Wrapping her hands around a warm cup might calm her nerves. When he moved to the counter, Mallory looked for a seat that would offer some privacy. No privacy existed in the crowded venue, but she chose a small, round table nearer to the back.

Elliott found her and set both coffees on the table. He smiled and shook his head. "I can't believe it's you. Remember tutoring me in advanced chem? I think I'm indebted to you."

She had almost forgotten those days when they met at the library. Elliott excelled in any subjects dealing with language. The sciences challenged him. He came to Mallory for help. Those were the days when she pined after him. Before the night in the backseat of his car.

"Yes, I do." Is that the memory that stood out in his mind? She remembered so much more than tutoring.

"So, what's important enough to bring you to our nation's capital? I don't imagine you're here with a political inside tip for me." He flashed her the smile that the cameras loved.

Mallory managed a forced chuckle. "No, I'm not into politics."

"A job?"

Her heart pounded faster with each moment of delay. "No, Elliott. I don't need a job." She closed her eyes and gathered her strength. If she didn't tell him, Jeremy Edwards would. "Elliott, I've done something that could get me in trouble, and it can hurt you. Hurt your career."

He lowered his coffee cup and sat up straighter, waiting, all traces of the smile gone.

She exhaled a deep breath, trying to calm the drumming of her heart. "I have a son. Our son." Mallory stopped there and allowed that to register. Elliott stiffened his squared jaw, a muscle twitching.

"Our son? First of all, that's never been confirmed. Secondly, you said you got rid of it."

She shuddered at the impersonal reference. "Him, Elliott. Not *it*. And I never told you I got rid of the baby. I told you I took care of things. And I did. I made plans and left you to have the future you wanted."

"So why now? Are you looking for money?" Gone was the smiling, reminiscing Elliott.

Mallory stiffened, remembering the last time he'd offered her money. "No. I didn't want your money then, and I don't want it now." She paused, dreading the next part. "I falsified the birth certificate and a journalist found out."

"Falsified, as in not mentioning my name? That happens all the time."

"No. Falsified as in naming the mother as Jolene Rae. I posed as her for the midwife, and allowed them to raise Samuel. Her husband, Mark, signed as the father. Samuel has no idea they're not his biological parents."

He gaped at her, his mouth slackening. "How in the world did you fool a midwife? Don't they check ID?"

"Jolene and I shared the same hair color and facial features. Her driver's license was five years old." The memory darted through Mallory's mind. Handing over the driver's license. The nauseating moments as the midwife examined the ID. The surge of relief when she handed it back with no questions.

Elliott sat back, dragging his hand across his face, emitting a low whistle. "So, what's this reporter want? He can't know of any connection to me unless you told someone. And let me remind you that paternity is still in question."

Mallory folded her arms across her chest, a protective barrier. She lifted her chin and glared at him. He had a sharp edge that hadn't been there in high school. The result of power and position? Gone were any feelings she had once harbored. One thing hadn't changed. Elliott remained self-protective at all costs. She reached into her handbag and pulled out the glossy 3x5 photo that had been taken shortly before Jolene's accident. She set it before him.

Time froze as Elliott stared at Samuel's picture. Finally, he picked it up, examining it through softened eyes. He set it back on the table. "I guess we don't need a paternity test."

Silence hung heavily between them. "So, what's with this reporter? What does he want?"

"I suspect he wants money and fame. Do you remember Jeremy Edwards? He was a year ahead of us in high school?"

Elliott nodded silently.

"He works for the *Charlotte Post*. I told him a reputable paper wouldn't touch this, and he said he has a source in DC that will print it."

"Yellow journalism." His ice blue eyes were mere slits as he practically spewed out the words.

"I don't know that term."

"A scandal press. Unresearched, sensationalized. It's a gossip tabloid. When's he planning to run this?"

"He's coming to see you tomorrow. I had to get here first."

He glanced at the picture, then turned steely eyes toward her. "You should have been here twelve years ago."

Mallory spoke through the tight line of her lips. "Maybe. But you made your wishes clear. You said I'd be on my own."

"What does this mean for you?"

"Possible five years and up to ten thousand dollars." Giving voice to the possibility heightened her tension.

Elliott planted his elbows on the table, his head propped against his hand, a distant look in his eyes. He abruptly pushed his chair back. "I'll call you tomorrow. I need to get this stopped." He slid a business card toward her, turning it to the empty back side. "Give me your number."

How would he stop it? What about Samuel? Would he tell Andrea? Mallory wanted to ask questions but his brusque dismissal made her pause. She remained quiet, jotting her number on his card.

When she set the pen down, Elliott picked up the phone number and stuck it in a pocket. "I'll call you tomorrow." He stood and took two steps from the table.

She hopped to her feet. "Elliott, wait. I need a way to reach you." Memories of the receptionist surfaced.

He dug another business card out, scribbled something on the back, and pushed it toward her. "That's my cell phone."

He turned to walk away, but stopped, pivoted, and picked up Samuel's picture. He tucked it in his jacket and marched toward the news center. Mallory watched until he turned the corner toward his office building, only then remembering that her car was directly across from him. She walked the same path that he'd just taken, then crossed the street to the parking garage.

Mallory drove out of the metro area toward Alexandria, and got a cheap hotel room. She'd wake before rush hour hit and head home to wait for Elliott's call. Could he stop this from hitting the news?

Chapter 14

Thankfully, Samuel was in school and Brady had left the house when Mallory returned home. She peeked in the garage to see if Savannah had taken the car away as she threatened. The Volvo remained in its place. Perhaps she needed to be more outspoken, to stand up to her sister more often.

The day passed with Mallory checking her phone constantly, even though it never left her side.

The squeal of school bus brakes announced Samuel's return. Mallory had hoped to hear from Elliott before school ended, but no call came. She regretted not calling Samuel last evening, but she hadn't trusted her voice to sound composed. Instead, they shared a dialogue of text messages, just to make sure Brady had arrived. She stood in the open doorway, watching him saunter up the sidewalk. When he looked her way, she gave a brief wave of one hand.

He came in and flung the heavy bookbag onto the kitchen table with a thud. "You're home."

"I'm sorry about yesterday. It was unexpected, but I had to see an old friend."

He scanned the kitchen looking for a snack, choosing an apple from the fruit bowl. "That's cool. Chloe?"

It took her a minute to understand. "No, not Chloe. How was school today?"

"Same." He bit into the apple. "Same every day. So, did you see Liam?" Samuel fluttered his eyes in a suggestive manner.

Mallory crossed her arms, but couldn't suppress a slight smile. "No, and what's that supposed to mean?"

"Just checking. That's good if it wasn't Liam cause Uncle Brady thinks you're a hottie."

This time there was no smile. Mallory's sharp voice told Samuel she meant business. "Samuel! That's an inappropriate comment. Besides, it's not true."

A pink blush climbed Samuel's neck and reached his ivory cheeks. "Sorry. But I do think it's true."

"Sit." Mallory pointed to the kitchen chair. She continued when they were both seated. "Samuel, your uncle loves you. He comes here to see you, not me. There is absolutely nothing going on, not even beneath the surface. Do you understand?" Even as she said it, memories of the beach surfaced. His hand resting on hers as they focused the telescope. Times when his eyes searched her with an intensity that made her turn away.

"Yeah, I guess."

"I guess doesn't sound convincing. Is there something he said that makes you think that?"

"No, it's just … well, I see the way he looks at you, especially when you're not watching." He squirmed in his seat, avoiding eye contact.

Mallory touched his hand. "Honey, your uncle's a nice man. He's sensitive to people around him. I'm certain he wants to make sure that we're all right. That everything's going well. Please don't read anything else into that."

"Okay. Sorry."

Afternoon turned into evening with no word from Elliott. A surreal normalcy filled the time. Dinner. Homework. TV. Mallory's stomach had formed a knot when the call finally came after nine o'clock. Mallory kept her voice low, even though Samuel was holed away upstairs.

"Mallory, it's taken care of. This won't hit the press."

How was that possible? The determined journalist who sat on her porch yesterday morning wouldn't be that easily deterred.

"How, Elliott? And how can we be sure?"

He also kept his voice low. Mallory imagined him in a closed-door office or stepping out onto a patio where Andrea couldn't hear.

"It seems that Mr. Edwards has a few vices. His own skeletons. A little reminder helped to change his mind."

She certainly believed that the low-rung journalist had vices, but she needed assurance. "Like what? I need to know."

"A mistress, gambling debts, and cocaine." He rattled off the list. "Our investigators only had one day. Who knows what they'd uncover given more time?"

Mallory closed her eyes and sank into the kitchen chair. Was it really over? She'd just dodged a poison bullet. "Thank you, Elliott."

A pause stretched between them. His voice lowered to a whisper. "I want to see him."

Her mind had been so focused on Jeremy Edwards that it took a moment to shift gears. Samuel. He wanted to see Samuel.

Nausea sprang to her stomach. "Elliott, please don't do this. That boy's been through enough. He lost the only parents he knew, and he's still grieving. I can't turn his world upside down again."

"I've lost twelve years already. I won't lose another."

She rose from her chair, rage replacing the relief that had come moments ago. "*You've* lost twelve years? *You* who wanted to abort him? Remember, I gave him life, and I lost the same twelve years."

His voice remained calm. He was accustomed to debating volatile issues and keeping his words even. "No, Mallory Rose. He was part of your family. Even if your sister raised him, you had the chance to watch him grow."

He didn't know how she'd exiled herself. How bitterness sent her running away. "I didn't. I moved away to make it easier on everyone. I didn't really know him until Jolene died."

"Well, that was your choice. I had no choice. You robbed me of mine."

"That was my sacrifice. That's what parents do. They sacrifice to do what's best for their child. Elliott, I'm begging you, please don't do this to Samuel."

She heard him sigh, and it kindled her hope.

"Andrea and I are working with a fertility specialist. We've tried for years, and it's not happening. Samuel may be the only child I'll ever have. I watch my wife cry every time she sees a baby. I see pain in her eyes when we're around friends with kids. How can I walk away now that I know I have a son?"

Panic shot through her sending a tremor to the hand holding her phone. Would he want Samuel? Would she have to fight for him? "You walk away because it's the right thing for him. That's what I did twelve years ago."

The silence lasted so long that she wondered if he'd hung up.

"Elliott?"

"I'm here. Okay, Mal, let's do it like this. I want to meet him, but he doesn't have to know I'm his father. We'll give him some time to adjust, maybe a few months, then tell him."

"Have you looked at his picture? It's like looking in a mirror. You can't meet him. He'll know. Everyone around you will know."

"If you'd have been honest with me twelve years ago everything would be different. Lies breed more lies, Mallory Rose. I intend to see my son. Work out a time and place. I'll call you tomorrow."

"Wait." She would never rest until this was settled. "Can we start by you seeing him, but not necessarily meeting him? He's playing baseball. You could come to Raleigh and see a game."

Mallory held her breath, waiting for his answer.

"All right. We'll do it your way. For now."

She breathed a sigh of relief. "Thank you, Elliott."

They hung up after exchanging e-mails and her promise to send him Samuel's schedule.

****

Mallory procrastinated, trying to buy a little time. Perhaps Elliott would change his mind, decide that it would be too upsetting for Andrea. After all, it meant that she'd learn of his unfaithfulness.

Saturday morning, a text message came. The swish sound woke her at 7:00. Elliott. She opened the text message.

Mallory, I'm still waiting for Samuel's schedule. I'm not a patient man. Please send it immediately or I'll make other arrangements to see my son.

Ignoring the problem wasn't going to work. If he made other arrangements, they'd certainly be less amenable. Samuel would sleep for at least another hour, probably more. Mallory went to the kitchen where Samuel's schedule hung on the side of the refrigerator. She snapped a picture and attached it to an e-mail. Before sending, Mallory typed a message. *The schedule is attached. His shirt number is twelve. Please remember that this is just a chance to see him, not to meet him. We'll talk about that when the time is right.*

She paused over the SEND key, but decided to add a nice closure. Anything to create a cooperative relationship. *Thank you for agreeing to do it this way. I'm grateful.*

She hit SEND, then hurried to put the schedule back in place before Samuel woke.

****

Mallory parked her car in the driveway of her parents' house for Sunday dinner. As she and Samuel made their way toward the front door, Richard pulled into the driveway behind her. All five kids exited the minivan. Zeke and Colin raced ahead to reach the door first.

Savannah carried the cake for their dad's birthday. Mallory watched Spencer signing to Lillian, followed by her reply. Their movements were so rapid and graceful, a language they comfortably shared. Mallory needed to learn some sign language so she could communicate with her niece. Perhaps the community college offered a class. She'd be able to fit in a few electives.

Mallory held the door, greeting each one as they entered. The clear lid on the cakepan showed frosty white icing with letters spelling out a birthday message. "Beautiful cake, Savannah. Did you make it?"

She narrowed her eyes as she answered. "They don't use stoneware cake pans at the bakery. Of course, I made it."

Richard placed a protective arm around her shoulder. As they passed through the doorway, Mallory held her hands, palms up, in question. She had no idea what her sister's problem was.

The temperature had dropped, so her dad and Richard began the task of inserting a board into the dining room table, creating space for eleven people to eat. Mallory tossed a salad while Savannah turned her attention to the two pans of lasagna that sizzled in the oven.

Wearing oven mitts, she placed each one on a trivet. "I brought these over yesterday so Dad could pop them in the oven." Her head craned around the kitchen. "Where's Mother?"

Mallory glanced through the wide archway to the dining room. "Must be in her bedroom. I'll get her." She walked through the living room where Richard and her father sat talking. A peek out the sliding doors to the patio showed Zeke and Colin running around in the backyard. Mallory continued down the hall and saw the teens and Samuel gathered in her old bedroom.

Her parent's bedroom door was closed. Rapping her knuckles on the door, she called, "Mom?" No answer came. "Mom?" She called again while turning the knob.

The door opened revealing an empty room. She swiveled and hurried down the hallway. "Dad, where's Mom? She's not in her room."

Her father leapt from the sofa to the front door. He turned the knob to find it locked. He hurried to the back door. It, also, was locked. "Lorraine," he called, running toward the sliding patio door. Mallory was steps behind him. The gate stood wide open.

Everyone sprang into action. Samuel, Spencer, Hannah, and Lillian ran from the bedroom to see what the commotion was about. Richard and Mallory started for the gate, stopping her father. "Stay here with the boys, Dad. We can go faster. She can't be far."

Savannah lost all composure as she grabbed an arm of each of the younger boys. "Who opened that gate? You know you're not allowed to touch the locks."

Colin started crying while Zeke adamantly denied touching the gate.

"Savannah Joy, it wasn't the boys. I was hurrying when I put the mower away. I may have left the gate unlocked," said their father.

Mallory couldn't hear the rest. She was out the gate. "Make sure you have your phone. You go that way. I'll go this way." She and Richard separated. She heard running steps behind her as Samuel fell into place.

"Aunt Savannah's coming, too. She went the other direction with Uncle Richard. Spencer, Lillian, and Hannah went out the front and are looking there."

After thirty minutes of fruitless searching, Mallory stopped her hurried steps, her heart pounding, her lungs feeling like they'd explode. She leaned over, hands on her thighs, taking deep breaths. "I think it's time to call the police. Let's head back." They continued searching on their return home, scanning every yard.

When they reached home, the gate had been relocked. "We'll have to walk around front." A narrow grassy strip between houses led them to the front door where Mallory rang the bell since she left without keys. Savannah opened the door to the living room where her mother sat on the sofa, looking perplexed. "You found her." Mallory ran to her mother. "Mom, you scared us half to death." She sprung her head around to her sister. "Where was she?"

"We found her two doors down in the neighbor's yard. She was sitting at their picnic table."

Two doors down? Mallory stood and squared her shoulders, filled with disbelief. "You found her two doors down? Why didn't you call me? I've been running frantically looking everywhere."

Savannah shrugged her shoulders. "Sorry. I didn't think about it."

Heat climbed to Mallory's head. She stepped toward her sister, fists clenched, fueled by anger. "You didn't think about it?" She stood inches from Savannah and repeated her question. "You didn't think about it? What's your problem, Savannah? What did I ever do to make you hate me?"

Savannah stepped backward. "Don't be dramatic, Mallory Rose."

"Listen." She poked her finger in her sister's direction. "You've been hostile to me since I returned from Wilmington. I want to know why."

"Girls. Enough. You're upsetting your mother." Her father's sharp voice silenced them.

Mallory unclenched her fists when she saw Samuel staring wide-eyed. She calmed herself with a deep breath, then stepped to the closet where she left her purse. "I think I've lost my appetite. Samuel, let's go."

Savannah stood erect, hands crossed over her chest, her narrow lips forming a thin line. Mallory passed by and leaned in close. With a whispered hiss, she said, "This conversation isn't over."

The first few minutes of the ride home were quiet. Mallory stole a glance at Samuel sitting wide-eyed. "Sorry you had to hear that."

"Why's Aunt Savannah so mean to you? She and my mom were pretty close. I never heard her being nasty before."

"That's the hundred-thousand-dollar question. I really don't know. I always knew that they were close. It's to be expected. They grew up together and I was much younger."

"She should've called you when they found Grandma."

"Yes, Samuel. She should have."

Chapter 15

Mallory dropped Samuel off at the ballfield early on Saturday morning. They always had warm-ups before the game started. That allowed her just enough time to run a few errands. After her trip to the post office and pharmacy, she slid onto the bench just in time for the first pitch. Samuel played shortstop. Even stooped over, ready to field the ball, it was easy to see how he towered above most of his teammates. The royal blue of his shirt was such a nice contrast to his light hair, still visible beneath his visor cap. Her heart swelled with the normalcy of the moment. She looked around at the moms seated around her and the dads, some seated and others standing near the fence. Had they taken for granted the privilege of moments like this? Moments that she had longed to be a part of.

As she scanned the fence, she saw him. Elliott stood between the outfield and the baseline on the side with the opposing team's dugout. He searched the field, his hands twined with the chain link. A visor cap covered most of his blond hair, and mirrored sunglasses shaded his eyes, but Mallory recognized him. She had spent too much time staring at him in high school, learning his mannerisms, his posture, the broadness of his shoulders.

Elliott made no attempt to find her. He had steered clear of any area where parents congregated.

Mallory found herself watching Elliott more than she watched the game. He moved down the fence line closer to the shortstop. How must he feel getting that first glance at a son he hadn't known existed? Did his breath catch in his throat as hers had? So many times she had imagined Elliott seeing his son. Now it brought her dread. She'd need to guard Samuel when the game ended. She wanted no contact yet. Samuel wasn't ready.

As it turned out, she didn't need to worry. At the end of the eighth inning, Elliott turned and retreated toward the parking lot. He was gone before anyone would have the chance to recognize the political pundit, co-host of his own show, Elliott Moore.

****

A few days had passed since the blow-up on her dad's birthday. Mallory had to resolve the tension with Savannah. It was a festering wound and now trickled down to impact her parents. She'd visit her sister while all the kids were in school.

Mallory turned her own car onto Savannah's narrow street. Very few of the small ranch houses had garages, including her sister's. Savannah's minivan was parked in the driveway, and Richard's car was gone. Perfect. Mallory took a loaf of pumpkin nut bread, a peace offering for them to share.

When the doorbell sounded, Mallory saw Savannah peek through the curtain before opening the door. She tipped her head sideways in question. "Please, come in." She swung the door wide.

Mallory extended her hands with the loaf of bread. "It's pumpkin. I was hoping you'd have some time to talk." Hopefully the bread would set the tone, letting Savannah know that she wanted a civil conversation, not an argument.

Savannah took the bread. "Please, have a seat. Shall I slice a piece for you?"

Synthetic hospitality. The right words. Words you'd use for a guest, not a sister. A sister wouldn't be shown to a chair. They'd gather in the kitchen and join forces setting up coffee, gathering mugs and silverware while jabbering about nothing and everything.

"Only if you're having some. Can I come and help you?"

"I'll just be a moment. Would you like coffee or tea?"

Sadness stole Mallory's voice. "No, thank you," came in a whisper. She shook her head and sat down.

Savannah returned after a moment, carrying a tray. "I brought you a glass of water."

Mallory looked at the tray where two plates held generous slices of the pumpkin bread, a fork, and a napkin. She had placed a small dish of mints in the center. Savannah lifted her plate and sat down, demurely crossing her legs at the ankle. "What can I do for you today?"

She hadn't practiced this conversation and wasn't quite sure how to begin. "I guess I want to continue the conversation that we started last Sunday. Respectfully. Not argumentatively."

"I'm not sure what more needs to be said. I told you I was sorry. With all of the confusion, I simply didn't think of calling you."

Savannah's practiced poise remained, sparking Mallory's annoyance. She leaned forward, resting her hands on her knees. "It's more than that and you know it. What have I ever done to you to deserve your anger?"

Savannah forked a tiny corner of the pumpkin bread and tasted it. "This is delicious. Thank you for bringing it." She set her fork down and dabbed her napkin across some invisible crumb. "I see no benefit from having this conversation."

"Well, I do. I'm not going to be your dartboard. Every time we're together, you throw little jabs my way. I need to know why."

"Really, Mallory Rose? Do you honestly not know?"

Mallory's mouth dropped open. "No. I honestly don't."

Savannah smoothed her napkin. "Well, that's typical."

"What's typical?" Mallory's arms rose, palms up and fingers splayed.

"That you'd have no regard for anyone but yourself. I shouldn't have expected a conscience. You just skated through life, ruining everyone else's plans, and you aren't even aware."

"Are we talking about Samuel? That didn't affect you. And Jolene's life wasn't ruined. She wanted a child. She loved him."

"Are you that naïve? Everything that brings changes to this family affects all of us."

Mallory took deep breaths, pushing back the irritation. She came to get an answer, not to argue. "Savannah, help me out here. I was sixteen and made a mistake. I handled it the way Mom and Dad wanted me to. I gave up my son so he'd have a good home, and so Jolene would have a child. I moved away so they'd have space, and so I wouldn't grieve seeing a son that I couldn't have. How did I ruin anything for anyone except myself?"

Savannah stood and looked out the window. "Do you remember our Charlotte home?"

"Of course, I do. I grew up there."

"No, not Mom's home, my home."

"You mean yours and Richards, on Cedar Road?" The two-story brick house sat on two acres of land. They all spent many days picnicking there, exploring the trails behind it.

She nodded. "And do you remember anything about Richard's job?"

Mallory tried to think, but not many details came to her. "He worked in some office building in the Industrial Park."

"He was Regional Manager of Marketing for all of the western Carolina area. He had twenty-four people working under him. His salary was more than twice what he makes now, twelve years later."

"Wait a minute." Mallory's temper began to flare again. "You didn't have to move. That was your choice."

"I had no choice. Unlike you, I needed my family. You managed to live a carefree beach life instead of being with your family."

"You think it was carefree? I spent years isolated from everything that mattered. I followed pictures of my son's life to see how he grew. I'd sit with Facebook opened just staring at him. I spent Christmases alone or with a friend who took pity on me, thinking of all of you together, thinking of my little boy's face Christmas morning, but never being there to see it."

"And that was your choice."

"No, Savannah Joy. That was my sacrifice. I did that for my family. It was less awkward for all of you if I was gone."

"That's a lie and a selfish excuse." She moved back to her seat.

"Charlotte's only a few hours from here. I had more reason to move than you did."

Savannah put her head back, resting it against the chair. Mallory watched all bravado drain from her self-imposed control.

"You knew why I was hospitalized."

Mallory nodded, though her sister's eyes remained closed. "Yes, after Hannah's birth. Postpartum depression."

"And again, after Lillian's. And again, after Mom and Dad moved."

Mallory's voice softened. "I didn't know."

"Of course, you didn't. You were self-absorbed and mother was secretive. No one knew."

She had no defense, knowing that both of those accusations were true. She had been fueled by bitterness, and her mother allowed no glimpse of imperfections in the Carter family.

"Depression can be a deep, deep hole. I wasn't always sure I'd come out of it." Expressionless eyes looked away, focusing on nothing visible. "Richard would have done anything to help me. Even leaving his job. He still worries that I'm going to crash again. Especially without Jolene Rae."

Mallory shuddered as Savannah spoke. She knew of one bout with postpartum depression, but never knew it had been that bad.

Savannah sat up straight, her momentary lapse of practiced poise ended. "And Daddy, he lost so much money from early retirement. They loved their home, and had to leave it. They lost all of their friends."

"It didn't have to be that way. Mother was so obsessed with appearances. Teen pregnancy isn't uncommon. We could have been honest and owned up to the situation."

"You knew that wasn't Mother's way. She'd have died telling her friends you were pregnant. Then, the stress of the deception and moving triggered her disease. She started forgetting things."

Mallory stiffened. "No, Savannah. I'll take responsibility for a lot, but not Mom's Alzheimer's. You know that's not linked to my circumstances."

"I'm not stupid, Mallory Rose. I didn't say you caused it. I said you triggered it. She may have gone years before it surfaced if you hadn't placed her under so much stress. It's a fact. Stress can cause brain lesions to form more quickly."

Mallory opened her mouth to argue, but no words came. Could it be true? Could her mother have gone years without signs of the disease? Her throat constricted, making breathing difficult. One mistake. One foolish, teenage crush. She stood, not sure if her legs would hold her as she made her way to the door. She opened it, looking back at her sister. "I'm sorry, Savannah Joy. I'm so sorry."

Chapter 16

With a cold, wet cloth across her forehead, Mallory attempted to calm the pounding tempest in her head. The last two weeks dished out more than she could handle. Jeremy Edwards. The hurried trip. Telling Elliott about Samuel. Her mother missing. Arguing with Savannah.

But even with all of that, the heaviest burden was Savannah's last accusation. Had she stolen healthy years from her mother? Was it her fault that the Alzheimer's hit her so early? She lifted the cloth and used it to catch the tears that wet her cheeks.

The phone on her nightstand rang, increasing the tension in her head. She picked it up and saw Brady's name, then silenced the phone. A moment later, a ding alerted her of a voicemail. She ignored it. Samuel would be home in less than an hour. She needed to pull herself together.

Mallory rose and made her way to the bathroom. She splashed water on her face, then added a touch of makeup to hide the puffy crescents below her eyes. She hoped Brady wasn't calling to say he was in town. The makeup might fool Samuel, but definitely not Brady. One look and he'd know something was wrong. She reached for her phone and pulled up the voicemail, then hit play.

"Mallory, I'll be in Chicago all next week. I thought I should let you know that I won't be around. Call if you need me for anything."

A bittersweet message. She didn't need anything else to deal with right now, and had no desire to explain her pillowed eyes. But the rest of this week and all next week meant ten days, a long time without the lightheartedness that he always brought. When Brady was here, they managed to laugh. His presence felt natural since Brady's time in Raleigh had continued to increase in frequency.

****

Samuel fixed a snack and sat at the kitchen table. He chattered on about the pep rally they'd had and about teacher workday tomorrow.

Mallory's thoughts traveled back to the day that she wished he could talk comfortably with her. That day had come, but would it last? Would he ever speak to her again when Elliott pushed the issue?

"So, what are your plans for your day off?"

Both of his arms bolted straight up above his head. "Sleeping in."

She laughed at the celebratory gesture. "Since you don't have to be up early tomorrow, do you want to stargaze tonight? We've just passed a new moon so it should be a dark night."

"Sure. Why do they call it a new moon when you can't see it at all?"

"The phases are a cycle. It waxes, meaning the visible crescent increases until it reaches a full moon. Then it wanes. That's when it begins the decrease. We identify the cycle by starting with the new moon."

"Even though it's the same old moon?"

"Yep." Mallory remembered Brady's voicemail. "Hey, your uncle left a message. He wanted you to know that he'll be in Chicago all next week, so he won't get here to see you."

"Bummer."

****

The night sky was as black as it could be in a populated area. The slightest sliver of moon hung in the darkness. Mallory perched her telescope on the deck and spent a few minutes pulling it into focus.

Samuel examined each of her movements. "What do you think we're going to see?"

"I'm hoping we'll see Jupiter. It should make a close approach to the moon. About four degrees. Venus is brighter, so if I can find that, we might be able to locate Jupiter."

"Why are we on this side of the deck? Last time we were over there."

"We need to look southwest. This gives us the best shot." She continued making miniscule moves of the telescope. "I've got it. Come here."

Samuel leaned in when Mallory stepped to the side.

"Don't move it. Find the moon. It's a skinny crescent, then look slightly to the left. Do you see the bright light?"

"That's Jupiter?" His tone filled with awe.

"That's what they tell me."

"Cool."

They spent the next thirty minutes searching the heavens. The vastness somehow made Mallory's problems feel insignificant. Especially when she saw them through the wonder of Samuel's eyes. He was so much like she had been when she first discovered her passion for astronomy.

"It's getting chilly out here. I think we better wrap it up."

Samuel took one last look before carefully lifting the telescope into the box. "Do you think I could make one of these?"

"Well, I'm certain you could, but you're welcome to use this one whenever you want."

"It'd be cool to make one. I'd need your help." He lifted his brows in hopeful expectation.

Mallory would love to help him. It would be a fun project. "I know a little more now than I did when I made this one. We could probably do better. Let me take a look at some models and we can plan it out."

He carried the box in and placed it on the table. "You want me to carry this upstairs for you?"

Mallory had stowed it in her bedroom closet. She looked into the mudroom. "No. I think I'll store it in my cubby. That way, it'll be close if you want to use it."

"You're not afraid I'd break it?"

"If it breaks, we'll make another one."

"I'll make room." He looked in and scanned the cubbies. Mallory saw his excitement fade as he looked at Jolene and Mark's cubbies. "I guess we should empty these."

Mallory stepped close and wrapped her arm around him. "That's up to you, Samuel. Whenever you think you're ready."

He touched his mom's silky pink jacket. "Maybe tomorrow. When I'm off school."

"Do you want to do it, or would you like me to?"

"I will." He swiveled toward Mark's cubby with the old, familiar sadness. A golf bag stood in the bottom below the shelf. "Do you think I could have these?"

"They're already yours, sweetie." She tried to lighten the mood. "Do you golf?"

"No, but Dad did. He loved it."

"I'm sure he'd be happy if you used them. Maybe your Uncle Brady would teach you."

"Maybe. I'll do this tomorrow and put your telescope somewhere safe."

"I'm here if you need my help."

****

The following morning, Mallory woke, remembering that there was no school. She rolled over and attempted to fall back to sleep. That didn't happen. She rose and felt the chill of the changing seasons and decided to slip a pair of socks on before heading downstairs. When she opened her nightstand drawer, she saw the folder from Jeremy Edwards. The handwriting samples and the analysis showing 99.04% confidence level. She had to shred them. If Elliott pushed the issue, Samuel would eventually know. But she'd protect him from the truth for as long as possible.

Mallory picked up the file and went downstairs to the office. She plugged in the shredder, lifted a page from the file and watched it feed in. Her phone sounded in concert with the whiz of the shredder.

"Hi, Dad."

"Mallory Rose."

His voice choked with emotion, reminding Mallory of the dreaded call last spring. "What's wrong, Dad?"

"Your mother. She didn't know who I was this morning and it frightened her. I explained, but I'm still not sure she understands. She looks at me with panic in her eyes."

"Oh, Dad. I'm sorry. Where is she now?"

"In the bedroom. She closed the door, but I took the locks off the inside doors long ago."

"Can I do anything? Would it help if I come over?"

"No, Mallory Rose. I just needed someone to talk to. I don't want to put her in the memory care facility, but I can't bear to think that she's afraid of me. Savannah Joy wants me to start the proceedings. What do you think?"

Mallory paced while she talked. The cold coffee pot reminded her that she hadn't started her day with the caffeine jolt that her body had gotten used to. She held the phone with one hand as she spooned ground coffee into the filter. "I don't have an answer for that. It might be good if you visit the facility. Savannah and I can help. One of us can go with you and one can stay with Mom."

"You come with me. Savannah Joy has her mind made up. You'll be more objective."

She sat at the table with her coffee, trying to imagine how hard the morning must have been for both of her parents.

****

Mallory folded towels in the laundry room adjacent to the mudroom, grateful that she didn't have to trudge to the laundromat like she'd done in Wilmington. When she finished, she turned from the work counter and moved Samuel's jeans from the washer to the dryer. She'd take the towels upstairs and bring down the basket with her own laundry.

Samuel had slept in, but by late morning, Mallory heard him working on the cubbies. As she crossed through the mudroom, she glanced at her telescope, carefully placed in Jolene's old cubby. Her jacket and slippers were gone. Mark's cubby was emptied of everything except his golf bag. Samuel wanted them, and they wouldn't have fit in his own space. It had taken five months, but she was determined to let him set the pace.

It had been a productive day. Even though she cleaned bathrooms and did laundry, it felt good to have Samuel home. He had worked on a school project in the study room adjacent to his bedroom. When he needed a break, he went downstairs to play a video game.

As she passed the family room, she peeked in, but didn't see him. She stepped in farther and saw him sitting at his father's desk in the office. He must be back working on his project. But how? All of his supplies were still upstairs. He never worked in the office.

She set the basket down and moved farther in. The familiar burgundy folder was open and Samuel read a page that he held in his hands. Mallory sprang into action, hopping over a pillow on the floor.

"What are you doing? That's private." She grabbed the paper from his hands and scooped up the file, lambasting herself for forgetting it. How could she have been so careless?

Samuel glared at her. "Why did you sign my birth certificate?"

She fumbled, almost spilling the contents. "This doesn't concern you."

He stood, shoulders back, challenging her. She watched as he set his jaw like she'd seen Elliott do. Anger turned his cheeks ablaze.

"It's my birth certificate." He pointed to the file. "That whole thing is about me."

Mallory attempted to calm the situation. "Don't worry about this, Samuel. Your mom and dad wouldn't want you to be fretting over something you can't understand."

"Can't understand? Like maybe you've been lying to me?" He pointed toward the file she held. "Those papers say that my mother couldn't have a baby." The red deepened. "Are you really my mother? And who's my real father? Was it you and my dad?"

"Of course not. I don't appreciate that accusation. Let's just calm down …"

"Yeah. As soon as you tell me the truth." He was yelling, leaning in close to her face.

"We can't discuss this now." Mallory needed space to think. This wasn't the way she wanted Samuel to find out. "We both need to calm down a little." She knew she'd have to tell him, but she needed to think through her words. She turned and walked away.

When she reached the forgotten laundry basket, Mallory placed the file in it and went upstairs. She closed herself in her bedroom and paced the floor.

How could she have been so foolish to leave the file in plain sight? Her response to Samuel had been insensitive. She had to tell him. Her carelessness brought the situation to a head faster than she would have liked. Should she tell him Elliott's name? Or did he already know. She searched the file but Elliott's picture was gone. She had shredded one page, but she didn't know which. Was Samuel holding Elliott's picture? Had it escaped her quick grasp of the file's contents or was it the one she'd shredded? Mallory tried to visualize the shredding, but only saw the blank back of the page.

A slamming door shocked her from her ruminating. The sound came from Samuel's room across the hall. She'd give him some time. Let him cool down. Then she'd tell him. Mallory went downstairs and out to the deck. The crisp air helped to clear her head. She rehearsed her words, and more importantly, her tone. She had handled it so poorly. Of course, it concerned him. Why had she suggested otherwise?

Sitting on the deck brought thoughts of stargazing, a reminder of their developing closeness. They could get through this. She would show Samuel that giving him up was an act of love.

Just after two o'clock, a little over an hour since their conflict, Mallory changed the neglected clothes from washer to dryer. There was no sound from upstairs. Samuel had either fallen asleep or was still sulking. She'd give him another hour.

At three o'clock, Mallory tapped gently on his door. "Samuel?" He didn't answer, so she knocked louder. "Samuel?" When no answer came, she turned the doorknob and peeked inside. The room was empty. The door to the Jack and Jill bathroom was opened. She moved to the door of his study room. "Samuel?" Her voice had gotten progressively louder with each call.

Mallory found his study area empty. Each nerve prickled. She bounded down the stairs and searched each room. Samuel was nowhere in the house. She checked the backyard. Then the driveway with the basketball hoop. He was gone.

Mallory went inside and paced the kitchen, her heart hammering. She drew in a deep breath, trying to put her fear to rest. She dialed his cell phone, but got no answer. He left of his own free will. Of that, she felt certain. He was twelve, not a small child. He had common sense. He'd cool off and then come home. But where would he have gone? Brady was too far away. Samuel would never go to Savannah's. Perhaps her parents, but that didn't seem likely. He loved them, but was uncomfortable with her mother's illness. She could call across the street to see if he went to hang out with Jake, but if he weren't there, that would raise questions that she wasn't prepared to answer. She couldn't worry about that. She had to find him.

Mallory went out the front door and down the walk toward the road, just as their garage door opened. The car backed out and turned onto the street. Jake was in the backseat with his sister. The parents smiled and waved as they drove away.

Fear began to resurface, trickling up the path of her spine. When did he leave? It was before one o'clock when she found him with the file. It was now 3:20. She must have been sitting on the deck, which meant that he went out the front door. Otherwise, she'd have seen him. Unless he left while she paced her bedroom. That meant he'd been gone over two hours. Mallory tried to calm her fears. She wouldn't panic. He'd come home.

By five o'clock, she couldn't wait any longer. A dozen calls to his cell went unanswered. She'd start making other calls. Her dad, Savannah, and Brady. She started with Brady. Her hands shook as she held the phone.

"Hi, Brady." She attempted to calm her voice. "Have you spoken to Samuel today?"

"No. Should I have?"

Mallory did her best to still her shaking hand. "I was just wondering if he called you."

"Why? Is something wrong?"

She hesitated, but had no option of protecting herself. "We had an argument and he ran away."

Brady hesitated before answering. "Okay." He stretched the word out. She could picture him thinking. Forming an answer. "So, if he needed to cool off, where would he go?"

"That's what I keep asking myself. I thought he might call you."

"Did this just happen?"

"He's been gone about four hours. I tried not to worry. I figured he'd cool off then come home." Voicing *four hours* aloud brought a fresh sense of alarm.

"Have you checked with his friends, your parents, your sister?"

"He's not at Jake's house. I checked. I know he wouldn't go to Savannah's. I'll try my parents next."

"Call Savannah, too. I'm on my way. I'll be there as soon as I can."

"Aren't you in Chicago?"

"Not yet. I'm scheduled to leave in the morning."

The thought of Brady hopping in the car and driving here, possibly missing his trip, renewed her sense of panic. He must be worried, which increased her own fear. How long until darkness stole the light? When was it time to call the police?

Chapter 17

Mallory paced the house, moving from the front door to the back door, hoping to see some sign of Samuel. At 7:30, Brady pulled in. He'd made the three-hour trip in two and a half hours. He sprinted to the back door where Mallory waited.

Brady met her with a question. "No word from him yet?"

"No. I keep calling his phone." Her voice cracked with emotion as she tried to hold back the tears.

"Yeah, so do I. No answer. Who all have you called?"

Mallory stepped into the kitchen. "My dad and Savannah."

Brady followed her inside. "Friends?"

"I wouldn't know who to call. He mentions names, but they're not kids that he hangs out with except in school. I only know some last names from the baseball roster. Savannah and Dad are calling me every fifteen minutes to check."

Mallory had held it together during her time alone. Now that she had someone to share the burden, she allowed herself to fall apart. She perched on one of the high stools at the kitchen counter and succumbed to the tears that threatened all day. With her face buried in her hands, she didn't see Brady come up behind her. He wrapped an arm around her and turned her toward him.

Brady's calming voice held no alarm. "Don't worry, Mallory. Samuel's a smart kid. And he's a good kid. He's not going to make stupid decisions." He took a deep breath, exhaling it in a sigh. "However, it may be time to call the police. Let me try contacting him once more."

He moved onto the stool beside her, speaking into his text message. IT'S TIME FOR YOU TO CALL US. EVERYONE'S PRETTY WORRIED. WE'RE GETTING READY TO CALL THE POLICE AND THEY'LL START A FULL AMBER ALERT SEARCH. PLEASE CALL US IN THE NEXT FIVE MINUTES SO WE CAN AVOID THAT.

Silence followed. They waited, watching the clock. Four minutes had passed when the text came in. DON'T DO THAT. I'M OKAY. THERE'S SOMEONE I HAVE TO TALK TO. I'LL CALL YOU TOMORROW.

Brady read it aloud.

Elliott! Was Samuel looking for his father? Mallory still hadn't figured out if he had the picture. Elliott's name had been printed on it.

Brady shook his head, his voice threaded with concern. "I still think we need to get the police involved. At least he communicated. Let me try one more time."

He spoke his message so Mallory would hear. "Sorry, buddy, but we need to call the police. Last chance. Call me now."

This time the response came immediately. PLEASE DON'T DO THAT. I'M FINE. I'LL BE STAYING WITH A FRIEND TONIGHT. I'M TURNING MY PHONE OFF NOW.

Brady dialed his number, but it went straight to voicemail without ringing.

She had to find out if Samuel tried to locate Elliott. "Brady, I need to run upstairs. I'll be down in a few minutes." Mallory hurried up the stairs and to her bedroom in the back of the hallway. She closed her door and called Elliott.

"Mallory." He answered with her name so he had obviously saved her contact in his phone.

"Elliott, have you ..." She didn't quite know how to ask. "Something's happened here. Samuel found out about the birth certificate and he's run away. Did he try to contact you?"

Silence.

"Elliott?"

"So, he knows I'm his father? He can't come here without giving me time to tell Andrea. I'm still not sure how she's going to take it."

A surge of adrenaline pulsed through her. "What? Our son's missing and all you worry about is Andrea?" Mallory stabbed the end call button. That was enough conversation to answer her question. Elliott hadn't heard from Samuel.

She trudged back downstairs where Brady still sat at the counter. "What do you think, Mal? He sounds okay. Should we give him a little time?"

She wished she had answers. "I don't think *a little time* will do. Sounds like he's settled in somewhere for the night." While Mallory spoke, her phone rang. Elliott. She silenced it without answering. Brady shot her a hopeful look, but she shook her head.

"I said it before. He's a smart kid. It sounds like he's with someone."

"I hope so." Images had been ripping through her mind, seeing him alone outside in the dark. "I guess we take him at his word. If we call the police and tell them what he said, they'll probably wait until morning."

With elbows on the counter, Brady perched his chin against steepled fingers. Mallory knew he was weighing all the facts. "What was the argument about? Do you mind me asking?"

Mallory went back to her kitchen stool, her legs too weak to hold her. Could she tell him? It was inevitable that he'd find out. If she didn't tell him, Samuel would. Twelve years of silence was coming to a crashing end. First Elliott. Now Brady.

She stretched the tightness from her neck before turning toward him. "It's a long story."

"It looks like we have a long night ahead." He stood and reached a hand to Mallory, motioning toward the family room. "Let's sit in here."

Her phone rang again. Savannah. She silenced the call. "I think I better let Dad and Savannah know he's safe. They're frantic and will keep calling." She sat on the sofa and texted them.

SAMUEL TEXTED. HE'S FINE. HE'LL BE HOME TOMORROW. IT'S BEEN AN EXHAUSTING FEW HOURS, SO I'M GOING TO TRY TO GET SOME REST.

Hopefully that would keep them from calling.

Mallory swiveled on the sofa, facing Brady. "What about Chicago?"

"I canceled it. This is more important. I wouldn't pry if it weren't for Samuel."

"I know." She took a deep breath and swiped at the ribbon of tears that had formed. "Do you remember when I told you that I went through a rough time when I was a teenager, and everyone made decisions for me?"

He nodded. "That's why you wanted to give Samuel choices."

She glanced away for a moment, suddenly filled with shame. Turning back, she made eye contact and shared the family secret. "I became pregnant when I was sixteen."

Brady's eyes softened. "I'm sorry. That must have been difficult."

Mallory nodded. "It was, and my mother made a bad situation worse. She couldn't handle the disgrace. We always had to look like the perfect family. No scars. No warts. Anything less was hidden."

"I know your mom. She's prim and proper, but sweet. I've always thought a lot of her."

"She is sweet. She has a soft heart. She continually told us that southern women should have a genteel nature. One more way that I disappointed."

"Mallory, you're …" He started to refute that, but she held up her hand to stop him.

"You said it yourself. I think you used the word *spunky*. I know I can have a snarky side. But back then, at that time, I needed them. All they could think of was how to hide the secret. That's why we moved from Charlotte."

His face registered surprise. "Really? I thought it was to be closer to Jolene when Mark took a transfer."

"Yes, but they hurried the move to accommodate my pregnancy."

"So, you gave the baby up for adoption?"

Mallory closed her eyes, reliving the day of Samuel's birth. The moment when the midwife held him high and her heart swelled with a love that produced a flood of tears. A protectiveness gripping her as she cradled him in her arms. Her hand resting on his chest, feeling the pulse of his heart as tiny lips puckered in and out. She laid her cheek against the sweet covering of light fuzz on his scalp, clinging to him as Mark attempted to lift him from her arms and place him in Jolene's.

"I gave him up. To my sister."

He looked confused, so she added, "Jolene."

The truth resonated with a shocked expression. "Samuel?"

A tiny nod of her head was all Mallory could manage.

He shook his head in unbelief. "They never told us he was adopted, so I'm guessing they never told him."

"No, he wasn't actually adopted. That would mean that our family was less than perfect. Did you know that Jolene miscarried three times?"

He raised a skeptical eyebrow. "I knew she miscarried once."

"They didn't tell anyone about the other two. And they didn't tell anyone that the doctor advised against another pregnancy. Here's where my story gets worse. My parents asked me, well practically told me, what they wanted. I delivered Samuel at home—at Mark and Jolene's home when they first moved here."

Brady was leaning forward now, glued to every word. It was his family, too, and he was hearing things that were new to him. "The rental?"

"Yes. We told the midwife that I was Jolene Donaldson. I signed the birth certificate with her name."

He sat back, expelling a large breath of air. "And you told Samuel?"

She flinched. "No, of course not. But he found out."

The silence hung heavily between them. Brady broke it with a shake of his head. "And my brother agreed to the deception."

It wasn't a question, and she offered no response. After another quiet minute, Brady moved beside Mallory and stretched his arm across the back of the sofa behind her neck.

"I'm sorry that happened to you. And I'm ashamed that my brother would agree to that."

"Jolene was in a bad place—emotionally."

"That's no excuse. There were other ways."

"I know. And I know that I could have refused."

"But you were sixteen." He said it as if that explained everything.

"They said that Samuel was an answer to their prayers."

Brady shook his head. "No, Mallory, not the way it was done. God will never accomplish His plan through lies and deceit. My brother may have compromised his values, but God does not."

Mallory wilted, stripped of the one thread of comfort in the whole situation. She'd rather believe that it was God's answer. That she had been part of a divine plan.

Brady stretched his neck, easing whatever muscle tension had set in. "Some things are beginning to make sense. Mark wanted no company when they moved here. I offered to help but he refused. Said they had everything under control. When they were settled, I came to Raleigh on business and we met for lunch. He told me Jolene wasn't feeling well so he'd rather meet me than have me stop by the house. Claimed it was too small and crowded."

Mallory smirked. "Crowded because I was living there."

"Of course, he didn't bother telling me that. When we received the call that Jolene had had a baby, we were stunned. He blamed his silence on their concern. Said they wanted to make sure the pregnancy was viable. When it got close and they felt confident that she wouldn't miscarry, they decided to make it a surprise."

They sat in silence, each lost in memories of twelve years ago.

"You know, that's why Savannah hates me. And that's why I moved away."

"That makes no sense. This whole family should have been grateful to you. You brought us Samuel."

"Jolene was grateful. She tried to make it right, telling me I was always welcome. She had my mother's tender heart. But she also embraced parenthood. Samuel was fully hers. That was too painful to watch."

Tears trickled, and Brady pulled Mallory toward him, stroking her hair as she leaned against his shoulder. She had years of practice in building a façade of self-sufficiency, but it crumbled with a strong arm around her. A shoulder to cushion the pain. She managed to speak through the tears. "Savannah said that's what brought on my mother's Alzheimer's."

Brady shifted, bringing her tear-streaked face up so she was forced to look at him. "Mallory, surely you don't believe that."

"It's true. I did some checking. Stress can increase the formation of brain lesions. It can trigger things like Alzheimer's."

"Trigger, Mallory. Not cause. Your mom was on her way to developing the disease long before any symptoms surfaced."

"Yes, but I caused it to surface. She lost years because of me."

"Is that what Savannah told you?"

Mallory answered with a nod.

"Honey, that's just not true. The stress may have been a trigger, but not by much. It could never have cost her twelve years. And Mallory, don't forget that your family has to share that responsibility. They didn't handle the situation right. You made a mistake, but who hasn't? Who can cast that first stone?"

He reached and pulled a few tissues from the box, handing them to her.

She blew her nose and cleared the stuffiness. "None of that matters now. I just have to find Samuel."

"And we will. How about if I make you a cup of tea, and you tell me about the argument. It will help if I know how he found out."

She nodded and Brady headed toward the kitchen. Now she'd have to tell him about Elliott.

Chapter 18

The cup of chamomile tea released apple-scented steam. Mallory breathed it in before taking a tentative sip to test the temperature. It was too hot to drink, but she liked the calming feel of the warm mug in her hands as she told Brady about Jeremy Edwards.

"I could go to jail. The penalty for falsifying a birth certificate is five years and up to ten thousand dollars."

Brady shrugged it off. "They're not going to send you to jail for that. You were a minor. I doubt there would be any charges at all. Besides, no paper would print a story like that. For certain, the *Charlotte Post* won't print it."

The time had come. She had to tell him. "Not the *Charlotte Post*. He's working with a scandal magazine."

"They're even less likely to run something like that."

"Yes, if it were only me. I'm not the parent of interest."

Brady's eyes widened. "Who's the father?"

His name tasted sour in her mouth. The name that had once made her heart soar. "Elliott Moore." She sipped the chamomile, breathing in the scent, praying for that sweet tranquility to return.

"Elliott Moore," he repeated. "The success story from our high school. Samuel's light blond hair. I should have guessed. Does he know?"

"He does now. That's where I went when I asked you to stay with Samuel. His network managed to squash the story. It seems that Jeremy Edwards isn't squeaky clean."

"Did he know about Samuel all these years?"

139

"No. He knew I was pregnant, but he wanted me to abort. I didn't tell him I did, but he made that assumption. He wants to meet Samuel. I begged him off for a while because Samuel's been through so much, but he assured me he won't be put off for long." A renewed stream of tears traveled down her cheeks. "What if he wants custody? I could never win in court."

Brady's arm came around her again. "Of course, you'd win. You're his mother."

"A single mother with no job, no skills, and no money for an attorney. Let's not forget I lied to him and I broke the law."

"Mallory, no one's taking Samuel. Don't worry about the money. Samuel's twelve. The court will consider his wishes."

"What if he chooses Elliott? Right now, he hates me."

"He doesn't hate you. He's had a big shock and he's angry. He needs time to think. I guarantee you when the dust settles in his head, he'll realize how much you've done for him. Not only in the last few months, but twelve years ago. As disappointed as I am with my brother right now, they were great parents."

Brady's confidence buoyed her. When he spoke with such assurance, it chased her fears away. "Yes, they were great parents."

Brady dabbed a lone tear from her cheek. "You're exhausted. Why don't you go up and try to get some sleep? I don't want to leave you alone. If it's all right, I'll just bunk on the sofa tonight."

"There are extra beds upstairs. You can use the front bedroom."

"No, I'm fine here."

"Do you think he'll call tomorrow? He has to call. I don't know what I'd do if something happened to him."

"He said he will. He's a trustworthy kid." He took the now empty mug from her hand. "I've got this. You go try to rest. Good night, Mallory."

She walked up the first few stairs, then turned. "You'll wake me if you hear from him?"

"Of course."

****

Sleep eluded her. Mallory kept changing positions, hoping sleep would claim her, providing a respite from her troubled thoughts. Where was Samuel at this very moment? Was he tucked away in a warm bed at a friend's house? Had he told them about the secret she'd protected for twelve years? She chastised herself for worrying about that now, but old habits were hard to break. She couldn't allow her thoughts to go in the other direction—that he had nowhere to go and was out in the cold, darkness of night, alone as he stared up at the stars.

That thought drew Mallory from her bed. The clock showed a little before two a.m. She stepped across the hall and into Samuel's room. Mallory stared at his empty bed and prayed. Surely God would hear her, if only for Samuel's sake. Then she tiptoed downstairs, hoping not to wake Brady. The French doors to the family room where he slept were closed. She continued past to the mudroom and retrieved her telescope.

Mallory slipped on her fleecy jacket and stepped out onto the deck. She positioned the telescope and looked up to the heavens. Somehow, it always served to calm her, to dwarf her problems. But tonight, it seemed to magnify them. The immensity of the universe served as a reminder that she had no idea where her son was. Should they have called the police even though Samuel said he was fine?

Muted stars dotted the sky, but Polaris beamed bright and proud. She didn't need a scope to locate it. Polaris, the North Star, constant, unchanging, a reliable guide to those who are lost. Samuel knew how to locate it. Perhaps he stared at the same sky tonight. Even that thought couldn't bring her comfort. Had God really counted the stars? Did He actually know each one and where they were, when she couldn't even find one little boy?

Mallory retraced her steps to the mudroom, past the closed French doors, and up the stairs. Instead of going to her bedroom, she returned to Samuel's room and curled up in his abandoned twin bed, praying until sleep came.

****

Bright sunlight woke Mallory, apprising her that the blinds hadn't been closed. It took a moment to remember where she was, and more importantly, why. *Samuel.* She was in his room, and he was missing. Mallory hurried across the hall and pulled on her robe. The sound of movement downstairs let her know that Brady was awake.

She found him in the kitchen, making coffee.

"Hope you don't mind me finding my way around your kitchen. Did you sleep okay?"

"I don't mind. Sleep? Not really. I guess at some point it kicked in because I woke to sunshine. What time is it?"

She glanced at the clock as he answered. "Eight-thirty."

"And no word yet?"

"I didn't expect to hear this early. The best thing we can do right now is to have some breakfast and wait. I'd suggest trying to call around nine or nine-thirty."

She nodded, still groggy. "What would you like? I could scramble some eggs."

"Why don't you let me do that?"

She hesitated, but acquiesced. "I think I'd like to get my shower before we call him. I want to be ready to go when we know where he is."

"Good idea. I'll have something ready when you come down. About twenty minutes okay?"

"Yes. Thanks."

Exactly twenty minutes later, Mallory came down to find scrambled eggs, toast, and fresh strawberries.

"Thank you." She stole a look at the clock. "Okay, almost nine."

He chuckled and handed her a plate. "Let's eat first. Sit."

She obeyed, too weary to argue. Brady served her juice to go with her breakfast. "Coffee or tea?"

"I'll have coffee, please."

He brought her a cup along with cream and sugar. "Not sure how you like yours." He reached for her hand. "Let's pray."

Brady prayed for Samuel, asking that this be resolved quickly so they could get him home, prayed for Mallory, that she would find peace and be comforted, and asked for God's blessing on their breakfast.

Tears pooled in Mallory's eyes, but didn't spill. She dabbed them with the napkin that Brady had left for her, feeling as fragile as bone china.

"How did you sleep, Brady?"

"I did okay. It's hard to keep my mind off of everything."

"I know." She attempted to smile.

He peered over the rim of his coffee cup. "That was a sad excuse for a smile. Is the breakfast that bad, or were you hoping for bacon?"

This time she managed a little grin. "Bacon would have been nice." A little levity helped to chase away unwelcome thoughts.

"I tried. There's none in your refrigerator."

They ate, then made the phone call at 9:15. It went directly to voicemail. There was nothing to do but wait.

Brady convinced her to refrain from calling every ten minutes. They tried again at 9:45 and 10:15.

After the 10:15 call, Mallory questioned their decision. "Are you sure we shouldn't call the police?"

"No, I'm not sure about anything. If we call them, it might generate an Amber Alert and be splashed all over the TV. And with everything you told me, there's a chance that might all come out as well."

"I'll have to deal with that if that's what it takes. I need to know if he's safe."

Just as Brady started to answer, Mallory's phone sounded its shrill ring.

She lurched from her chair to grab the phone. Chloe. She set it on the table, disappointed. "An old friend. I can't talk to her now." A moment later, a ding alerted her to the voicemail that Chloe apparently left. Mallory scrolled to it, not because she was anxious to hear it, but because the morning was way too idle. She needed something to occupy her mind.

Chloe's cheerful voice came through. "Hey, girl. Hope you're doing well on this sunny morning. I didn't know you were in town, but I saw that sweet boy of yours yesterday. I hope you're going to stop in to see me. I'll be here till four today. I've got a vanilla latte with your name on it."

She gasped.

"He's in Wilmington. Listen." Hope kindled as she hurriedly hit speaker and played the message for him. When it finished, she hit redial. It rang at least ten times, but she knew firsthand that Chloe couldn't always answer when she was in the store. She also knew that she kept her phone silenced, only on vibration while she worked.

Brady hopped to his feet. "Let's go, Mallory. I can be ready in five minutes."

"Good. I'll keep trying her number."

****

Brady hopped on I-40 while Mallory continued to call Chloe and Samuel. "How in the world did he get to Wilmington? What if he's not there anymore?"

"Buses run between these two cities."

"Would they let a minor buy a ticket?"

"Possibly. It's in-state. You can always find a way."

Mallory clutched her phone, feeling the vibration when she heard the ring. She grabbed it without looking at the screen.

"Mallory, why haven't you called me or answered my calls? You left me hanging here, worrying about my son."

Elliott. Why hadn't she looked before answering? "I'm on my way to pick him up. I'll call you when I'm home."

"I told Andrea. We talked through everything. She's thrilled and wants to meet him too."

"No." Mallory practically shouted the word. "Do you ever think beyond yourself and Andrea? Elliott, he lost the parents who raised him. Then he discovered that I'm his birth mother. He doesn't need anyone else in the mix. Not yet."

She stole a glance in Brady's direction. His face remained stoic, but his hands clutched the steering wheel, stripping all color from his knuckles. She saw the firm set of his jaw.

Elliott's voice shifted her attention back to the phone call. "Don't make this difficult. I can play hardball."

Mallory interrupted him. "I can't tie this phone up. I said I'll call you when I know something." She ended the call without a good-bye.

"A text came in while I was talking." She opened the icon. "It's Chloe." She read it aloud. HEY, GIRL. I SEE YOUR CALLS, BUT THIS STORE'S ROCKING TODAY. HARD TO TALK. ARE YOU STILL IN TOWN?

Mallory's fingers flew over the keys. CHLOE, I HAVE AN EMERGENCY. I NEED YOU. PLEASE GET FREE AND CALL ME. HURRY.

Barely two minutes passed before her phone rang, showing Chloe's ID.

"Chloe, thank you."

"What's up, girl?" Her musical voice brought a flood of relief, even before asking about Samuel.

"I'm putting you on speaker. Samuel's uncle is with me." She hit the icon and continued. "When did you see him? Did you talk to him?"

"I sure did. He came in last night, somewhere around seven-ish. He was looking for Liam."

"Liam? Why in the world … Never mind. What did you tell him?"

"Ha! I told him you can't pin Liam down. He goes where the wind blows. He'd likely find him at the beach, in the beach shop, or at his home. He wanted Liam's phone number but that made me laugh. I told him phones aren't Liam's style. They lead you to commitments. I gave him the address. What's going on, honey?"

"Samuel and I had an argument. He's missing. We're about thirty minutes away. If he comes by, will you call me? And try to keep him there?"

"I'll do my best short of kidnapping. Don't you worry none. Arguments have a way of smoothing out when tempers calm down. If anyone can calm him, Liam can. Nothing rattles him."

"Thanks, Chloe. I'm going straight to Liam's unless I hear from you."

When Mallory had disconnected, Brady asked, "Is that the surfer?"

"Yes. Samuel liked him, but it makes no sense. Not now."

"Sure it does. Could just be that he wanted distance. Once he was here, it makes sense that he'd look for the only person he knows."

"I guess. Follow the signs to Wrightsville Beach."

Chapter 19

When they crossed the causeway to South Harbor Island, the speed limit dropped drastically. The town set limits to 35 mph unless otherwise noted. Mallory loved the unhurried pace when she lived here, but today it raised her anxiety. She just wanted to see Samuel. To know he was still here and hadn't hopped a bus to somewhere else.

They passed the shops on Causeway Drive and the surf shop where Liam sometimes worked refurbishing old surfboards. "Turn left at the next intersection. Then go two blocks."

The speed limit had dropped to 25 on the narrow side streets. They crept along until she could see his place up ahead. "It's that corner house with blue siding. Turn left and his room is around the back."

Liam lived in a one-room rental on the lower level of a beach house. The out-of-town owner gave him free rent for maintenance. Trim the bushes, mow the tiny patch of grass, and do minor repairs. He was also the contact for renters if they needed anything.

As Brady made the turn, Mallory saw Liam sitting on a webbed chair, a surfboard on two saw horses in front of him. A roll of fiberglass was propped against the leg of his chair. When she lived nearby, Mallory had watched him repair dings by patching and applying some type of epoxy.

Today she had no interest in surfboards. Samuel wasn't with him. She felt nausea begin to grip her stomach. Brady parked and Mallory bolted from the car.

Liam raised his eyes, a grin forming. "I figured you'd be coming by sooner or later."

"Where's Samuel?" She had no time for niceties. "Was he here?"

Liam used his foot to hook a nearby webbed chair and draw it closer. "Sorry. I only have one extra."

"Liam, where's Samuel?" She practically shouted it.

"Chill, Mal. He's sleeping."

"Here?" Her head sprung around to the closed door.

"Yeah. On my sofa." He tipped his head toward the door. "But don't go in. He's exhausted. We were on the water all morning."

Relief and anger merged. "In this weather? It's freezing."

Liam ignored her and stood. He reached his hand past her. Only then did she remember Brady.

"Liam Bergman."

Brady shook the offered hand. "Brady Donaldson, Samuel's uncle."

Brady placed his hands on Mallory's tense shoulders as he leaned in to whisper. "We're here, and he's safe. Just take a deep breath."

She turned toward Liam. "I won't wake him. I just need to see him."

His grin returned as he shook his head in mock annoyance. "Come on." He walked to the door and turned the knob, gingerly pulling the door past whatever hindrance caused it to stick. He blocked her entrance with his arm. "Just a peek."

Samuel was curled on his side on a frayed sage green sofa, a blanket pulled up to his chin. His hair stood up in disarray. Even from this distance, Mallory heard the soft purring snores. Brady's hand touched her back as he craned his head to see his nephew.

"Satisfied?" Liam asked as he closed the door.

"Thank you." She turned and hugged his shoulder. "I'm sorry I snapped at you. But you could have called me."

He shrugged and went back to his work on the surfboard. "I don't do phones. Besides, he said he'd call you when he woke up. And for your information, I wouldn't let the boy freeze. He wore my extra wetsuit. He's a good kid. Even asked me if I had sunscreen."

The crisp September air sent a shiver to Mallory's arms. Brady must have noticed. "Let me get your jacket from the car."

The moment he was out of earshot, Liam shifted the surfboard aside and leaned forward. "Samuel told me what's going on. I didn't know if I should say anything in front of your friend."

"It's fine. Brady knows everything."

"Do you know why Sam came to me?"

Mallory shook her head, and refrained from correcting the nickname. "No. I just figured he needed space."

Brady returned and held the jacket for her to slip her arms into.

"He asked me if I was his father."

"What? Why would he think that?"

"I asked him the same question. Basically, I'm blond, he's blond, we both love surfing, and he thought that you and I seemed pretty close."

"I'm sorry, Liam."

He leaned back, his arms hooked behind his neck. "It explained a lot to me. When I first met you, I knew you were hurting. I didn't know why and figured it wasn't my business. You needed a friend, so that's what I tried to be."

"And you were. You've been a good friend."

"I'm not one for sticking my nose where it don't belong, but that boy needs to know who his father is."

"I know. I plan to tell him, but right now, he's so angry with me."

Liam's casual grin returned. "I think he's had time to get over that."

He pulled the saw horses close again. "I'm repairing some divots and told the owner he'd have it back tomorrow. You can stay and keep me company or sit in the coffee shop if you want to keep warm." He tipped his head in the direction of the shop that had changed hands a dozen times in the past decade. No one tried to remember its name anymore.

"Sorry, I'm not going anywhere until Samuel's with me."

Brady had been focused on the surfboard and Liam's skilled hands doing the repairs. "How about if I go and bring us some hot coffee or tea?"

"That sounds good. Tea for me. Liam?"

"Nothing. Thanks."

Mallory knew he wasted no money on anything but his water sports. "You sure? My treat. I know you like the chai."

"Well, you twisted my arm. Chai Tea Latte would be fine."

Mallory realized her purse was in the car. "Wait just a minute." She stood, but Brady was already in motion, his back to her.

He waved a hand in the air. "I've got it."

****

The tea warmed her. Liam and Brady chatted about surfboard repairs and fiberglass patches. After about forty-five minutes, Mallory heard sounds from the one-room flat. She sat upright in her seat to listen.

Liam lifted his chin. "I think Sam's awake. Go on in."

Mallory stood and glanced at Brady, waiting for him to join her.

"Go ahead, Mallory. I'll give you two a few minutes."

She wasn't sure if she wanted to be alone. Brady was a safety net. After a moment's hesitation, she gave a slight knock and opened the door. Samuel walked from the bathroom, his hair still jutting out in crazy directions. He stopped in his tracks when he saw her.

"Hello, Samuel."

"How'd you know I was here? I was going to call you later."

"I know. I was too worried. I had to find you."

"I guess Liam called." He walked back to the sofa and began folding the blanket.

"Nope. He informed me that he doesn't do phones. I spoke to Chloe. She told me she'd seen you."

He placed the folded blanket on the sofa, then turned toward her. "I need to know the truth."

A line drawn in the sand. A question that would decide how they'd move forward.

"It's not Liam." She tried a testing smile to lighten the moment, but he remained stoic, waiting for an answer. His expression demanding it.

"I'm going to tell you, Samuel. I promise I'll tell you everything. But I'd rather do it at home. Would that be all right?"

He stared without answering, then finally asked, "And you promise?"

"Yes. I promise." She made a *cross my heart* motion.

He took a few awkward steps toward her. Mallory was the first to reach her arms to embrace him. He hugged her back. "I'm sorry I worried you."

She was sorry for so many things, things buried deep inside her guilt. She prayed that time would take away the sting. "I'm sorry I wasn't honest with you."

Samuel stepped away. "It's really hard to think about it. You know, that my mom's not my mom."

"No, Samuel. I gave birth to you, but my sister will always be your mom. She loved you so much."

"I know. I'm just not sure I can call you Mom. It feels like I'd be forgetting her."

"You call me Aunt Mallory. I'll love you the same way whether you think of me as your aunt or your mother."

A rap on the door was followed by the scraping sound of it opening. Brady poked his head in. "Safe to come in?"

Samuel's ears reddened and he lowered his chin. "I guess I'm in trouble."

Mallory pondered that response. He stood up to her, demanding answers. But he cowered to his uncle's authority. Which would she prefer? Freedom to have open communication, or to be a respected authority? There was no question that he loved his uncle, and Brady loved him. She'd have to muse over that at another time.

Brady didn't answer. He closed the space between them and hugged his nephew. "Just don't ever do that again. You had us worried sick."

"Sorry."

"Your Aunt Mallory and I are ready to go home. I think you owe a thank you to Mr. Bergman."

Confusion crossed Samuel's face, and Brady motioned outside. "Liam."

****

Samuel had rented a bicycle yesterday to ride from Wilmington to the beach. Today they would return it to the rental store and stop to see Chloe before returning to Raleigh. Brady loaded the bicycle in the car and they headed for the causeway toward Wilmington.

All awkwardness seemed to be gone. Samuel couldn't wait to talk about surfing, wearing a wetsuit, and helping Liam sand the surfboard. Mallory pumped him with questions about traveling, what he'd eaten, and where he slept. She discovered that he had taken a bus, as Brady suspected. He found Liam at the beach and spent the night on his sofa.

"He's really cool. I wanted to stay in touch with him, but he doesn't have internet."

Mallory chuckled. "Or a car. Or a phone. Or a job."

"Yeah, but he leads a cool life, always having the beach there and surfing whenever he wants."

Brady maneuvered through the historic district to reach the peer at the Cape Fear River. "You know what else he doesn't have? He doesn't have a wife or children. No family around him, and no way to see friends unless they happen to pass by his little strip of beach."

Samuel shuddered. "Yeah. I guess that part's not cool."

They returned the bicycle to the shop, then went a few doors down to the Emporium. When they opened the door, the chimes sounded and Chloe looked up, ready to call out her welcome. When she saw them, she rushed over and hugged Mallory first, then Samuel. Brady had hung back. Chloe leaned in close with a conspiratorial whisper. "Is that the uncle? He's quite the hunk." Her eyebrows rose in question.

Mallory quickly ended Chloe's speculation. "It's not like that." Even as she said it, she recalled his arm circling her when Samuel went missing. The comfort of his nearness as she sat on the sofa, spilling her story for the first time. He held no judgment, only compassion. Mallory trusted his words when he said everything would be all right.

Mallory motioned for Brady to join them. Chloe was right that he was easy on the eyes. She shook that thought away. Brady was here for Samuel—not for her. "Chloe, this is Samuel's uncle, Brady Donaldson. Brady, Chloe owns this shop. I used to work for her."

Chloe flashed her brightest smile his way. "Well, well." She drew her arm around Mallory's shoulders. "You all are one lucky family having this lady around."

A grin filled Brady's face. He looked Mallory's way when he answered. "No argument here."

****

When they were back in Raleigh, Brady gathered his things. "I think I need to leave you two alone." He leaned over the back of the sofa and whispered something to Samuel, then went to the kitchen door.

Brady had been Mallory's lifeboat on a stormy sea. No words were adequate. She wanted to cling to him, stop him from leaving. "Brady, I can't thank you enough. I don't know what I'd have done without you."

"No thanks needed."

"I'm sorry about Chicago. I hope it's not a big problem at work."

He reached and drew Mallory into a hug. "You have enough on your plate. Don't worry about me." He looked like he wanted to say more, but he touched her cheek with his fingertips. "Just take care of our boy."

The touch was so light, barely discernible. Yet the absence left a void. When the door closed between them, she touched her cheek wanting to hold on to the feeling. Mallory stayed at the closed door for a prolonged moment before going to the family room.

She had promised Samuel the truth. She eased herself into the chair facing him. "I'm sorry I wasn't honest with you. I hope you can forgive me."

"Yeah, but I want to know what happened. Who's my real father, and why didn't my mom and dad tell me I'm adopted?"

With a deep inhale, Mallory readied herself to tell her son why she gave him away. "You weren't technically adopted. I lied when I signed your mother's name on your birth certificate. I was sixteen when I got pregnant with you. My sister—your mom—desperately wanted a baby. She had three miscarriages and the doctor advised her not to try again. My parents and your parents devised a plan that would avoid the embarrassment of a teenage pregnancy, would put you in a good home, and would answer my sister's prayers.

"Samuel, I didn't want to give you up. It was the hardest thing I've ever done. But I knew I couldn't raise a baby on my own." She couldn't even take care of herself by standing up to her parents. How could she parent a child?

Samuel sat quietly through Mallory's explanation. An unnatural stillness for a twelve-year-old boy. His blue eyes muted and serious. "Yeah, Liam told me that. He called you a sad, little bird. He told me that it was the greatest act of love."

"Liam said that?"

"Yeah, and some other nice stuff about you. I guess he was like a best friend or something to you."

"Yes, he was." A prolonged silence stretched between them. "I guess you want to know about your biological father."

"Yeah, I do." He leaned forward, a hint of tension returning to his body.

Mallory's energy waned with the heaviness of memories. "We went to school together. I had a terrible teenage crush on him. Football player. Handsome. Smart." Samuel didn't need to know that it was a one-night fling, that he was conceived in the backseat of a car. A rebound when Andrea left. The product of a drunken party. "Do you know the name Elliott Moore?"

Samuel thought for a minute. "Sounds a little familiar, but no, I don't know who he is."

Mallory explained what a political pundit was, and told him about the cable network's show.

"So, he's famous?"

"A little bit."

"How come he never tried to see me?" His jawline sculpted to firm lines, so like his father's.

Mallory paused before condemning herself again. "Because I lied to him, too." The confession rode in a whisper.

Samuel eyes widened. "You lied? That's wrong, even for adults."

"Yes, it is. It's wrong at any age. In my situation, I didn't actually lie to him. I just led him to believe …" How did you talk with a twelve-year-old about abortion? Did he even know what it was?

He answered that question for her. "He thought you got an abortion."

"Yes, Samuel. But I couldn't do that. I'd never do that."

He smirked. "Thanks. I wouldn't be here if you had."

She responded with a grimace. The reality of that choice sent a chill through her. "I can't imagine you not being here. Elliott knows now. He wants to meet you. How do you feel about that?" The question twisted her stomach even through her attempt to sound calm.

"It'll seem weird, but yeah, I'll meet him."

"If that's what you really want, we'll plan something. Let me think about the best way to do that."

Chapter 20

An hour after arriving home, Mallory caught a flash of black passing outside the window. She peeked out and saw a black BMW in the driveway. Her hands clenched as Elliott stepped out of the car.

Mallory hurried outside, hoping Samuel hadn't seen. Elliott's long stride brought him quickly before her.

"What are you doing here? I said I'd call you." Her voice held a whispered fury.

He met her hushed rage with a calm, even tone. "You said you would, but you didn't. I warned you, I won't be pushed aside." He stepped closer, invading her space. His clipped words were filled with resolve. "Now, I've come to meet my son. I suggest you invite me in."

Mallory took a step back. She tried to match his determination, but her shaking hands betrayed her. "We've had two brutal days. This isn't the right time. Let us get through today. I'll call you to set something up."

He firmed his stance, his determination unwavering. "I'm here now. I don't plan on leaving until I meet my son."

"No, this is not the time." She hissed the words through clenched lips. "He's been through too much. You're a stranger to him. It will be better if we plan something that he enjoys."

He crossed his arms and continued in his even tone, but with eyes intent on intimidation. "I'm a stranger because of your deceit. Now, make this happen, Mallory Rose. You can take me inside or bring him out here. I'll take him out for ice cream or something."

"You will not take him out. And don't you dare talk about my deceit." When he stepped toward her, she poked him in his chest to back him up. "You wanted him aborted. I saved his life. You said to handle the problem and I did. You told me I'd be on my own, so I gave you the freedom you wanted." Her voice rose with each word.

His eyes were steel flints. "We were sixteen years old. We didn't know what we wanted."

She moved her hands to her hips. "You always knew exactly what you wanted, and that didn't include Samuel. Or me."

"Is that what this is about? A woman scorned?"

"Don't flatter yourself." Elliott hit too close to the truth. She had no such feelings for him today, but the memories of that sixteen-year-old girl still stung. The days she'd pined after him, yearned to be with him. The ache when she saw him with Andrea after she'd so foolishly given herself to him.

"I don't intend to stand here and argue. I am going to meet my son. The only question is whether you make that happen or the courts order it. Your choice."

"Aunt Mallory?"

Samuel's hesitant voice came from the deck behind her. How long had he stood there? What had he heard? He stared at Elliott but spoke to Mallory. "It's okay, Aunt Mallory."

Mallory glared at Elliott, poking a finger in his direction. "Stay here." She walked toward Samuel, stepping up onto the deck. "Samuel, it's been a long two days. I can make him go away for now."

"No. I want to meet him."

She sighed. She had hoped to orchestrate this differently. "Okay, Samuel. Will you go inside for a few minutes, and I'll bring him in?"

Samuel's eyes were riveted on Elliott. He didn't break eye contact until he turned to go in the house.

Fear fueled Mallory's anger. Would Elliott's presence in Samuel's life crowd her out? With clenched fists, she stepped down from the deck.

"Thirty minutes, maximum. And I'll be with you. No discussion of our teenage years. Just tell him about yourself and ask about him. He loves baseball and video games. He does well at school and enjoys astronomy. Keep the conversation there."

Elliott grinned for the first time. "Astronomy? I know where he gets that."

She took him through the front door. Back doors were for family and friends. As far as Mallory was concerned, Elliott was neither.

Samuel sat on the sofa, waiting. He stood when they entered.

"Samuel, this is Elliott Moore."

"Nice to meet you." Samuel extended a hand as he'd been taught to do.

After shaking Samuel's hand, Elliott took the chair closest to him, leaning forward in a relaxed posture. He followed Mallory's instructions and kept the conversation casual.

"I hear you like baseball. What team do you root for?"

"The Braves. I've been to Atlanta to see them twice."

Elliott nodded. "I grew up following them. I'm more of a hockey fan these days. Washington Capitals."

"Oh yeah, I like the Hurricanes."

"Are you interested in politics?"

Samuel shook his head. "Not really. People just fight all the time."

"I didn't follow it much when I was your age. My interest grew in college. I dual majored in broadcasting and political science. Don't think of it as fighting. It's kind of like sports—people playing a game. Opposing candidates can be friends. They know the deal. When they're campaigning, they expect the competition. What's your favorite subject in school?"

"I like most sciences."

Elliott sat back, looking quite relaxed. "Oh, it figures. Your mother loved science. She used to tutor me."

Samuel's eyes widened. "You knew my mother?" Samuel quickly realized what Elliott meant. "Oh, you mean my Aunt Mallory."

Mallory seethed at Elliott's insensitive faux pas.

Elliott looked between the two of them. "You said he knew."

Samuel answered for her. "I know Aunt Mallory's my birth mother."

Elliott leaned in, his hand on his knee. "And you know that I'm your biological father?"

Samuel's eyes darted back and forth, between Elliott and Mallory. "Yeah, I know."

"Have you ever been to Washington, DC?"

"Yeah. I was eight when we went. My dad liked the museums."

Mallory watched Elliott stiffen at the reference to Mark.

"How would you like an insider look? I can take you some places that tourists can't go. You could come and watch us film our show."

Mallory tensed, ready to pounce like a stalking cat. But stopped when Samuel answered.

"That'd be so cool."

Elliott reached in his wallet and pulled out a business card. "Here's my phone number and e-mail. What's your number? Do you have a cell phone?"

Mallory bristled as Samuel recited it and Elliott entered it in his phone.

Thirty minutes turned into forty before Mallory could usher him out. She stepped outside, one hand on her hip. "You had no right inviting him without talking to me first."

He shook his head and chuckled. "You're not calling the shots here, Mallory Rose." Without another word, he got in his car and closed the door.

Five days later, a subpoena was delivered by registered mail. Elliott was suing for full custody.

Chapter 21

Twelve years without her son. Now when she had a second chance, Elliott planned to steal him away. Elliott, the man who wanted to abort him. The man who held Andrea and career in highest importance. Where would Samuel fit in that hierarchy? Was this for Elliott, or did he acquiesce to Andrea's desire for a child?

She couldn't tell Samuel. Couldn't let him know that his world was about to spin out of control again. In the deepest part of her, she harbored a fear that Samuel would want to live with Elliott. Would he reject her as his father had done years ago?

Mallory needed to stop the negative thoughts and form a plan. She drew a line down the middle of a page and began to list pros and cons. Top of the list, she was Samuel's mother. Courts typically favored mothers. But what about mothers who lied and broke the law? That went in the right-hand column. Under that, she had no income. She had no significant work skills. She lived off of Samuel's inheritance. Elliott had a lucrative career. A two-parent home. He'd been cheated out of the knowledge of his son.

The left-hand column was sadly sparse. Mallory tried to find other positives, but came up empty. She needed a lawyer. A good lawyer. The money was available in Mark and Jolene's estate, but that added to the left column—Samuel's inheritance paying her legal fees. Would Savannah even agree to release the funds? How would it look in court?

She could ask her father but the decision to move her mother to the memory care had been difficult. Could he handle one more family trauma? She remembered Savannah's warning. *Do you want him to have a heart attack?*

Brady? He had received a portion of his grandfather's estate equal to Mark's. Would he loan her money? How would she ever repay him? She could get a court-appointed attorney, but she had to do better than that, or she would lose her son.

Mallory chose the option that would be best for her case. She couldn't use Samuel's money. She picked up her phone and dialed Brady, hoping he wouldn't grow weary of coming to her rescue.

Her voice cracked as she tried to get the words out. When she told him about the custody suit, the phone line went silent. For a moment, she thought he had hung up. Then she heard his voice. "I'll be there in the morning. Don't worry, Mal. This will never fly."

When Samuel was asleep, Mallory pulled out the picture album of Samuel's life. With the book propped open on her bent knees, she flipped pages, looking at Samuel in every stage of the life she'd missed. Only one picture included her. She held her one-day old son as Mark snapped the photo. Samuel's eyes were closed as Mallory's lips brushed the sweet, fuzzy head that leaned against her. The scent came back to her. The sweet smell of a newborn baby. The one and only memory representing her in this book.

She turned the pages of Samuel's life, a life she hadn't been a part of. Would she be finishing this photo album distant from him? Would she follow Andrea's Facebook postings to watch her son become a teenager? To see him graduate?

A Christmas picture showed Samuel at seven years old. He flashed a smile that couldn't be staged for a camera as he held up his new baseball glove. The picture captured his excitement. Christmas was three months away. Would he be celebrating with Elliott and Andrea? It was a very real possibility, and she might be powerless to stop it.

When morning came, a heavy fog lay across the neighborhood as the school bus took Samuel away. A dark mood hovered in the clouds above her as she waited for Brady. Mallory pressed her fists against sleep-deprived eyes.

Brady arrived looking as somber as the sky. He hugged Mallory and gave her hands a squeeze before sitting across from her, speaking words far more confident than she felt. "No judge would move a kid who just lost his parents and place him with strangers."

Mallory pictured her list. That would go on the left, in the positive column.

"But what about the birth certificate? I lied."

"That's a slap on the wrist. You had just turned seventeen. They'll issue a corrected certificate and possibly fine you."

Her shoulders went limp with the word *fine*.

He reached across the table and lifted her hand into his. "Mallory, stop worrying about money. Please. Take that concern off the table. We need to do everything possible to keep Samuel here where he belongs. After you called me, I started a search of attorneys who work custody suits. Malachi Hughes is top of the line. If you're in agreement, I'll call him."

Mallory nodded. For once, she was thankful for Brady's take-charge personality.

****

Mallory and Brady were ushered into the office of Malachi Hughes. He motioned to the two chairs across from his massive wooden desk, and got right down to business. "Okay, folks, how can I help you?"

Twelve years of cautious silence, and now Mallory found herself telling her story over and over.

Malachi's face registered no surprise, no judgment. Just passive listening. Every now and then, he jotted something on the yellow legal pad.

When she finished, the attorney sat up, his brown leather chair returning from the tilted position. He scribbled a few more things on his paper. Then looked up, his eyes traveling between Mallory and Brady.

"A few things you should know. The courts will have to deal with the false birth certificate. It's a misdemeanor against a minor.

I'm not too worried about that in and of itself. They'll probably throw it out. Worst case would be a fine, possibly probation. Nothing significant. The bigger issue is how it affects the outcome of the custody petition.

"Next, be aware that custody battles between states have their own unique challenges. It's unlikely that a joint custody agreement will be made. Typically, when distance is an issue, one parent will be awarded primary, physical custody.

"The single parent status is less of an issue. It's fairly common."

That had been one of Mallory's big concerns. She hadn't realized the extent of her tension until that assurance helped her to relax. It made sense. Most custody battles would involve single parents since they typically followed a divorce.

Malachi continued. "Of greater importance is your ability to support the child. Let's talk about your income and job stability."

The tension returned. Her mind scrambled to think of a way she could put a positive sway to her answer. There just wasn't one. "I'm not employed, but Samuel's estate is sufficient to provide living expenses until he's of age."

His attempt at a passive expression was compromised slightly with a miniscule rise of his brow. He quickly recovered. "So, your living expenses are covered by his inheritance? Where are you living?"

Brady jumped into the conversation. "My brother's estate is adequate to cover living expenses without impacting Samuel when he's of age. The family, both the Carters and the Donaldsons, asked Mallory if she would stay in his home to minimize changes in Samuel's life."

Malachi's steepled fingers were tapping together while he appeared to be analyzing the facts. His head moved in slow nods. "I see. Much rests on the judge's impression of that situation. It may be viewed in a positive light—doing what's best for the child." He turned toward Mallory. "Or it may be viewed as Samuel providing for you instead of you providing for him."

Brady crossed his arms over his chest. "That's not what's happening here. Mallory left a job and moved to Raleigh to take care of Samuel."

"Good. Give me that information. Where you lived, your employer, and your income. That will help to show your commitment."

A rush of heat climbed Mallory's throat, traveling to her face. "I lived in Wilmington. I worked in retail."

He poised his pen and glanced over his glasses at her hesitation. "Employer?"

He jotted Cape Fear Emporium down before looking up, one eyebrow raised. "Annual salary?"

The heat climbed to her ears. "I was hourly. Minimum wage."

Malachi's passive expression returned. He jotted that information. "Did you have health care benefits?"

"No."

"Who provides Samuel's health care?"

Brady leaned forward, crossing his arms. "That's provided from my brother's estate. Give us your honest opinion. What's the chance that Mallory could lose custody?"

"Honest opinion? I think it's going to be a tough battle. Falsifying the birth certificate, no job, and living off of the child's inheritance. Factor into all of that the status of the father. Elliott Moore is well known, probably has a healthy income, and may be seen as the victim since he wasn't informed about his son for twelve years. His attorney's a bulldog. I know his reputation."

He held his hand out, palm open. "Now, before you despair, you have some positives that factor into the equation. We can make some convincing arguments that you've always had your son's best interest in mind. You refused abortion, which the father wanted. He told you you'd be on your own, which explains your silence. There was no lie. You told him you were pregnant, and he said leave me out. There's evidence of you making the best decisions for Samuel from the time of his birth when you were a teenager, to the time of your sister's death when you stepped in to raise him. Since he's twelve years old,

Samuel's wishes will be heard. If he wants to stay with you, most judges will take that into consideration."

Mallory didn't trust her voice. The negatives weighed heavy, a boulder crushing her. They were factual. Undisputable. The positives were subjective, dependent on how convincing her attorney could be. Her life was in the hands of an unknown judge's opinion. She looked at Brady and saw the same worry etched across his face. He asked the question. "So, give me a number. What are our chances?"

The attorney hesitated, his eyes on the yellow legal pad. He looked up, leaned back in his chair, and answered. "Fifty-fifty. It all depends on the judge."

Chapter 22

A few days later, Samuel noticed the album. He pulled it to the kitchen table to browse while he ate his breakfast. He scooped a spoonful of cereal into his mouth.

Mallory watched with unease. "Careful with the album. It took years to pull that all together."

He scooted the album away from his bowl. "This is so cool, that you saved my pictures all these years."

Mallory ruffled his hair playfully. "I lived for those pictures, Samuel. There wasn't a day that I didn't think of you. I hope you know that."

"I know. It's too bad my dad didn't know about me."

Mallory stiffened at the mention. His dad? "Do you mean Elliott? Remember that your parents were Mark and Jolene Donaldson."

"I know. I just don't know what to call him. I can't say *Elliott*. It doesn't sound right. I don't want to call him Mr. Moore."

"Did you ask him?"

"Yeah. He said he'd like *Dad*."

Mallory tensed with anger. Of course, Elliott wouldn't be sensitive. "You could tell him what you told me—that you miss your parents, and it's too hard to call someone else Mom or Dad."

"That's because I have something else to call you. I can't call him Uncle. I guess I'll just call him Dad. We talked last night. He wants me to come to DC next weekend."

Her chest tightened. "Sorry, buddy. You've got a game."

"I could miss just one."

Mallory swallowed her frustration, trying to keep an even tone. "And let your team down? That's not the right decision. You have to be responsible to your commitments."

His excitement morphed into a pout. She hadn't told him about the custody suit. Had Elliott? If he had, Samuel would definitely be talking about it. If they spent the weekend together, Elliott might tell him. He'd have time to convince Samuel to choose him.

She lifted his empty cereal bowl. "It's always good to have something to look forward to. Can we put the visit off for a few weeks? Fall baseball will be ending soon."

"I guess. That'll give me time to map out the things I want to see." His face lit up. "Maybe he'll come see my last games."

****

Malachi called with an update. He filed her response form and the initial hearing date was set for two weeks from today.

"Can you walk me through the procedure? What should I expect?"

"The preliminary hearing will present the case. Unless there's some compelling reason to throw out the petition, which there isn't, the judge will most likely order temporary visitation until the final hearing. He may order mediation, although I suspect some of the extenuating circumstances may work against that."

"Wait. What do you mean by extenuating circumstances?"

"Mediation is ordered in situations where couples are able to work things out with the help of a mediator. If tensions are too high, or if the case has complicating circumstances, the judge is less likely to order it."

Her heart plummeted. "Complications like falsifying the birth certificate?"

"Possibly. And the lack of income. We drew a short straw with the judge. Sheffield is known to be an advocate for paternal rights. Now, before you throw in the towel, there's also the possibility of the judge granting you custody with child support from the father."

It always came down to money. Mallory didn't want anything from Elliott. "I can get a job."

"I'm afraid that's too little, too late. They'll look at your income over a three-year span."

"Seriously, Malachi, am I going to lose my son?"

A moment of quiet stretched before his answer. "You won't lose your son. Both parents will be granted time with Samuel. The uncertainty is primary physical custody."

Mallory heard what Malachi didn't say. He expected her to lose. She felt the color drain from her face as she struggled not to fall apart. Brady was her first thought. The lifeline that she'd been clinging to. But was she leaning on him too much? He paid for the attorney and deserved an update. Mallory opened her laptop and typed an email, outlining her conversation with the attorney, and sent it off to Brady.

****

Even before rising from bed, Mallory reached her phone and tapped her e-mail. Nothing. Her phone and e-mail remained silent for three days after her call from Malachi. The initial hearing would be in ten days, and she'd had no word from Brady. She had allowed herself to rely on him. His wisdom and encouragement. Sooner or later she had to stand on her own. It was wrong to depend on Brady to be the cavalry. Not fair to either of them. A friendship developed, but that didn't allow her to run to him with every problem. She had depended on herself for the past twelve years. His silence told her she'd have to face this alone.

Ten minutes after the school bus pulled away, Mallory heard a knock on the back door. Only Savannah or Brady used that door. She hurried to the kitchen and found him waiting on the deck.

"Come on in. I didn't know you were in town."

He walked with a heaviness; worry etched at the creases of his eyes. "I came in last night. I want to talk with you while Samuel's not home."

He motioned to the kitchen table. Mallory pulled a chair out and sat. Brady took the seat beside her, turning his chair backwards and straddling it to face her. His hands rested on the back of the chair, and he kept his head down.

"Brady, you're scaring me." His eyes remained downcast. Was it worry about the custody suit, or had he come to tell her she was wearing him out with phone calls and text messages? To ask her to stop?

He righted himself and met her eyes. "I'm afraid we're going to lose this custody suit."

As his words unfolded in her brain, Mallory's pulse pounded like a blowing wind whooshing through her head. In every step they'd been through, Brady had remained positive. When Mallory took guardianship—*You're the perfect person.* When Samuel was missing— *He's a smart boy. He'll be okay.* His optimism had kept her from crumbling. She needed him to tell her all the reasons why everything would be okay. But now, Brady was worried. Did he blame her for how she'd handled everything? Mallory held onto the table to keep the room from spinning.

"I can't lose him. I can't have him taken from me a second time." A wall of tears pooled in her eyes. She pictured Samuel packing his clothes, his trophies, everything belonging to him, and moving to a new city, a home with two strangers. Having his world ripped out from under him again.

"I know, Mal. My mind keeps reliving the meeting with Malachi. Asking myself what we can do to make the case stronger."

"So, what are you thinking? I'll do anything."

Mallory listened to the ticking of the clock, waiting for something, anything that could be done. Finally, his eyes met hers. "I think it would help if you were married."

Her hope drained away. "Malachi said that doesn't matter. He said being a single parent wouldn't be a detriment."

"No, but the finances will. We're at the mercy of a judge and don't know how he'll view the current situation. Will he look at what you've done and decide you've made the best choice for Samuel. Or will he think ..."

At his hesitation, Mallory finished the thought. "That I'm a gold digger living off of my son's inheritance."

His eyes softened. "None of us think that."

"But a stranger might."

"That's my concern. I know this house is paid for, so if you were married, you could stay here, but without using Samuel's inheritance for living expenses. If those funds weren't being touched at all, it would be a non-issue."

Mallory had no response. She wasn't married. Had no prospects for marriage. At eighteen years old, all of her time and energy had been spent proving that she could make it on her own. Aside from working at the Emporium, she spent weekends cleaning rental houses at the beach. Work allowed no time for relationships. A few casual dates failed to develop into anything serious. She held back the part of herself that she'd given to Elliott—both physical and emotional. There'd never been anyone with whom Mallory could imagine a happily ever after.

Brady's eyes held hers. "Mallory, I could provide for you and Samuel. You could both go on my healthcare. I'd cover the utilities and all living expenses. We wouldn't need to touch Samuel's inheritance."

Was she hearing him correctly? Was he really implying they marry for the sake of custody? She thought he'd come to tell her good-bye. To soldier up and figure it out on her own.

"Are you suggesting we marry?"

A sheepish grin replaced a tiny bit of the heaviness. "Not the proposal every girl dreams of."

Massive understatement. "Why would you do that?"

"We can't lose Samuel."

Brady was nothing like the few men she had briefly dated. He perfectly matched her image of the man she'd someday love. Handsome, thoughtful, successful. But those adolescent fantasies died years ago, buried in the grave along with her senior year, college, and career.

Surely Brady had plans of his own that didn't include a pity wife. "Can I ask why you've never married? I imagine you had ample opportunities."

A smile, heavy with regret, came before his answer. "I spent too many years with the wrong person. Her name's Lisa. It was easy to fall into a comfort zone. We dated for four years. I had no reason to break up with her. She's sweet, and I liked her company. It gave me someone to spend time with—go to dinner, movies, concerts— things you don't want to do alone. It just never moved to love. After four years, we both realized the relationship wasn't going anywhere. We went our separate ways about six months ago."

Mallory propped her elbows on the table, cradling her chin in her clasped hands. "You didn't marry her, and yet you're offering to marry me to help the custody suit?"

"Lisa was the wrong person for my future. All things happen for a purpose. Maybe the timing of this situation is to save Samuel." Brady brought it right back to the heart of the matter. Marriage for a purpose. One that had nothing to do with her. Nothing to do with love.

"Do you really think it would make a difference? What if we married, and still lost the suit?"

A slight smile found its way to his lips. "I could do worse."

A flush warmed Mallory's cheeks. "And you could do better." They were down to one-liners. A moment of silence stretched between them. "Samuel said you think I'm a hottie."

Brady sprang upright from his slouched position. "What? He actually said that?"

"Don't worry. I reprimanded him."

An embarrassed grin replaced the surprise. "I hope you weren't too hard on him." He looked at the fruit bowl at the center of the table. "It's just naming a truth. I think the apple's red because it is."

Mallory had no response but felt the heat intensify on her cheeks. Was that Brady's attempt at a compliment, designed to be flirtatious?

Her silence brought his return to the practical. "We've grown close over the last few months. I enjoy spending time with you and Samuel."

Close like friends, but friends don't marry. Then memories flooded her mind. His hand tucked around hers on the telescope. The touch of his fingers brushing her cheek. His arm gathering her close as they sat on the sofa. His eyes holding hers, drawing her in. She fidgeted, her hands moving to her lap.

"I know we're good friends. And I know you're good for Samuel. But marriage?" Such an enormous decision.

Brady reached for her hand. "Mal, if we had time, I'd do this differently. Take you out, test our feelings, give it time to grow. But we don't have time. Samuel doesn't have time."

The clock ticked away the minutes. Mallory looked up, moisture gathering in her eyes. "I can't lose him, Brady."

He gave a nod of agreement. "I'll take that as a yes."

It was surreal. Was this really happening? Would it be in name only? Would he still live in Charlotte? So many unspoken questions collided, jumbled together in her head.

Brady was willing to change his whole life in order to help her. To protect Samuel. She once put all of her hopes in Elliott Moore. Look how that turned out. Still, what were her options? She'd do anything to save her son. Even a marriage of convenience.

"Yes. But there are so many questions."

"We can sort them all out in time. Mal, I think this has to happen sooner rather than later. If we plan ahead and have a wedding, that will push us too close to the final court date. It might be seen as a ploy."

"You mean, the ploy that it is?"

He ignored the question. "I'm suggesting that we do this right now. Privately. Then we can tell everyone. Let's go downtown today to apply for the marriage license. Find a JP to marry us in the next day or two. As soon as that's done, I'll call Malachi and give him updated financial information. And Mallory, just to answer one of those many questions—I won't expect anything from you. Maybe in time that will happen." He reached for her hand, holding its softness in his. "That will be completely up to you."

She could so easily bask in his hand holding hers, allowing him to take charge. The familiar image returned. Sitting on the sofa with Brady's arm around her. His fingers brushing her cheek. She must not go there. Those thoughts led to heartache. This was not about her; it was all for Samuel's sake. "I can't think of letting a man in my heart. Right now, there's only room for Samuel."

He nodded, still holding her hand. "Why don't you go get ready and we'll head downtown. The courthouse opens at nine."

****

Mallory hadn't been to her parents' home since the day her mother went missing. She hadn't seen Savannah since the visit to her home. Her only contact had been when Samuel ran away. When she brought him home, she had called and downplayed the situation, telling them that he stayed overnight with a friend, with no mention of Wilmington. They knew nothing about the custody suit. Nothing about her hurried trip to Washington, DC. Now add to that, a surprise marriage. Her mother once had keen instincts. If it weren't for her dementia, she'd have known there was more going on. At the end of this month, they'd be moving her into a room at the Birchfield Memory Care Home.

After securing their marriage license, Mallory asked Brady to stop at her parents' home with her. They wouldn't tell her dad until after they married, but it might not come as a complete blindsided shock if he knew that she had been spending time with Brady.

Even though her dad had given her a house key, Mallory knocked on the front door.

"Hi, Dad. I wanted to stop in to see Mom and to check on you. Brady's in town so he said he'd tag along."

Her dad shook his hand. "Good to see you, Brady." He turned back toward Mallory. "She's having a bad day. Don't expect much."

Her mother's frame appeared dwarfed in a wingchair in the living room. Even seated, Mallory could tell that her slacks were too loose and her blouse didn't want to remain tucked in. She had the fragile look of a porcelain doll.

"Hi, Mom." Mallory leaned down to kiss her wrinkled cheek, but her mother shrank into the chair, fear in her eyes. "It's Mallory Rose, Mom." She didn't try to introduce Brady. That would be too much. She caressed her mother's hand, as delicate as a bird's bone.

"We'll only stay a few minutes. How are you holding up, Dad?"

He shook his head in despair. "Seeing her fear has been the hardest."

"Mr. Carter, when did you first see signs of Alzheimer's? Was it sudden or gradual?"

"Well, that's an interesting question. I knew we had a problem about six years ago, but after she was diagnosed, I thought back to signs that could have alerted me. We all get forgetful, so I had no reason to get alarmed. But once she was driving and got lost. It was in Charlotte on roads that she'd known all her life. She said it was the craziest thing, but she just blanked. We laughed about it at the time. Mallory Rose, do you remember when she didn't show up for your parent-teacher conference?"

"Oh yeah, that was the beginning of my junior year. She was so mad at herself."

"Your mother was passionate about your education. She never skipped those. When she found out she'd missed it, she was troubled for days. She kept saying, 'I can't believe I forgot that.' There were signs about three or four years before it became obvious."

Alzheimer's was at work stealing her mother's memory before Mallory's pregnancy ever occurred. It hadn't been dormant. It was making a slow entrance into her mother's life. Savannah was wrong. This really wasn't her fault.

As they were leaving, her dad patted Brady on the shoulder. "Don't be a stranger. You're welcome anytime."

The car eased into traffic heading toward home. "Thank you, Brady. I know why you were asking about my mother."

He didn't look her way, but she could see his smile in the profile of his face. "You have enough worries. You don't need to add that one."

Her eyes traveled to the marriage license tucked on the driver's side visor. Brady was a good man. Another day, different circumstances, their marriage might have been good. But not like this.

Her future wavered as unpredictable as the wind.

Chapter 23

Samuel left for school, and Mallory went upstairs to dress for her wedding. What did you wear to an appointment with a JP to sign papers binding you together as husband and wife? It really didn't matter. No one would be there to see them. No photographer would capture happy faces dancing, cutting a three-tiered cake, and drinking champagne from fluted glasses.

Mallory shook off those destructive thoughts. She had no time for what ifs. Today wasn't about her. It was about Samuel. She pulled a casual skirt from the closet and stepped into it before sliding her feet into comfortable flat shoes. A pull-over top with three-quarter length sleeves finished it. Nothing noteworthy, which she deemed appropriate.

Brady picked her up, dressed as insignificantly as she, and they drove downtown to the office of a Justice of the Peace, arriving a few minutes before their appointment time.

The receptionist, Kenisha Fredricks according to her name tag, ushered them into the adjacent office of Geoffrey Gorman. Mallory guessed him to be fifteen years past retirement age. His snow-white hair was carefully combed in an attempt to cover splotches of age-spotted skin. He stood to greet them without the aid of the cane propped against his desk.

"So, this is the big day." He attempted a smile. "Do you have the marriage license?"

Brady pulled the folded paper from his shirt pocket. "Yes, sir."

Mr. Gorman slid his glasses on and read the document. "Looks in order. We can do this a few different ways. You only need to sign the appropriate papers to make it legal. Or I can talk you through traditional vows that you'll repeat. Or if you'd like, you can say your own vows to each other."

Brady looked her way. "Mallory?"

She saw no reason to say vows that may end up being broken. "Let's just sign."

"Since you have no one with you, I'll have Kenisha witness." Mr. Gorman called to her as he placed X's on the lines that needed their signatures. Then he tilted the pen toward Mallory.

Her left hand tremored as she poised the pen over the blank line. This wouldn't really be a marriage, so she'd be falsifying another document. At least this time, she'd sign her own name. She scribbled Mallory Rose Carter and handed the pen to Brady. He took it and added his signature, before handing it to the receptionist. She signed with a flourish. Mr. Gorman was the last to sign. He picked up the official seal, adjusted the paper inside and pressed the embedded seal of authenticity.

"Okay, folks. You are officially man and wife." He motioned to his assistant. "Kenisha, will you take a picture?" He slid a desk drawer open and lifted out a camera. "We can use this and she'll mail you the picture, or if you have a phone camera, she can take one with that."

Mallory wanted to scream. No pictures. She wanted no reminder of the sham ceremony. But Brady handed the assistant his cell phone, and moved beside Mallory, his arm resting on her shoulder.

"Everybody, smile," Kenisha instructed before snapping two photos.

When he tucked his phone back in a pocket, Brady reached for his wallet. "What do I owe you?"

"Thirty-five dollars, please."

Brady peeled some bills from his billfold, handed them over, and they left.

No one spoke on the ride home. Mallory resisted the tears as long as she could, but by the end of the ride, a few insistent drops had stained her cheek. Brady pulled into the driveway and opened his car door. Mallory held up her hand, motioning to stop him. She didn't want him walking her in. She needed time alone. Time to mourn.

Two momentous events, marriage and childbirth. She'd made a mockery of both. This was not the life she expected. "I imagine you have work today. I'm good."

He ignored her and came around to her side of the car as she stepped out. "We have to tell Samuel. We should do that together."

"He won't be home for hours."

"Please let me come in and talk to you."

"Brady, I'm emotionally drained right now. I need a little time."

He reached for her hand and held it. "Okay, Mal. I'm sorry it had to be this way."

Tears were threatening, and she wanted to escape inside before they broke through. But the irony of his words hit her. He was apologizing for the hurried ceremony, for the marriage itself, but it was her fault. He stepped up and married someone he didn't love to save Samuel for her. When he freed her hand, she started to speak, to thank him. Instead a sob escaped in place of her words. As he pulled her toward him, she wrapped both arms around him and allowed the tears to come. He held her until they quieted, then placed a kiss on her forehead.

She lingered for a moment before moving back, out of his hold. "Thank you. Come back in an hour or two. I'll be better then."

****

Mallory pulled her emotions together and formed her questions. What would they tell Samuel? Did they tell him Elliott filed for custody? He didn't have to attend the preliminary hearing, but eventually he would have to know. Should they tell him theirs was a marriage of necessity for the lawsuit? That would make him feel as guilty as Mallory felt, knowing they'd been trapped in an unwanted marriage. No, they had to let him think it was the real deal. He already thought Brady had his eye on her.

She had questions about the marriage itself. He indicated that it wouldn't include romance, but implied that he might want that in the future. Did he intend this marriage to be permanent? Would he move into this house, or want to move them to Charlotte? Or perhaps neither of those. Maybe he'd live in Charlotte and see them from time to time, just as he had been doing.

By the time Brady returned, she had changed into comfortable jeans, washed the streaks from her face, and covered her puffy eyes with make-up. The coffee pot was set up, ready to brew, and she pulled cookies from the freezer. Somewhere in the last hour, a new determination gripped her. She had to be strong and decisive. She had taken care of herself since she was eighteen. She couldn't fall apart now.

"I set coffee up. Would you like a cup? I have some turtle brownies. They're Samuel's favorites. I learned that through trial and error."

He moved toward the family room. "In a few minutes. Can we talk first?"

"Let me start brewing. I'll be right in."

She turned the coffee on and pulled two mugs from the cupboard before joining him in the family room. She sat on the sofa, as far from Brady as possible. "I guess we have some big decisions to make."

He moved from his chair and came to sit beside her. "We do, but first let me call Malachi. I thought it would be better to be together in case he has questions."

He placed the call. "Malachi, Mallory and I have some updated information for you. Can I put you on speaker?" When the speaker was activated, he set the phone between them. "Mallory and I were married this morning."

After a hesitation, he responded, his voice tight with suspicion. "No kidding? Why didn't you mention that was going to happen?"

Brady looked at Mallory, but she had no desire to answer. "It wasn't in the works then. It was going to happen eventually. We just moved it up some."

She shot him a surprised look. More lies. Weren't they?

Malachi blew out a loud breath. "So, does this result in financial changes?"

"Yes. I'll be fully supporting both Mallory and Samuel."

Mallory imagined Malachi opening the yellow legal pad and writing as he spoke.

"And living where?"

"Same house. It's the best thing for Samuel. It's paid for, but I'll be covering all living expenses—utilities, insurance, healthcare, and Samuel's private school."

Mallory's mouth dropped open to protest, but she held back. They could discuss school when the call ended.

"Okay. That should help immensely. Can I get some figures?"

"Sure. Annual salary, $125,000. Additionally, I have some passive income."

"What's the source?"

"Interest and dividends."

"Rough estimate?"

"Approximately 900K, depending on the economy."

Malachi let out a slow whistle. "Okay. Got it."

"And this will help our case?" Brady asked while Mallory held her breath.

"It will. Custody isn't about the richest parent. But my biggest concern was the inability to financially support the child. Well, congratulations to you two. I'll get this in the report."

"Just holler if you have any questions." Brady put his phone away and turned to her.

Mallory was speechless. She knew about the inheritance, but putting numbers to the interest income was staggering.

With a reach into his pocket, Brady pulled out a jewelry box and opened it. The velvet case held both a diamond ring and a wedding band. "I know today was hard. Brutally hard. I wish things could have been different."

The round-cut diamond shone brilliantly, catching the light through intricate facets. "They're beautiful. You really didn't have to do that."

"I wanted to. We don't want anyone questioning the legitimacy of our marriage. I bought a band for myself." He held his left hand open to show her.

The words stung as much as the morning's wedding had. Of course, the ring would be for the sake of appearance. Everything about this arrangement was. She allowed him to slip it on her finger and reached deep to hold on to her new determination.

"Thank you. They fit perfectly."

"Good. I guessed, but the jeweler said you can come in for adjustments if necessary."

She flayed her fingers open and admired the beauty. If it couldn't hold the true meaning associated with wedding rings—a circle with no beginning and no end, eternal as love should be—at least she could admire the physical beauty.

"Let's talk about Samuel before he gets home. I'm not sure I'm ready to tell him about the custody petition. I'm carrying a boatload of guilt that you had to marry me to increase my chances. I don't want him to feel guilty, too."

"You need to let that go, Mallory. I'm the one who suggested we marry. And I'm not at all unhappy with the situation. I expect Samuel's going to be happy with the news."

Not unhappy? Had she heard right? "I think so, too. Unless we tell him about the lawsuit. Then he'll know it's not real."

He breathed a heavy sigh. "It is real. Legal and binding."

"You know what I mean."

Brady brought the discussion back to the custody issue. "What if we don't tell him and Elliott Moore does? You saw how he reacted when he found out we hadn't been truthful. He wants facts."

Mallory noticed that he said *we*. He shared responsibility for a lie he had no part in. Brady was right. She had to be upfront with Samuel. She couldn't afford to anger him to the point that he'd run to Elliott. "All right. That means we hit him with two surprises today."

"It has to happen. I think it's best coming from us."

The coffee pot had long ceased its dripping, sizzling sound. The aroma reminded her. "I can smell the coffee. I'll go pour us some."

She filled the two mugs and opened the fridge for cream, then set the steaming cups on the coffee table before asking her next question.

"We need to talk about living arrangements." He had answered one of her questions in his conversation with Malachi. He had no plans of moving them to Charlotte. "Are you planning to stay in Charlotte and visit here occasionally like you've been doing?"

He sipped the hot coffee and set his mug on a coaster. "I'm not sure. I'll keep my condo in Charlotte, but I'm thinking that I should spend more time here. Have a more constant male presence in Samuel's life. It might help if the judge knows there's a male role model. Are you okay with that?"

"Back when the accident happened, you weren't able to take custody because you couldn't live here. How has that changed?"

"Nothing's changed. I still travel. I'll continue to be in Charlotte for meetings. That's not conducive to raising a child on my own. But that wouldn't stop me from spending more time here."

"Okay." Mallory tried to form the next awkward question, but Brady answered before she had to ask.

"Why don't you move into the master bedroom and I'll take the smaller one?"

Relief and disappointment mingled in the same thought. Not that she had any intention of sharing his room. It was one more reminder of the charade their marriage would be. First, she falsified a birth certificate. Now, she falsified a marriage. "I'm settled in and comfortable. You can take the bigger room. Samuel's been pretty possessive of things that were his parents. He'll do better with you taking their space."

He raised an eyebrow in question. "Why would you think that?"

Mallory grinned. "He likes you better."

"Ha. Not for long. I'm more of a disciplinarian than you are."

Her eyes widened. Was he planning to trump her parenting decisions?

He stretched his arm across the back of the sofa. "Don't worry. You get to be good cop."

The conversation indicated that Brady planned to become more present in their daily lives. It did not sound like he intended to return to the old routine where they'd see him a few times each month. Yet Mallory still tested the boundaries of this new reality.

"I have to tell my dad and Savannah. Would you mind coming with me when I do that?"

The hand that had been stretched behind her moved to her shoulder, his fingers stroking it in soft circles. "Of course, I'll be with you. I planned to. I'm hoping you and Samuel will come to Charlotte when I tell my folks. I can promise you they'll be thrilled."

A knot formed in her stomach at the thought of telling Brady's parents. With the pending custody hearing, they'd learn of her teen pregnancy. "Thrilled that we eloped and they didn't have to deal with a big wedding?"

"No, they'll be ticked about that. Thrilled with their new daughter-in-law. After all, you're a Carter girl. I know for a fact they love Carter girls." She didn't exactly know what to make of his smile.

****

Mallory kept checking the clock, practicing the words in her mind. She heard the screeching sound of the school bus's brakes. Samuel came bounding in. "Uncle Brady's here?"

Brady called from the family room. "Guilty. What gave it away?"

Samuel hurried in. "Duh. Your car."

"Did you even say hello to your aunt? I think she fixed you your special snack."

"Turtle brownies?" He swiveled around and dashed to the kitchen. "Sorry. Hi. Was I right?"

She gave him a mock pout. "I know. I'm second fiddle when your uncle's here. But he isn't the one who made these." She held up the plate of turtle brownies.

"Thanks, Aunt Mallory. This calls for milk." He poured himself a tall glass. "Okay if I take them in the other room?"

"Sure."

He went in and headed toward the video game.

"Not now, buddy. We want to talk to you."

Mallory was about to sit in the wingchair until Brady gave a small movement of his head, and tapped the cushion beside him. She switched to the sofa, leaving a small space between them.

Samuel's eyes darted from one to the other. "You look serious. What'd I do?"

Mallory laughed. "You didn't do anything." She looked toward Brady because every word she'd practiced had fled from her brain.

"Samuel, I don't know if you realized, but over the past few months, I've grown very fond of your aunt. Actually, from way back when I first saw her last spring."

Samuel sent Mallory an *I told you so* look.

Brady reached for Mallory's hand. "I asked her to marry me, and she said yes."

His mouth opened wide enough to swallow a golf ball.

Mallory wasn't sure if that shock was happy or just plain disbelief. "I know you've had a lot to deal with. How do you feel about that?"

"Cool." His face expressed pleasure, then quickly dropped. "Do we have to move to Charlotte?"

"No, Samuel. I'll come here, but I'll have to make trips to Charlotte frequently. We'll work it out so you can stay in your school."

"Good. It would stink to change schools." He grabbed for another brownie and placed it on the napkin Mallory had given him.

"Samuel, there's something else we have to tell you. I said yes, but for many reasons, planning a big wedding wasn't a good idea."

"You mean because of Grandma?"

She was glad he latched on to that. "That's one reason. What I'm trying to say is that we got married today, just privately. You're the first person we've told."

"Oh, that's a bummer. I thought I'd get to be best man or something."

Mallory's eyes fixed firmly on his. "You are the best man. Never doubt that."

Brady shuffled uncomfortably. "Now that I've been put into second place, we need to tell you something else. Your biological father would like you to come live with him. We don't want that to happen. You're twelve years old, almost a teenager, and we'd like your thoughts."

Samuel suddenly looked like a little boy. Uncertainty on his face. "Is this because you got married?"

"No. He doesn't know that."

"I mean, are you asking me because you got married? Like, do you want me to go?"

"No!" Brady and Mallory answered in unison, their words rushing together. Brady motioned for her to speak.

"Absolutely not. We want you here with us. We're a family. We've sort of been growing into a family for the last few months."

Brady moved to stand beside Samuel's chair, and clapped him on the back. "We're hoping you don't want to go. You're one of the two reasons I want to be here." He looked back and forth between Mallory and Samuel.

"Okay. Good. I'd like to visit my dad, but I don't want to live with him."

Brady gave his shoulder another squeeze. "That's what we wanted to hear."

Now Mallory delivered the bad news. "Samuel, do you know what custody means?"

"Yeah. Lots of kids at school go between their parents' homes. You know—when they're divorced."

Mallory looked back to Brady, a silent request to finish.

"Custody is usually decided in court. That's what … that's what Mr. Moore is planning to do. He's taking it to court, and we're opposing his request. We don't want you to worry because we're certain that the court will keep you right here where you belong."

Samuel's hands tightened around the napkin, crumbs escaping onto the coffee table. "I just won't go."

Brady chuckled. "You won't have to be a passive resister. The court's not going to make you go. We're sure of it."

Mallory hoped those words were prophetic.

Chapter 24

Mallory decided to wait and tell her whole family together. Brady agreed to join her at the Sunday dinner. They planned to share the news of their marriage, but not the custody suit. Before leaving for dinner at her parents' home, Mallory broached the subject. "Samuel, you know that we're planning to tell Grandpa and the rest of the family about Uncle Brady and me. I try not to worry Grandma and Grandpa, so I haven't mentioned the custody issue."

"I'll zip my lip. My mom used to tell me that a lot when she didn't want them to know stuff. She'd say, 'Zip it, Samuel.' Then she'd pull her fingers across her mouth like a zipper."

Mallory pictured Jolene's expression. She'd seen it from her own mother many times as a child. Mallory understood all about keeping quiet. She'd grown up in a house that held secrets inside their walls. "Actually, I haven't mentioned that you met your biological father. They don't know who he is. Can we keep it that way until things are settled?"

"Yeah, Grandma won't know what we're talking about anyway."

Seeing Brady at Sunday dinner would be enough of a surprise. If she'd told them ahead of time, Savannah may have called her out. *This is family time. Mother doesn't need other people seeing her this way.* However, in Brady's presence, she'd be the perfect hostess.

"Brady, you know that in my mother's house, I'm Mallory Rose. You might be corrected if you forget that."

He grinned as he parked the car. "I'll just say *hey, you.* That will avoid a mistake."

They were the last to arrive. Savannah stopped short in her steps when she saw Brady, but quickly recovered. "How nice that you could join us today. Let me set another place at the table."

Mallory swallowed the lump that seemed to block her breathing. "Actually, before you do that, I'd like to gather the family. I have something to share."

Savannah switched to full alert. The straight line of her lips tightened beneath steely eyes. But she played the role of hostess. "Of course. Please, have a seat and I'll call everyone in."

Mallory didn't have a seat. When the whole crew gathered, there wasn't enough seating in the living room. Brady stood beside her as each one came in and filled the sofa and two chairs. The younger boys plopped on the floor, and the teenagers perched on the sofa arms.

"Brady and I have something to tell you." She looked at him pleadingly, keeping her ringed hand behind her.

He draped his arm around her shoulder. "Mallory Rose and I have grown closer over the last few months. I asked her to marry me, and she said yes."

Mallory's gaze fell on her dad. A smile filled his face, bringing creases to the corners of his eyes. Her look darted toward her mom. She sat with hands folded in her lap, looking confused.

Savannah didn't wear her usual stiffness. No daggers came from her eyes. She wilted with a defeated look.

Mallory stepped in closer to Brady. "There's more to our news. With everything that this family's been through over the past year," she stole a glance her mother's way, "we decided that a big wedding wouldn't be a good idea. We were married in a private ceremony earlier this week." The word ceremony tasted bitter, but the best she could do.

Her dad's smile drooped. "I would have liked to give you away."

"I know, Dad. I didn't think it would have been good for Mom, having all her old friends see her." How duplicitous, blaming her mother's illness.

Her dad rose from his seat and came toward them, wrapping Mallory in his arms. "You're right. She would've hated that." He correctly spoke of her in the past tense. The old Lorraine Carter would have hated that. "I'm so happy for you." He turned toward Brady and shook his hand with a vigor Mallory hadn't seen in a while. "Welcome to our family. I've prayed for someone like you for our Mallory Rose."

Savannah hopped up and darted toward the kitchen. "Let's eat. Our dinner will be a celebration feast."

When Mallory stepped in to help, Savannah shooed her away. "I've got this. I guess you're the guest of honor. I'd throw a wedding shower for you, but I'm sure you'll want for nothing." Mallory wanted to think her words expressed kindness, but she knew better. They wore a sharp edge.

Oh Savannah, if you only knew.

****

Mallory and Brady shifted the clothing in the master bedroom only enough to provide a little space to hang his things, and emptied two drawers in the dresser. If Samuel noticed that they kept separate bedrooms, he made no mention of it. He was typically asleep before they went upstairs, and wasn't an early riser.

Samuel left for school Tuesday morning without knowledge that the preliminary hearing would occur. They attempted to downplay the entire issue. He didn't need to worry about another upheaval.

As soon as the bus pulled out, Mallory and Brady hurried to his car. They made the trip into town and parked near the Wake County Courthouse. They approached the stately building, its rows of narrow windows recessed in the concrete columns. An emblem of the state seal was centered above the doors. The American flag and North Carolina flag were flying, one on each side of the courtyard.

Brady motioned toward the building. "This is a great piece of architecture." He began pointing, naming architectural terms that defined the structure. Any other day, Mallory may have had an interest.

She caught sight of Elliott standing off to the side near a grassy area, the first she had seen him since he filed suit. A rush of adrenaline surged through her. Her hands shook until she flexed them, squeezing them open and closed. Fingernails embedded into her palms leaving angry indentations. A quick movement propelled her in his direction.

Brady reached for her shoulder. "No, Mallory. Don't."

She shook his hand off and marched over to Elliott. "Mallory, don't lose your cool. We can't give them reason to question our character." Brady's words followed her, but they tumbled to the ground, overpowered by her rage. Her hands needed a release from the tension. As she reached Elliott, she placed both hands on his chest and shoved him backward.

"Who do you think you are? You have no right to try and take my son."

Elliott recovered from the stumble and appeared unfazed. He widened his stance, giving him more balance, then smoothed his suit coat. "Don't you mean our son?"

Brady wrapped his hand around her arm. "Don't do this, Mallory." Again, she brushed his hand off of her.

"Why are you doing this? You know what that boy's been through." She stepped toward him, poking the air with her index finger.

He leaned in, refusing to back up. "And I know what my wife's been through."

"So, this is for her? You'd rip a child out of his world so she can play mother? Get her a dog."

Firm hands gripped her shoulder, swiveling her around. Brady's authoritative voice held whispered fury. "Stop it! You're going to hurt our case." When a few steps separated them from Elliott, he loosened his grip, positioning an arm across her back and ushered her to the door. Before stepping inside, he faced her. "You can't lose your cool like that. Take a deep breath."

Mallory inhaled, then released the air.

He rubbed her arm. "Did I hurt you?"

She shook her head.

"We're going to win this. We can't afford to lose control."

Her heart still raced. "You're right. I'm sorry."

His mouth curved into a grin. "I see you've still got spunk."

****

The room was smaller than a traditional courtroom, and rich with oak. Two rows of four pews for spectators which remained empty, two tables for attorneys and clients, a witness stand and a judge's bench, all in a rich grainy oak. The only break from the off-white walls and oak was an American flag flying in the front of the room. Both she and Brady sat at a table with Malachi. He cautioned them that Brady would not be permitted a seat at the defendant's table for the final hearing. Today was less formal.

Elliott sauntered in with Andrea at his side, like nothing had happened. His wife had not been with him outside, but of course they would come here together. It was just like high school, the perfect couple. Blond, beautiful, successful. Elliott nodded toward Mallory as if this were the first he'd seen her today. He shook hands with his attorney and sat. So casual, exuding confidence.

The solid oak door on the side of the room opened. A man in a casual golf shirt and black slacks entered. Malachi stood and motioned for them to do likewise.

The man walked to the bench and slid his arms into a black robe. "You may be seated." He shuffled a few papers, finding what he wanted. "I'm Judge Sheffield and this is a preliminary hearing for the purpose of deciding custody for the minor child Samuel James Donaldson."

Mallory estimated him to be in his mid to late fifties. His once-dark hair had faded and gray streaked through it. Heavy brows hovered over tortoise-shell glasses resting low on the bridge of his nose.

"I've reviewed the brief as well as a motion to dismiss by the defendant. That request is denied. A final hearing date will be scheduled. Today we will set guidelines for temporary custody until the permanent arrangements have been determined. Additionally, the defendant is charged with a misdemeanor for falsifying a birth certificate." He looked over his glasses, directly at Mallory. "I'm sure your attorney has counseled you on the possible repercussions?"

She nodded. "Yes, sir."

Malachi whispered. "Your Honor."

"Yes, Your Honor."

"How do you plead?"

"Guilty, Your Honor." Malachi told her to expect this. There was no merit in denying it.

"Sentencing will be ordered at the time of the final custody hearing." He shuffled papers and selected another. "Temporary custody is granted to the child's mother, Mallory Rose Donaldson. Because of the distance, the child's father has visitation rights twice monthly, the second and fourth weekend. The second will be in the state of the child's residence and the fourth in the state of the father's residence. Any holidays that occur prior to the final hearing will alternate beginning with the father, Mr. Moore. Inclusive holidays are noted on the court order. I remind you, these are temporary orders."

Mallory saw whispering at Elliott's table. His attorney stood.

"Your Honor, if we may, on visitations where Mr. Moore cannot take Samuel to Washington, we'd like to request that they be permitted to travel to Charlotte where he can visit with his extended family."

The judge tipped his glasses and looked over the top rim. "The court order says, in the state of the child's residence. The last I checked, Charlotte and Raleigh were in the same state. You'll be notified of the final hearing date. This session is dismissed."

He clunked his gavel on the wooden surface and it was over.

Malachi gathered them outside the courthouse. "Not bad. It's what we expected."

Mallory shuddered. "He wasn't very friendly."

"Judges aren't supposed to be friendly. They're supposed to be fair. You kept custody for the short term. That's huge and a positive sign."

Elliott wasted no time staking his claim. A text message sounded during the drive home.

THE FOURTH WEEKEND IS IN TEN DAYS. I'LL PICK SAMUEL UP AFTER SCHOOL, AROUND 3 AND HAVE HIM HOME SUNDAY EVENING BY 9.

****

Later that week, Savannah met Mallory at their parents' home. They needed to be with their dad while he moved their mother into the Birchfield Memory Care Home. Dad's stoic manner didn't fool Mallory. This was the hardest thing he'd ever done. Theirs was an enduring love, surviving forty-two years of marriage. Dad had always treated her with china doll fragility. Today, he would give her care into the hands of strangers.

The open suitcase was almost full. Savannah had selected which clothes to take. She was folding them neatly, symmetrically, matching sleeves to sleeves with perfect folds. Not a hint of a wrinkle remained.

"How can I help?"

"Shoes and slippers. We're limited to two pair of shoes. Pick the most comfortable. Something easy to slip on and off."

The task seemed to soften the hostility between them. Mallory knew she had to tell her family about the custody suit. It was public record, and would be terrible if they heard the news elsewhere. The timing was wrong to tell her father. He didn't need another worrisome burden. But she may never have a better opportunity to tell her sister.

She took a deep breath and prayed this wouldn't begin another battle. "I've never really talked much about my pregnancy. Lies have a way of crumbling, letting the truth seep out. My lies started a slow crumble last summer, and now it's become a massive rock slide."

Savannah stopped folding clothes and turned toward her sister. "What are you talking about, Mallory Rose?"

Mallory pushed the suitcase back and sat on the bed beside Savannah. "Samuel knows."

"What?" A rise in her vocal tone. "Why in the world would you tell him now?"

"I didn't. But he found out. His biological father pushed the issue and they've met."

"The boy you've protected with your silence all these years."

"I made mistakes, Savannah Joy. I admit that. My silence was to protect Samuel, not the father."

Savannah lowered her head, studying her sister. "Are you sure about that? Maybe you were protecting yourself."

Who were her lies really designed to protect? Not herself. She knew that. She hadn't been proud of her actions, but she'd never have chosen to be hidden away. Mallory replayed the scene in her mind, the one when she told her parents. A look of unadulterated fear had filled her mother's face.

"Mother." Mallory said it with full assurance. "I knew the gossip would crush her."

A bitter look fleetingly crossed Savannah's face. "You're probably right. She was terrified that someone would find out about my ... my illness."

Mallory ventured a rare touch, reaching her hand to her sister's shoulder. "I'm sorry I didn't know. Do you still struggle with depression?"

Savannah stared at her hands and allowed the silence to answer for her.

Mallory slid closer and stretched her arm around her sister's back. Savannah leaned against her, covering her face with her hands. "I miss Jolene Rae so much. She always knew how to help me."

"I know. You two were so close." Realization gripped her. Savannah may be older, but with Jolene gone, the responsibility fell to her. She needed to bridge the gap between them. Depression was an illness, and her sister needed her. Her energy was depleted, but she'd reach deep and find what was required.

Savannah sat up straighter. "I've been hard on you."

"I never realized how far reaching the consequences would be. I only knew how much I wanted to be with Elliott. Who knew how that would domino to this?"

Savannah's head sprung up. "Elliott? Do you mean Elliott Moore?"

"Yes. He's Samuel's father."

Savannah released a rush of air.

"He's suing for full custody." The words came out of Mallory's mouth in a broken cry.

She had feared telling Savannah. She expected the fullness of her wrath. *How could you let this happen? I should have known you couldn't be trusted with guardianship.* But she heard none of that.

Instead, her sister grasped both hands in hers. "He can't win that. They'd never take Samuel away after all he's been through."

"I hope you're right. I haven't exactly been a model mother."

Savannah released her hands. "Neither have I. Neither has our mother. We all make mistakes. We won't allow Elliott to do this."

A common enemy threatened their family, bringing the sisters together. They shared a rare hug just as their dad stepped into the doorway. "Girls, I've been waiting a long time to see this."

Chapter 25

A somber aura cloaked the room as they waited for Elliott. At the sound of the doorbell, Brady asked, "You or me?" Mallory stood. "I'll do it."

"You're not planning to push him or call him names, are you?" While it was spoken teasingly, Mallory saw a fragment of concern in his eyes.

She chuckled, her attempt to lighten the moment. "I'll try to behave."

She opened the door to see Elliott waiting and Andrea craning her neck from the passenger side of the car. Mallory intended to keep him waiting outside but, without an invitation, he stepped into the foyer.

"Samuel's gathering his things. You can wait here. He'll be right down." She would not welcome him into the family room.

He peered in and saw Brady. "I didn't have a chance to congratulate you on your marriage. The timing was … interesting."

She bristled at the suggestive response. It hit too close to the truth. "My mother's very ill. It wasn't the right time to have a big wedding."

"I'm glad to see you're well taken care of."

Of course, Elliott would have his team of investigators dissecting every aspect of her life. "What are you implying?"

"I'm congratulating you, Mallory Rose." His hard smile was more of a smirk.

The sound of footsteps shifted their attention. Samuel bounded down the stairs, a navy-blue duffle bag slung over his shoulder. Brady stepped into the foyer to say good-bye.

He nodded to Elliott but turned toward Samuel.

"Call us when you get there. Remember your manners. We love you, buddy."

Samuel stepped in and hugged his uncle, then turned to Mallory. He hugged her, and her arms clung to him a minute too long. He squirmed out of them. "It'll be cool, Aunt Mallory. I'll see you Sunday."

Mallory took a reluctant step back. "Call me, Samuel."

He gave her a thumbs up and hurried toward the black BMW. Mallory waited until the car turned the corner and disappeared from view. Then she closed the door. Brady stood behind her, his arms reaching. She stepped into them and tried to draw comfort.

"It's going to be fine." He pulled his head back to look at her. "I guess I was somewhat of a hypocrite telling Samuel to have good manners. I just couldn't make my arm reach to offer a handshake. I was afraid I'd deck him instead."

Mallory managed a slight smile. "A sight I may have enjoyed seeing."

Brady kept his hands draped lightly across her shoulders. "What would you like to do while Samuel's in Washington? It's rare that we have a chance to go out."

She hesitated, choosing her words carefully. "I'm not sure I want to celebrate that."

"Honey, this is our future. The court will allow Elliott visitation. That's not going to change. And frankly, it's the right thing. Samuel needs to know his father. He seems fine with this, so we need to acclimate our lives. Let's plan something. I'll check to see what's on stage at one of the local theaters. Or maybe we can go somewhere for a few days. Wilmington or Carolina Beach."

He had begun to call her honey, mostly at moments when she needed encouragement. A night out was so rare for Mallory. Even when she lived in Wilmington, she never had extra money for extravagances. The most she did was nurse a soft drink at the Rococo Lounge with Chloe. "Gosh, I can't remember when I last saw a play."

Brady took that as a yes. "Great. Let's see what's available. We'll have dinner out and make a night of it."

****

Malachi called early Saturday morning. They had a court date. In two and a half weeks, it would all be over.

"Maybe the ruling will change and Samuel can be with us for Thanksgiving and Christmas."

Brady shook his head. "Don't count on that, Mal. It's going to be shared holidays. We've got to accept that."

She frowned. "I guess you're right. I just hope I'm not in jail."

Brady laughed. "You're not going to jail."

That evening, Brady took Mallory to dinner at Mandolin's. After seating them, the maître d' handed them menus. Despite Samuel's absence, Mallory felt lighthearted as she spread her napkin across her lap. She'd had very few dates in her life, and none with a man like Brady Donaldson. "I think we have this backwards. Most people date before they get married."

"Yes, and after. It's healthy for a marriage."

She leaned in, teasingly. "And you know this how?"

"Common sense. Would you like wine?"

"One glass. Don't get a bottle unless you plan to drink it and give me your keys."

"Yes, ma'am, and I'll be keeping my keys."

It was a rare, relaxed time when they could talk. Brady had asked her for an evening without discussion of the lawsuit. Instead, she shared pieces of her conversation with her sister.

"I didn't realize how hard it was for her to hide her depression. She needed to talk about it, deal with it. But Mother made that impossible. I'm starting to understand more every day how hard that must have been for Savannah. It answers a lot of questions."

"You mentioned her difficult finances. I don't understand how that can be. She served as executor of a large estate. The fee would generate a sizeable return."

Mallory puzzled over that for a moment. "I didn't think about that. I know they have medical expenses from Lillian's auditory issues, and probably from Savannah's hospitalization."

"Mallory, we're talking five percent on over eighteen mil."

Mallory mentally did the math. "That would be … about $90,000?"

He chuckled. "And I thought math was your strong suit. Add a zero, my dear."

She recalculated. "Oh, my goodness. You're right. That's $900,000."

He sipped his wine. "Yes, it is. We didn't grow up wealthy. That happened in the last ten years of my grandfather's life. He worked in a manufacturing plant but always tinkered in his garage. He could take just about anything apart and put it back together correctly— sometimes better. Over the years, he developed three separate systems that streamlined processes. People wanted to buy his patents for years, but he wisely held on to them. Before long, they were in use in manufacturing plants and eventually, the auto industry. When he sold them, they were worth a small fortune.

"All that to say, the amount of revenue from the executor fee would have been life-changing for us when I was growing up."

That explained some things for Mallory. Mark and Brady never appeared to be spoiled, rich kids. Their family didn't live a wealthy lifestyle. "Do you think Savannah took the fee? Maybe she didn't realize she was entitled to it."

"If she didn't know, she had the world's worst attorney."

****

After dinner, they went to the Duke Energy Center and saw *The Lion King*. Mallory hadn't been to a musical since high school. Somehow, Brady managed to secure excellent seats at the last minute. The spectacular costumes and music took her to another world, a carefree place where she was able to stop thinking about Samuel in Washington, DC with Elliott.

Partway into the show, Brady tucked her hand in his. It felt natural, his larger hand cocooning hers. Was it coincidental that the song on stage was "Can You Feel the Love Tonight?" Brady was such a good man—thoughtful, caring, attentive. It would be easy to allow herself to feel the love. But their marriage wasn't built on that. There was no promise of permanence. No words of love had been spoken. Mallory's heart was too fragile to withstand a lost love. She had to protect it at all costs. Still, he seemed contented, almost happy, about the marriage.

When they exited the center, Mallory reached for her silenced phone. She had a missed call and voicemail from Samuel. She put the message on speaker so Brady could hear.

"Really cool day today. I went to see my dad's work and we toured the National Air and Space Museum. He said he knew I liked astronomy. It was cool. You'd like visiting there. I'll see you tomorrow night."

"Sounds like he's having fun." Brady said the right words, but his face remained rigid.

It should have been a good phone call. Samuel was safe, happy, and would be home tomorrow. Yet it put a damper on the evening. Mallory hated that Samuel called Elliott *Dad*.

When they walked into the mudroom, Brady reached for Mallory's coat and hung it up. He had never taken or asked for a cubby of his own.

He caught her hand and turned her toward him. "I know you're planning to see your mother tomorrow. Would you like me to come with you?"

"Oh, Brady. It's always a hard visit. You don't need to do that. She won't know you."

"I wouldn't be coming for myself. I'd be coming for you. To support you."

"Thank you, but I'll be fine. And thank you for tonight."

His shoulders dropped slightly. "If you change your mind, I'm happy to join you. Did you enjoy the musical?"

"Very much. It's been too long since I had an evening like that." A strained silence followed. Should she encourage him, or step back and protect her heart? He still held her hand. She glanced at the clock on the kitchen wall. "It's after eleven. I'm usually asleep before now."

He leaned closer and Mallory wasn't sure if he planned to kiss her. If this were a typical date, they'd be standing at the door saying goodnight. A kiss would be an appropriate ending. Even an expected ending. But his kiss only reached her forehead.

"Goodnight, Mallory."

She climbed each step feeling the heat of his kiss on her forehead, reminding herself that this wasn't a real marriage. It held no promise of permanence. He never even took a cubby.

****

Mallory drove Samuel to Malachi's office where Elliott's attorney would be present. "They're going to ask you some questions. They may record your answers as well as writing them. Just be honest. Try not to be nervous."

"Are they going to ask me where I want to live?"

"Probably."

Samuel turned his gaze to her. "I already told my dad I don't want to live there."

Mallory kept driving, trying not to show her reaction. "Really, what did he say?"

"He said I shouldn't worry about it, that everyone wanted the best for me."

A platitude. Just enough to lull Samuel into complacency. Elliott had no intention of listening to his wishes.

"Samuel, may I suggest something? I certainly don't want to put words in your mouth, but when you refer to Elliott as your dad, and refer to me as Aunt Mallory, that makes it sound like you're closer to him. Like you two have a better relationship."

"What do you think I should call him?"

She caught herself biting her bottom lip. "Maybe just Elliott."

"Oh. I'll try, but I've kinda gotten used to Dad."

She tried not to let her jealousy show. "Just for now. For the next thirty minutes. It would help."

When they arrived, Samuel was taken into the office, and Mallory directed to a waiting area. After thirty minutes, the office door opened and Malachi approached her with Samuel at his side. "He did well. You have a very polite young man here. I'll meet with you and Brady Tuesday morning before court."

She and Samuel got back in the car and headed toward home. "That was a long time just to tell them where you wanted to live. What else did they ask you?"

"It wasn't all questions. We just talked about things."

"Things?"

"You know, like my baseball team and friends at school. A little bit about my mom and dad. Oh, and they asked about you and Uncle Brady getting married, if that was a surprise to me."

****

The men were in the living room while Mallory and Savannah cleaned up from dinner. The issue of the executor's fee still puzzled Mallory. She broached the subject. "Savannah, can I talk to you about something?"

They had an undeclared truce, but still didn't have the sisterly closeness that the two older siblings once had. Mallory had to word this carefully so Savannah wouldn't become defensive.

"I know that Mark and Jolene's estate was substantial. I just want to make sure that you've received all that's due you for your work as executor."

Her eyes rose defensively. "I would never take Samuel's money."

Mallory lifted her gaze in surprise. "Do you mean that you haven't taken your fee? Any of it?"

"Of course not. I didn't do this for the money. Jolene was my sister. I'd do anything for her."

"If that's true, then take your fee. She named you to do a task, and she'd want you to have it."

Savannah backed down slightly. "It doesn't feel right. I never intended to be paid to help her. I had no idea what their net worth was until she died."

"All the more reason for you to take what's due you. Samuel will be well provided for."

Savannah lowered her head, obviously thinking over what Mallory had said.

Mallory touched her shoulder. "You were such a good sister and her best friend. If you can't take it for yourself, take it for your family. She loved those kids."

"Yes, she did. I'll think about it."

"Do more than think. Call the estate attorney and request your full fee. You've earned it and I'm certain that's what Jolene Rae would want."

****

Samuel sulked when they told him he couldn't attend the hearing. "Why? It's all about me."

"Because you have school." Mallory knew it was a lame answer, but she and Brady discussed it. Neither thought he should be in the courtroom. There was no telling what sordid details might be said.

"I want to hear if they play the recording of me talking."

"They won't. Malachi told us the judge will hear it privately and receive the written transcript. Now get ready so you don't miss the bus."

"This sucks."

"Samuel!" Brady's raised voice caught his attention.

"Sorry." In a lower voice, he whispered. "But it does."

Fifteen minutes later, Samuel hopped on the school bus and it made the wide swing around the corner. Once out of sight, Mallory and Brady got in the car and headed toward town.

Brady drove through rush hour traffic, weaving in and out of cars on the I-440 beltline. They parked midway between Malachi's office and the courthouse, and planned to walk the distance after their meeting.

"Okay, folks. This is the big day. We're in good shape. Your boy was pretty decisive on where he wants to be. He was also respectful talking about his father. That bodes well for you. Judges don't like to see parents causing dissention. You can read the transcript." He pushed a copy their way.

"I never relax at these hearings until they're over. The outcome is subjective, dependent on the judge's opinion. All other trials are decided based on the law. In custody, there's no law that says who will be the better parent. But this is pretty solid considering the last year of Samuel's life."

Chapter 26

The oak door opened and everyone stood as the judge entered. This time he already wore his robe. He walked to the bench and wasted no time getting started.

"Today is the final custody hearing between Mallory Rose Donaldson and Elliott Moore, regarding the minor child, Samuel James Donaldson. We'll start by addressing the misdemeanor charge for falsifying a government-issued document."

He tipped his glasses and looked directly at Mallory. She and Malachi stood. She wanted to glance behind her where Brady sat, but instead, kept her eyes focused on the judge.

"Those charges are hereby dismissed due to the minor age of the defendant, the lapse of time since then, and the conditions leading to the defendant's duress."

A weight lifted from Mallory when she heard the word *dismissed*. One hurdle crossed.

The judge continued in his monotone voice. "However, I remind you that the deliberate and premeditated act not only resulted in an inaccurate government document. It also had a significant impact on a child. A new birth certificate will be issued showing the mother as Mallory Rose Carter and the father as Elliot Moore. The legal name of the child from this date forward will be Samuel James Moore."

A chill rippled through her. It took every ounce of restraint for Mallory not to scream. They stripped Samuel of his name, the name of Jolene and Mark. The name that was now hers. That would cut deeply when he found out. Mallory longed to see Brady's expression but she knew better than to turn around.

Both attorneys were granted time to state their cases. Malachi laid out the whole picture of a teenage pregnancy, Elliott's desire to abort, and the statement that he wanted no part of being a father. Justification for Mallory's years of silence.

Elliott's attorney argued that the words of a sixteen-year-old, a minor in the eyes of the law, were not a valid reason to be denied knowledge of his son.

When both sides had exhausted their arguments, the judge frowned, wrinkling his forehead. He looked from Mallory to Elliott, tapping an absentminded rhythm with a pencil. Mallory's eyes remained fixed on him, deliberating, deciding their future. After a few moments that felt like a lifetime, he stilled the pencil and sat up straight.

"First, we'll discuss visitation for the non-custodial parent." The temporary terms closely mirrored the permanent order. The detailed visitation schedule was outlined, including times, holidays, and summer. "The non-custodial parent will have the child for one month each summer, to be agreed upon by both parents. In the event that an agreeable arrangement cannot be determined, the court orders that it will be the month of July."

He laid aside the page he had finished and shuffled them into a neat pile. "Now, for primary, physical custody. This case had many factors to consider. I'm an advocate for joint custody, but with the distance between homes, that proves unfeasible. I considered the changes that this child has already endured with the loss of the couple who raised him. Additionally, I've read Samuel's transcript, his involvement in the school and the community, and his desire to remain in Raleigh.

"However, I can assure you, as a parent of two sons, watching them grow from infancy to their teenage years has been the best part of my life. That opportunity was denied to Mr. Moore, intentionally and with duplicity. Considering all factors and the knowledge of a child's resiliency, primary physical custody is awarded to the plaintiff, Mr. Elliott Moore. The transfer must be made within one week's time."

Mallory grasped the table, caught in a strong wind swirling around her. It whooshed through her ears and clouded her vision. Voices were talking but she could make no sense of the sound. A hand landed on her back. She turned toward it, but it wasn't Brady. Malachi's hand, one on her back and one holding her water, telling her to sip. Brady. He was nowhere in sight.

She forced herself to drink the water, hoping to restore her senses. The wind in her ears began to ebb and her vision came into focus. Malachi's words became comprehensible. I'm sorry. Never expected that. In her peripheral, she saw Elliott hugging Andrea excitedly. This couldn't be happening. She couldn't let them take her son.

"What can we do now? Do we appeal?"

He shook his head sadly. "In my experience, this is the end of the road. Unless there's new information, most judges won't overturn a valid custody ruling."

"Valid? How can that be valid? Samuel doesn't want to go."

His face held compassion, but he offered no hope. "Let's move out of here."

She talked while they wove their way through people in the hall. "I want to appeal. I have to try."

He pursed his lips. "Don't do it, Mallory. You'll waste time and money. And you'll need a new attorney. I don't take cases I know I'll lose."

She walked to the courtyard where people meandered and traffic passed. There was no sign of Brady. He'd abandoned her. The hour of her greatest need and he was gone. Mallory walked in circles, not sure what to do. She moved in the direction of the parked car, midway between Malachi's office and the courthouse. The car was there, right where they had left it. Empty. Finally, she saw the sign for a bus stop. Should she leave knowing Brady was somewhere in the area? Somewhere, but not with her. She stepped toward the bus stop where others waited its approach. She'd have to ask the driver where it went. If it didn't get her to the Cary area, she'd have to call a cab.

It didn't take long for a bus to appear. As Mallory stepped forward, she heard her name. Brady jogged toward her. She looked back and forth between him and the bus, but then stepped backward and motioned for the driver to go.

"Mallory, what are you doing?"

She wrapped her arms around herself. "You were gone."

"I'm sorry, Mal. I didn't trust myself to see him. I went back inside but you weren't there."

That was when she saw his hand, scraped open with traces of fresh blood. "What did you do to your hand?"

He brushed off her concern. "It met a brick wall. Let's go home."

When they buckled and started moving, Brady looked her way. "Mallory ..."

"Don't talk." She stared straight ahead. "Just drive."

Mallory leaned back against the headrest and closed her eyes. She was sixteen again, cradling her newborn baby. She tried to hold on as Mark lifted him from her arms, handing him over to Jolene. Powerless. She had no options. For one brief, beautiful moment, she had him back. Until history repeated itself. Elliot would take him, and she couldn't stop it.

When they reached home, Mallory glanced at the fresh blood seeping from the scrapes on Brady's knuckles. "Come here and let me clean that up." She rinsed it and doused it with an antiseptic. "There are softer things you could've punched."

"Like Elliott Moore's face? That's why I left. I didn't trust myself." He pushed away the bandage she prepared to wrap around his hand. "I don't want to wear that. Samuel doesn't need to know I lost it."

She continued to cut the bandage and lifted it to his hand. "Just until the blood stops seeping. It's swelling. You need an x-ray."

"We'll see. Right now, we need to decide what our next step is."

"We have no next step. Malachi said it's over. He won't appeal."

Brady flinched as she began wrapping his hand. "He's not the only attorney out there."

"He said we'll lose. No judge will overturn the decision unless there's new information."

"Okay, so we get new information. We can hire an investigator."

Brady mirrored her initial reaction. Do something, anything, to change the outcome. He hadn't yet reached her present state of hopelessness. "Save your money. I guarantee you, Elliott Moore's squeaky clean. He'd never jeopardize his career."

They sat in the kitchen, Brady's bandaged hand resting on the table.

Heaviness weighed Mallory's numb limbs. She expected tears but her eyes remained dry. "I understand why parents abduct their own children. I want to take Samuel and run."

Brady's vacant eyes reflected her defeat. "How do we tell him, Mal?"

She heard the pain in his question, but had no answer. She was empty. Mental fatigue stole every ounce of energy.

Hours later, by the time the school bus came, Brady had removed the bandage.

Samuel bounced in the door and Mallory's breath caught in her throat. Elliott followed behind him. "My dad tried to pick me up, but they wouldn't let me ride with him cause his name's not on the pick-up list."

Brady stood with a wide stance and hands on his hips. "You're not welcome here."

Samuel's eyes darted between the two men, confusion stamped on his face. "What? Why?"

Elliott ruffled Samuel's hair. "I want to be here when you tell him."

"Oh yeah, the hearing."

Mallory wore a stony glare. "I think it's best if we talk with Samuel alone. Let me show you out."

"I want to be here. We have to discuss arrangements and frankly, I don't want you to put a negative spin on this."

Samuel still looked from one adult to another. "Why can't he stay?"

Mallory lowered herself back into her chair. Elliott took that as a cue and pulled out a kitchen chair. Samuel followed suit, and only Brady remained standing, every muscle tensed, lips tight with anger.

Mallory took over before a full-blown fight broke out. She left the chair and stooped down before her son. "Samuel, you're going to have a chance to spend time with all of us. The court decision made sure of that."

"Good. It was a blast going to Washington."

"The judge …" The words lodged in her throat as tears pooled in her eyes. She tilted her head up, looking to Brady for help.

He stepped closer, putting a hand on Samuel's shoulder. "The judge awarded primary physical custody to … to Elliott." A stranger may have missed the choked emotion in Brady's voice, but Mallory knew him well enough to hear it.

Samuel's head swung around to his father, and back to Brady. "But I don't want to live there, I just want to visit."

Elliott scrambled to change the tone of the conversation. "Listen, Samuel. I know it will be a hard adjustment, but I promise you'll get used to it and love living there. Andrea's already fixing your bedroom. We're very excited."

"But my school's here, and all my friends." His eyes remained wide.

"We're looking into schools. We'll find a private school like the one you're in now. I know there are loads of little league teams."

"No. I'm staying here. I'll visit, but I'm not moving."

Mallory took his hands in hers. "Samuel, we don't want you to move. Your uncle and I are heartbroken. But this isn't an option. It's court-ordered, and we all have to comply."

A loud, scraping sound came as he pushed back his chair, yanking his hand from hers. Samuel jumped up, his face turning crimson. "I'm not going." He fled the kitchen and they heard his steps pounding each stair tread, followed by a slamming door.

Elliott hopped up and started to follow. "I'll talk to him."

Brady quickly closed the distance and blocked his path. "Not unless you'd like my fist in your face."

Elliott hesitated, then backed up. "He'll adjust. The sooner we make the transfer, the better."

Brady's fists clenched. "Not one hour before we have to. Now, it's time for you to go."

Mallory held the front door open, glaring at him.

****

One week passed too quickly. The tears that hadn't come the day of the hearing appeared almost daily. The weight of grief squeezed her heart. She sat on Samuel's bed and imagined the room empty. There was so much to pack up, but she couldn't do it. She couldn't load things into boxes and have Samuel return from school feeling like they were booting him out. He'd have to decide what to take and what to leave.

Anger consumed Brady. It was a side of him that she'd never seen. He made no eye contact when he spoke to her, always in clipped sentences. No wonder he was angry. He'd entered into a loveless marriage for Samuel's sake. Surely, he regretted that decision now. There was no reason to stay married. It wasn't like they'd made vows to each other. They would end the marriage when the transfer was complete. When Samuel was gone.

Mallory woke by six, following a restless night. As she walked past Brady's room, she heard the rush of water from his shower. Samuel had thirty more minutes to sleep before she woke him for school. Mallory went down and started brewing the coffee.

About fifteen minutes later, Brady came down, fully dressed, his damp hair combed neatly, carrying his briefcase. He set it on the table, then went to the cupboard and reached for a to-go coffee cup. "I have to be in Charlotte for a few days." He poured coffee and replaced the carafe. Then he sealed the lid and picked up his briefcase. "I'll be back early next week."

Mallory's mouth dropped open. Samuel would be gone. Brady wouldn't be here.

"He leaves Saturday." The statement held an imbedded question.

"I can't be back by then."

He gave no reason. This was intentional. He didn't want to be here. "Aren't you even going to say good-bye to him?"

He stopped in the middle of the open doorway. "He's sleeping and I need to go." He stepped outside and pulled the door closed between them.

Every time Mallory opened her heart—Elliott, Samuel, Brady—she found herself alone. She tried to protect herself from loving Brady, tried to hold him at arm's length, but somehow love had trickled in, speaking lies of hope. Clearly, love only trickled one way. Brady had abandoned her.

****

Thursday evening, they shared a somber dinner at her dad's. He and Savannah wanted a chance to say good-bye to Samuel. Mallory tried to wriggle out of it. "But Dad, he'll be back here in a couple weeks. It's not like he's gone from our lives."

"It won't be the same, Mallory Rose."

"Okay, but no teary good-byes. In fact, no good-byes at all. It's been hard enough on him. Just hug him and tell him you'll see him in a few weeks."

Her request for no teary good-byes was forgotten. Both her dad and Savannah cried when they hugged him.

Friday morning, Samuel dressed for his last day at school. He made the same decision that Mallory had made many years ago. He chose not to tell his classmates or teachers. He didn't want questions. Didn't want to talk about it. Mallory dropped him off, remembering the feeling. Looking at all that was familiar, knowing it would soon be part of the past. Her heart ached for him. This would be a difficult day. Almost as difficult as tomorrow.

At the end of the school day, Mallory joined the car line, inching forward to reach the pick-up spot. Samuel stood waiting, his backpack bulging, filled to capacity. He opened the back door and tossed it in, then buckled himself in the front passenger side.

Mallory forced a smile. "How was your day?" Stupid question. She knew how it was. She had lived it.

He grunted an "Okay," then turned toward the window. He didn't want to talk. Mallory drove, recalling the early days when she took guardianship. She had asked stupid questions trying to force conversation. Samuel closed himself off, avoiding eye contact and positioning himself tight against the door. They'd come full circle.

****

Mallory wanted every minute that she could spend with Samuel, but he isolated himself in his room. She had tried to talk about packing, asking him what he wanted to take, but he brushed her off.

"I'll take care of it before Saturday," he told her. It seemed to Mallory that the Donaldson men handled problems the same way— by isolating themselves. But then she remembered, Samuel wasn't a Donaldson at all. At least not genetically.

By six o'clock, Mallory sat in the family room alone, her feet tucked up under her. The evening news couldn't hold her interest, but at least it broke the quiet. No sound of packing came from the upstairs. The mechanical click of a turning key caught her attention. She bolted to her feet as Brady came in the back door.

Mallory stood in the threshold of the family room as Brady tossed his bag on the table. His wide stride closed the distance between them. "I'm sorry, Mal. I didn't think I could face tomorrow, but I was wrong to leave you alone." He reached to hug her, but she stiffened. She had no capacity to handle another painful loss. She'd melted into his comfort many times in the last few months. But that was before. Before he left her at the courthouse, then retreated from facing Samuel's last few days. She refused to allow herself to depend on him.

"I've been alone before. I'll have to get used to it again." She withdrew to her spot on the sofa. Brady gazed at her, rubbing the back of his neck. Mallory turned away.

"How is he?"

She shrugged, refusing to look up. "In isolation. As of this morning, he still hadn't packed anything."

"Can I go up and see him?"

Mallory moved her head in a slow nod. "You don't have to ask that question." Brady had already assumed the role of a guest.

****

Saturday came, and Elliott would be there by noon. Brady had been in Samuel's room helping him. He came downstairs carrying a full duffle bag.

"Do you need help carrying things down?"

Brady placed it by the door. "He said this is all he's taking."

"None of his sports equipment? Books? Trophies?"

"He said no. I told him I'd pack up the video game system. He said he's not taking it."

"I'll see him in two weeks. If he changes his mind about anything, I can take it up there."

Brady stared at Mallory, but she couldn't read his expression. She had used the word I, not we. She assumed nothing, and she couldn't worry about his feelings right now. The next few hours would hold enough pain.

Mallory watched the window for Elliott's car, as one would watch for an approaching hurricane—knowing it was coming, and bracing for the arrival. At ten minutes after noon, his black BMW pulled into the driveway, close to the garage door.

Mallory stubbornly refused to open the garage. Let him walk around front and ring the bell. When it sounded, she walked to the door and let him in. A flinty nod was all he got in the way of a greeting.

"I parked close to the garage so we could load his things in the car."

Mallory's toe gave a slight tap to the duffle bag.

"Okay. Is the rest in his room? I'll go up."

"No, you won't go up. He'll be down in a minute. You may wait here."

She went back to the kitchen and left him standing there alone. A few minutes later, she heard Samuel and Brady make a slow trek down the stairs. Mallory returned to the entry carrying a box. She set it on the floor. Neither Samuel nor Brady acknowledged Elliott.

Elliot couldn't have missed the somber mood. His attempt at cheerfulness fell flat. "Hey, Samuel. You ready? Where's the rest of your things?"

Samuel glanced at the duffle bag. "That's all I'm taking. I'm not staying."

Elliott's lips clenched together. He started to say something but changed his mind. "Okay. We can buy whatever you need."

Samuel turned his back to him and faced Brady. "I'm not staying. And I'm not using the name Moore."

"Samuel, you need to promise me you won't run away."

When he didn't answer, Brady placed a hand on each shoulder. "I mean it, buddy. It's not safe. I need a promise."

Samuel shuffled from one foot to the other. "All right."

"I need to hear it. Tell me."

His shoulders went limp, melting into defeat. "I promise I won't run away. But I'm still not changing my name."

Mallory heard Samuel's desperation to hold on to some tiny shard of control. She recalled the feeling vividly.

"Remember how much we love you. You call us if you need anything, even if you just need to talk." They hugged, holding on to each other until Brady broke the hold. "Remember who you are. No matter what anyone calls you," he tapped Samuel's heart, "in here you're a Donaldson."

He nodded and turned to Mallory, who held the box. "I want you to have this." She opened the flap to reveal the telescope. "We never got around to making you one."

His eyes widened in surprise. "Are you sure? Don't you want to keep it?"

Elliott's words cut through the moment. "We can buy you a real one."

Samuel glared at him. "No. I want my mom's." He set the box on the floor and hugged her. "I'll take care of it. It means so much …" His words caught in his throat.

"I love you, my sweet boy."

"I love you, Mom. I'll see you in two weeks."

Mom. She knew it was spoken for Elliott's sake, but it still touched her heart. They parted, both with teary eyes.

Elliott reached for the box, but Samuel snatched it, twisting his body so the telescope was out of reach. Elliott picked up the duffle bag, and opened the door.

When it closed behind them, Mallory turned and went up the stairs, leaving Brady behind. She fell on her bed and sobbed.

Chapter 27

Sunlight streamed in through the slatted blinds. Mallory laid on her side, knees drawn close, her arms crossed tightly beneath the blanket. She saw no reason to get out of bed. The digital clock said 9:48. Sleep had been elusive most of the night, and now her body crashed hard. She welcomed the oblivion.

A light rap sounded on her bedroom door. She ignored it until the sound increased. "Mallory?"

She reluctantly swung her legs over the side of the bed and sat up. "Yes?"

"May I come in?"

She wanted to say no, but her failure to answer resulted in a turn of the doorknob. Brady opened it inches. "I brought you coffee."

"Thank you. I didn't mean to sleep this late."

He pushed the door open fully and carried the mug to her nightstand. "That's fine. I'm glad you could sleep."

The dresser mirror across from her reflected her wild hair, dark as a midnight sky, straggly and unkempt. Shadowy rings sagged below her eyes. In contrast, Brady wore gray woolen slacks and a dress shirt. His hair was combed neatly and slightly damp. She caught a scent of his minty breath, and lowered her head, imagining how awful her own would be.

"I'll be down in a few minutes."

"Take your time. I was just checking to make sure you were all right. I'm going to church, but I didn't wake you earlier. I figured you needed some sleep."

She bit back the words that sprang to her mouth—that she wasn't feeling particularly thankful this morning. She'd be a fraud sitting in church trying to sing and act joyful. It always amazed her that her mother could leave home after a frenzied morning of sibling arguments, paste on a believable smile, and look like the happiest mother in the world. Mallory hadn't mastered that level of disguise.

She made a feeble stab at brushing her hair and splashing water on her face. What was Samuel doing now? Did Elliott and Andrea go to church? Elliott's family did. She knew they went to the Presbyterian church back when she knew everything she could learn about Elliott Moore. Back when she kept his picture hidden in her bedroom so she could stare at it every spare minute. Back when she'd been young and stupid. How could she have been so gullible?

She imagined Andrea dragging Samuel along, showing him off to her friends. Would she tell them that he was Elliott's illegitimate child? Mallory smirked at her own question. She'd have no choice. He was Elliott's mirror image.

Mallory took her half-empty cold coffee downstairs and popped it in the microwave. The newspaper waited on the kitchen counter where Brady must have dropped it. She slid it from the green, plastic cylindrical bag and took it to the table with her reheated coffee. Time to look at real estate rentals. This house belonged to the estate of Mark and Jolene. The only reason she lived here was to take guardianship and keep Samuel's life as normal as possible. Another abject failure on her growing list. She couldn't continue to live here. She'd move out before Savannah asked her to. They had smoothed their relationship slightly, but that was before she lost Samuel.

After seeing the price of rentals in Raleigh, Mallory turned to the want ads. It would be a stretch to afford something in a nice area of town. She found a highlighter in the drawer and marked jobs that she would be qualified to do. Telemarketer. Waitress. Retail.

She closed the paper and went to the office. Opening the laptop, she logged onto a site with rental property in the Washington, DC area. Nothing kept her in Raleigh. She was certain her family held their hostility in check for Samuel's sake. If she'd have stayed in

Wilmington, he'd still be here. Savannah or Brady would have found a way to take him if Mallory hadn't. Despite the difficulty, they'd have never allowed social services to place him in foster care.

The prices in Washington were out of her reach. She wouldn't take money from Brady. Mallory closed the laptop, knowing what she had to do.

****

Brady returned home carrying a white bag. "I hope you haven't had lunch. I stopped at the Greek Kitchen." He pulled out two salads, an order of hummus and pita chips. "I didn't want you to worry about cooking something." He set them on the table beside the newspaper.

Mallory moved to the table and eyed them cautiously. "I'm not sure if I can eat anything. My stomach's a little off."

"Try, honey. You've got to eat something."

She picked up a chip and scooped a little hummus, then toyed with her salad, taking small bites. Brady ate his salad and pushed his dish aside.

Seeing the highlighted ads, he flipped the paper over. "What are you looking for?" It opened to the real estate section. "Mallory?" His tone held a question mark.

"I can't stay here. I was allowed to live here as Samuel's guardian. Now that he's gone, I have to find a place of my own."

"Is that what Savannah said?"

Mallory looked away from his probing eyes. "No, but under the circumstances, I can't stay here."

He pushed the paper aside. "I? You know, you do have a husband."

A melancholy smile. "Not really."

Brady sat back and crossed his arms. "What's that supposed to mean?"

"I think that's obvious. The marriage was staged."

"It's not staged. It's legal."

"You know what I mean. It was always for a reason—to keep Samuel. I guess you could say it lost its purpose."

Brady uncrossed his arms, propping elbows on the table. His hand still showed scabs from the healing process of his encounter with the brick wall. He stared at nothing for a few moments. "So, you're saying you want a divorce?"

Did she want a divorce? Mallory was afraid to want anything. It came with disappointment. "Wasn't that always the expected outcome?"

They stared at each other, Mallory trying to read his silence. He remained poker-faced. He had plenty of time to refute it, but silence was his only response.

She broke the silence. "I'm moving back to Wilmington. I called Chloe and she'll give me back my job."

His mouth tightened. "Running away again. Why do you need a job? You'll be a rich divorcée." He pushed back and stomped away, anger fixed over every part of him.

Now Mallory stood and folded her arms across her chest. "What's that supposed to mean? I have no intention of taking your money."

"Well, my dear, we live in North Carolina. I believe that half of what's mine, is yours."

Her hands reached for her hips. "Brady, you suggested marriage, not me. I resent the implication."

He stopped walking, his back still toward her. After a pause, he turned around, his features softened. His arms hung limp from slumped shoulders. "I'm sorry. I never thought that. Of course, you'd want a divorce. I'll start the paperwork immediately. And Mallory, I know you're not asking for it, but I intend to take care of you financially." Brady resumed his path to the stairs. "I need about thirty minutes to pack up." He started toward the stairs then turned. "If you're sure that's what you want."

Was it? She never allowed herself to think of their marriage as permanent. She had said the marriage lost its purpose. Brady could have countered her remarks, but he didn't. He had never suggested there was any reason but Samuel. She knew he was willing to stay with her, but she didn't want *willing*. She wanted more than that. She searched his face, trying to read it. He looked like a kicked puppy, but was it about the marriage or Samuel? He waited, but when she said nothing, he turned and climbed up the stairs.

Mallory studied her hand. The rings were more beautiful than she ever imagined she'd have. Perfect in all ways but one. They lacked meaning. He as much as said that when he held that velvet box. *We don't want anyone questioning the legitimacy of our marriage.* A sorry reason for a wedding ring. She slipped the diamond from her finger, along with the gold band. She had no box. If Brady saved it, it would be in his possession. She went to the office for an envelope. After writing Brady's name on the front, she placed the rings inside and sealed it.

When he came down thirty minutes later, he set an overnight bag and a suitcase on the floor, and went back up for the last of his things. Mallory had intended to hand him the envelope, but this would be easier. She unzipped his overnight bag and tucked the envelope inside. The bedroom door closed as she rezipped his bag.

Brady came down carrying a garment bag with his suits. "I think I have everything that's mine. Is there anything you need me to do before I go?"

"No, but Brady, about the money—we can have an annulment. That will protect your assets."

He held up his hand like a stop sign. "No discussion. I'll continue monthly deposits in your account. It's what I want to do."

"I won't use it."

"That'll be your choice."

****

Samuel called that evening. Mallory grabbed the phone. "Samuel?"

"Hi." He kept his volume low.

"I'm so glad you called. How are you? I can't stop thinking about you."

"I'm all right. I hate it here."

Mallory's heart hurt thinking of his pain. She knew how it felt to have life ripped from you. To be thrown into a new unfamiliar world. "I know, sweetheart. It'll get better."

"You should see this room. The bedspread is Washington Redskins. And she has trains on the wall."

"Trains?"

"Yeah. These wooden plaques like I'm five or something. The food's gross. She can't eat gluten, so apparently, none of us get real food. It tastes like cardboard."

"Tell you what. You start a list of foods you want, and we'll eat them all when I'm up there. Just hang in there."

"If I ever get out of the house without them, I can buy food. I have money. I took some from my mom's stash. I mean … my first mom. I'm sorry I didn't tell you about it. I took some when I ran away, too. You have to get the step stool. It's in the cupboard above the refrigerator, way in the back. There's a tin with cookie cutters, and an envelope hidden under them. It has lots of money—like a thousand dollars or something."

"Thank you, Samuel. I don't intend to use it, and I'm glad you took some of it."

"Can I talk to Uncle Brady?"

The question caught her by surprise. What should she tell him? He didn't like secrets, but that might be one surprise too many.

"He's not here tonight. He had to go to Charlotte." Samuel was accustomed to Brady coming and going.

"Oh, okay. I'll call his phone. Love you, Mom."

An hour later, Mallory received a text message from Brady. JUST SPOKE WITH SAMUEL. I DIDN'T MENTION ANY CHANGES. PLEASE LET ME KNOW WHEN YOU PLAN TO DO THAT.

****

Cleaning energized her. Mallory scrubbed and vacuumed every inch of the house. When she left on Wednesday morning, the wooden furniture glowed with a reflective waxed surface. The kitchen and bathrooms sparkled with polished chrome and the scent of lemon. Savannah would find nothing amiss.

She texted her sister. Since I'm no longer Samuel's guardian, I'll be vacating the house today. With your permission, I would like to use the house on the weekends that I bring Samuel to Raleigh, and during the summer month when Samuel is here. Other than that, I'll be in Wilmington.

She loaded her car with boxes and her one lone suitcase. Clothing on hangers were draped over the boxes. Before leaving, she had to face the call to her father.

After greeting him and a moment of small talk, she told him she was leaving.

"Why Wilmington? What about Brady?"

"Dad, surely you knew that our marriage was staged. We thought it would help win the custody suit. Clearly, we were wrong."

"One wrong doesn't have to lead to another. Marriage is marriage. It's not meant to end."

"This one's different. We made no vows to each other. I won't hold him in a marriage that wasn't meant to be."

"Are you telling me that he asked for it to end?"

"It doesn't matter. Would you have me stay in a marriage without love? Is that what you want for me?"

"Mallory Rose, I've seen you two together. You can't tell me there are no feelings there."

"Dad, there's nothing there. The end."

They hung up without any real closure. How many times had she disappointed him? A teenage pregnancy. Leaving home at eighteen. Losing Samuel. A failed marriage. Surely, he'd be glad to have her gone.

Before that final flick of the light switch, Mallory made one more trip through the house. The first day she walked in, dying hydrangeas met her. Samuel avoided eye contact and answered her questions in one-word replies. Change was slow, but it came. As she prepared to leave, she saw images everywhere. Samuel and Brady playing video games. Samuel bounding down the stairs, often leaping over the final two steps. Stargazing on the deck. Brady kissing her forehead after their date. Samuel calling her *Mom*. Maybe she had done something right. Why did it have to be ripped from her?

Mallory made one stop before hitting the interstate. It would prove easier than the conversation with her dad. Her mother had no idea that a tsunami had hit their family, throwing everything into chaos.

Natural light filled the lounge area where she found her mother seated in an upholstered wingback chair. She was ambulatory while others in the large room were wheelchair bound. Mallory stepped close, hoping for recognition. Her mother made eye contact, slightly opened her mouth, but closed it soundlessly.

"Hi, Mom. It's Mallory Rose."

Her mother's head tilted in confusion, but then, emptiness clouded her eyes.

Dropping into the chair beside her, Mallory lifted her mother's silky hand, cradling it in her own. She rubbed her thumb over the translucent skin. As a child, she had stretched her own stubby fingers wide and held them against her mother's long, graceful fingers, always wishing hers could be like her mother's. She'd seen her hands dance over piano keys, grip casseroles cushioned by pot holders, and felt them skillfully create a French braid in Mallory's thick hair. She recalled a hand resting on her fevered forehead. Tears sprung to her eyes. "I'm sorry I wasn't here, Mom. I'm sorry I was so angry. I know you loved me."

Mallory ached to hear her mother's voice speaking words of forgiveness. Yet she was doing it again. She would leave today and run away to her coastal sanctuary, hoping the space between them would ease her pain.

When Mallory left her mother's room, she saw a missed call from Samuel. She sat in the lobby and returned his call, anxious to hear his voice

"Hi, Mom."

It never got old, hearing Samuel call her mom. "Hi, sweetie. How are you doing?"

"You mean, do I still hate it here? Yes! I'm not in school yet, and I only met one kid my age—a dorky neighbor. At least they keep pumping me with books. It's the only thing I do. They keep wanting me to play a game or watch a movie with them, since I'm not allowed to have a TV in my room. She said too much screen time, that's what she calls it, isn't good."

He never referred to Andrea by name. He always relegated her to a pronoun.

"You know, Andrea's right that too much is never healthy. I told you that, too." Mallory had determined she wouldn't become that parent who verbally sullied the other. If Samuel had to live there, she would try to help him make the best of it. "My real question is, why aren't you in school yet?"

"They said I'll start in the second semester. They thought too much special stuff would be going on over the holidays. Plays, concerts, and stuff like that. Nobody wants to be the new kid and come in during the middle."

"Speaking of holidays, I spoke with Elliott about Thanksgiving— or I should say we've e-mailed. They legally have custody from the afternoon and evening. Instead of trying to squeeze in a morning visit and another meal, he agreed to let you come for an extra weekend in December if I'd give him the whole day on Thanksgiving. His parents are spending the weekend in DC and they'd like you to be there. I've been staying in Washington when I see you because it's so hard to take you to Raleigh and have you back to DC in a weekend. Elliott agreed to a four-day visit. It makes better sense than spending so much time in a car. How do you feel about that?"

"Are you still coming next weekend?"

Mallory heard the plea in his voice. "Of course. I wouldn't miss it."

"Then okay. Hey, can you sneak me some snacks?"

She chuckled. "Why? Don't they let you have snacks?"

"Oh yeah, if I want hummus or yogurt." Samuel's tone held disdain.

"You like yogurt."

"Not theirs. It tastes sour. I was told we don't eat things with processed white sugar."

Mallory laughed. "Well, eating healthy won't hurt you."

"Mom, sometimes you just gotta have a cookie."

Mallory chuckled, almost seeing his expression. "I'll see what I can do."

When their call ended, Mallory nursed a smug satisfaction that Samuel hadn't readily taken to Andrea. That he wanted to come home. As she made her way to the car and headed for the interstate, those feelings faded to the familiar ache. She took the road to Wilmington, escaping again to her refuge.

Chapter 28

A semblance of déjà vu grew as the little Civic turned into Liam's driveway. Somehow it felt right. His friendship met Mallory at a needy time many years ago. Maybe she'd find comfort for the fresh wounds today. As she approached the house, she found him awkwardly using the clippers, scissoring errant branches that fell to the ground—a task he hated. Liam allowed very few concessions to his life of ease, but this was one of them, necessary to keep his one-room apartment.

Liam formed an easy smile as she approached. "Well, well. I knew you couldn't stay away from the coast for long. Where's your sidekick?"

"He's gone, Liam. I lost custody." The solemn words denied a return of his smile.

He kept clipping as if she'd said Samuel was out for a stroll on the beach.

"But you'll get to see him sometime, won't you?"

"Yes, twice a month."

"Good. Bring him around. He's almost ready to try a bigger wave."

Mallory took the clippers from his hand. "You're butchering that shrub. I'll trim. You can bag the clippings." He made no argument. He'd readily give up what he hated to do. She resisted trying to make him understand how devastating this had been for her. And for Samuel. Liam just didn't get it.

He stepped into the garage and came out with a black trash bag for the yard cuttings as she finished trimming. When the few shrubs were nicely shaped, he put the clippers back inside and tied the trash bag.

"Want to come in?"

"No, thanks. I just wanted to stop by and say hi. I'm working for Chloe again, so I'll see you from time to time."

"Hey, Mal. Remember what I told you. Don't get yourself bogged down by this. You'll see the kid often. It's a good home, isn't it?"

The cool air brought a shiver. "Good doesn't mean it's the right one for him."

"Doesn't mean it's the wrong one either."

It was the same as saying, *Chill, Mallory*.

****

"Welcome to Cape Fear Emporium." Mallory called to the only patron in the last hour. Fewer customers came in the souvenir shop in the fall, and fewer still wanted ice cream. Chloe assured her that she wasn't a pity hire.

"Girl, you know the scoop. Those college kids love working summer, then they're outta here come fall. I'm tired of working from morning till night by myself. You came at the perfect time."

"That will help when summer comes again. You won't forget I'll need a month off?"

"Got it. Two long weekends each month, and one month in the summer. I told you we'll work around that."

"I promise I'll look for a rental as soon as I get the time. I can't thank you enough for letting me stay with you."

"Honey, you just crash at my place as long as you need to. When I'm a feeble old lady, you can take me in."

Mallory managed a laugh. "You're forgetting that I'll be a feeble old lady by then."

Chloe waved the comment off with a flip of her hand. "Naw. I've got a few years' head start on you. Hey, Thanksgiving's right around the corner. You headed back to your dad's place?"

"I don't think so."

232

"Up to see Samuel?"

"No. He'll be meeting his new extended family."

"Well then, you just plan on coming to Hickory with me. My mama will be happy to have one more plate at that table."

"Chloe, I'm just not up to it this year. Would you mind if I stay at your place while you're gone?"

"My home is your home. What I mind is you spending the day alone."

"That's exactly what I want to do."

****

Rental property near the Emporium was way out of Mallory's price range. Her bank balance was healthy thanks to Brady, but she didn't plan to use that money for herself. She decided that she would use it to see Samuel. That would help with fuel, a hotel room, and possibly airfare for visits when she brought him to Raleigh. The five-and-a-half-hour drive would be eleven hours both ways, then another eleven to take him home two days later. She hoped to drive up once a month when she stayed in DC, and fly when he was coming to Raleigh. Eventually, she might be comfortable with him flying alone, but not yet.

Working her way out of the historic section, Mallory took highway 117 toward UNC Wilmington where ample apartments were available. She paid a deposit on a furnished efficiency that would be available December first. The check took her balance down leaving only the amount of Brady's deposit. It was all she had left until she got her first paycheck.

****

The weekend before Thanksgiving, Mallory made the drive to Washington DC. She rang Elliott's doorbell, but never stepped inside the house. Samuel bolted out the front door and hugged her.

"Where's Uncle Brady?"

The question took her by surprise. Mallory should have anticipated it. "You know, Samuel, it's a long drive for a short visit. Your Uncle Brady was out of town all week."

"Oh. Let's go." He started toward her car. "You should've brought the Volvo."

She was going to have to tell him, but not this visit. Perhaps over the longer visit in two weeks. She turned and called to Elliott. "I'll have him back Sunday evening."

Elliott stood watching, his hands on his hips. Samuel had no words of good-bye. He just hurried to the car, tossed his bag on the backseat and buckled into the passenger side. "Now, let's find someplace with a big juicy burger, fries, and a Coke. In case you couldn't guess, sodas aren't allowed either."

Mallory tried not to undermine Elliott and Andrea, but Samuel made her laugh when he mocked their house rules.

"You know, when I came up the first time to visit, it was like I was company or something. It was cool and we had fun. But as soon as I got here to live, there were all these rules, like they want to change everything about me. And I think Elliott's henpecked."

Mallory laughed. "Where'd you learn that word?"

"I don't know. But sometimes he'll start to let me do something, and she'll correct him. Like once we stopped in a restaurant for lunch. I was all ready to order fries. Elliott nodded like it would be okay but then she corrected him." Samuel mimicked Andrea's voice and mannerism, flinging an unseen lock of hair over a shoulder. "But Elliott dear, they're deep fried. We need to help Samuel develop good habits." Elliot closed the menu and said, "How about a salad instead?"

The time went too fast. They visited the Air and Space Museum, ate out, went to a movie, and the weekend was over with no resemblance to real parenting.

"Do I have to go back? I really want to come home."

He sounded like he might cry. Mallory's heart broke all over again, but she tried to keep her response light. "You do, sweetie. Unless you want them to put me in jail for abducting you. Remember, next week's Thanksgiving. You'll stay here and meet Elliott's parents. I'll be here the following weekend. Then your next visit will be in Raleigh. That one will be four days."

"They check my phone to see how long I talk to you and Uncle Brady. They said I have to start limiting my calls."

Mallory's jaw clenched. She didn't respond. If they attempted to isolate her, she would undermine them. She'd buy him a TracFone to keep hidden.

****

On Wednesday, the day before Thanksgiving, Brady texted her. The sight of his name brought a catch to her throat. It was the first she'd heard from him since he left the Raleigh house. WOULD YOU MIND IF I COME TO SEE SAMUEL WHILE HE'S IN RALEIGH FOR THANKSGIVING?

A wave of disappointment followed. He wanted to see Samuel—not her. Samuel must not have told him about the Thanksgiving arrangement. She replied immediately. I'M SORRY. SAMUEL ISN'T COMING FOR THANKSGIVING. I ALLOWED ELLIOTT TO HAVE THE FULL DAY. IT WAS TOO MUCH TRAVEL IN TOO SHORT A TIMEFRAME.

The moment she hit send, she regretted her reply. She hadn't asked how he was or wished him a happy holiday. She could have invited him to visit on their four-day weekend. Why had she been so hasty? She'd wait for his reply, then send an invitation. But no reply came. Maybe she should have called him to explain instead of replying with a text. It was too late now. She'd already responded. His silence unnerved her. Was he angry?

Mallory spent Thanksgiving alone. She told herself it was no big deal. She'd spent holidays alone before. She would enjoy the quiet. She baked turtle brownies and made Rice Krispies treats for Samuel. She'd freeze them for her next visit.

When she finished cleaning the kitchen and packaging the treats for the freezer, Mallory sat on Chloe's recliner and pulled the footrest up. She closed her eyes thinking of what this day might have been. Brady and Samuel laughing and teasing each other. She'd be baking pies or a sweet potato casserole to take to the family dinner. It would have been her first holiday with her family in years. Her dad had left numerous messages asking her to come, but then she'd have to endure their disappointment. Samuel had been with them for all of life's hallmark moments. They would face this holiday without Jolene, Mark, Samuel, and Mother. Even if her mom was physically there, she was mentally and emotionally absent. Not the person they'd always known her to be.

If she had her telescope, she'd head to the beach. The magnitude of the heavens usually managed to make her worries feel small. Except at the times when it reminded her of how alone she truly was.

****

Early December brought frigid temperatures to Washington DC. Mallory found her wardrobe insufficient. She'd need a warmer winter coat since DC was now part of her routine. The winter season stretched before her. She hated the drive, the traffic, and the climate. Weekend visits allowed her to be a small part of Samuel's life, but they denied her the opportunity to be a parent. She missed their after-school conversations, helping with homework, stargazing. Instead, they tried to find fillers for their time so they didn't have to sit in a hotel room.

A waitress showed them to their booth, and Mallory slid across from Samuel. He tugged off a new coat that she didn't recognize. She had once known all of his clothing. Washed it, dried it, folded it, and packed up what no longer fit. The new coat was one more reminder of her loss.

They placed their order and the waitress brought drinks.

"I'm a little confused here, Samuel. Why did you start a new school? I thought they were going to wait until after the holidays."

Samuel took a large gulp of his root beer. "She's always changing something. Guess she changed her mind about school too. Last week they just told me I was starting school the next day."

"I'm glad you're in school. I was just surprised to hear it."

"He signed me up for the Afterschool Club without even asking me."

Mallory held the cup of tea, allowing the mug to take the chill out of her hands. "So, what do they do at Afterschool Club?"

"Different stuff every day. One day a chess instructor taught us to play. I already knew how. I used to play with my dad. I mean, my real dad. Sometimes we go out to the field and play stuff like flag football. I wish we'd do baseball."

This didn't sound like the school clubs that Mallory knew. She'd been a member of the Science Club, cheerleading, and track. Clubs founded for a purpose, focused on a theme. "What's the main purpose of the club?"

"They call it a club, but it's for the kids whose parents work. You know, so they don't have to go home when nobody's there."

Aftercare. Mallory stuffed down her anger for Samuel's sake. "Isn't Andrea home?"

"Who knows? She doesn't like me."

Fury formed a knot in Mallory's stomach. It took restraint to keep her voice even. "Why do you think that? She was anxious for you to come."

They halted their conversation as the server placed their meals before them—a pepperoni pizza for Samuel, and a chicken salad croissant for Mallory.

Samuel popped a loose slice of pepperoni in his mouth, closed his eyes, and let out a satisfied sigh. "Ahh, real food."

"Samuel, what makes you think Andrea doesn't like you?"

"I guess some days she does and some days she doesn't. She talks to me like I'm three or something. Then she gets mad and doesn't talk at all. And they're already changing my bedroom."

"Changing it like getting rid of the train plaques and letting you pick what you want in there?"

"No, changing it like moving me to another room."

"Why?"

"They said they need to paint the room I'm in now. I'll have the little room at the end of the hall. I hope they don't move the trains in there."

This made no sense to Mallory. They prepared the room before Samuel came. Her only source of information came from Samuel himself. She'd need to keep a careful watch. No child should live in a home where he felt unloved.

****

The office store carried cardboard mailing tubes in various sizes. Mallory held two of them up, nesting one inside the other, testing the smoothness of the slide. It needed to move easily, but snugly. As she gazed at the variety available, she thought of Brady. *If you ever need mailing tubes, I can get you plenty.* She shook the image from her mind, forcing her thoughts from Brady back to her son.

Mallory learned painfully that any delay could result in a missed opportunity. She wouldn't miss a chance to nurture Samuel's desire to build a telescope. She'd have all of the materials ready for his next visit to Raleigh.

All she needed now were the lenses, one concave and one convex. She recalled Brady's laugh when she'd explained about the lens sizes and focal points. *You've already lost me.* She pictured the three of them working on this project. But that wouldn't happen. His words were prophetic. She'd already lost him.

Chapter 29

The December wind stung the exposed skin of Mallory's cheeks as she sat on the isolated beach. The temperature was too cold for beachgoers, but she wrapped a blanket around herself, clutching it tightly. She'd grown to love the crashing waves. They were so predictable, rising to whitecaps, breaking and climbing the shore, leaving broken shards of shells, then rolling back to sea, carrying gritty sand. And always, another wave waited in its wake.

Why did the constant motion of the sea calm her? Maybe because it left no decision to her. It moved of its own accord. She had no power to hurry it or slow it. No ability to make it better or worse. There were no what-ifs.

During the peak season, people would bring radios, stretch out on the sand and listen to canned music. She never understood that. The ocean played its own symphony, one that couldn't be matched by man. It held rhythm, dynamics, and a steady tempo.

She was so focused on the music of the sea, that she quickly heard a break from the normal cadence. The rustling of footsteps in the sand came from behind her. A wave of apprehension caused her to swivel around the wide expanse of beach. Her father stumbled toward her, tottering in the sand, carrying a folded chair.

"Dad!" She hurried to offer a steadying hand. "What are you doing here?"

"I was told I might find you here." He positioned his chair facing her, his back to the wind coming off the sea.

"Why didn't you call me? I'd have met you somewhere."

He motioned toward the tote bag under her chair. "If you had heard the phone."

"Sorry. It may be silenced." She began to worry about the reason for his visit. "Is everything okay? Is it Mom?"

"You're mother's fine. Well, let's say, she's the same. She'll never be fine again. Mallory Rose, I think it's time we had a heart-to-heart talk."

Mallory had been perched at the front of her chair. She sat back, wishing she had only the predictable sound of the sea again. "I know I messed up, Dad. Again."

He nodded, not disagreeing with her. "Every action has a consequence. Some are far-reaching."

Did he really come here to remind her? "Do you think I don't know that? I've suffered the consequences of a teenage mistake for twelve years."

"I'm not talking about that, Mallory Rose."

"Can we finally drop the Rose? Mother's not here to care." Her clipped voice struck back, designed to hurt.

He stared her down, and she shrank before his eyes. She wasn't accustomed to talking back to her father.

"Mallory Rose." He emphasized the middle name. "I'm talking about you living like a martyr. Thinking you're a victim. I know that what happened twelve years ago was hard for you, but you have to assume some responsibility for taking us all down that path."

"I did take responsibility. I moved away to make things easier for all of you. Jolene didn't have me in the way, mourning over my loss. Do you have any idea how hard that was? Did you ever spend a Christmas alone? I spent years of them away from my family so it would be easier for all of you."

"So, you were the martyr. What did that help? Every Christmas when people left and we were alone, your mother cried."

A fresh load of guilt wrapped its way around her shoulders. "I always called. And you always drove here a day or two later."

"It's not the same. We missed you. Your sisters missed you. You didn't get to know your nieces and nephews. Jolene knew what she was getting into when they took Samuel. She welcomed you to be part of their lives. It was your choice to isolate yourself."

"It was hard, Dad."

"Yes, it was. As I said, every action has consequences. But you weren't the victim, Mallory Rose. You could have gone to college, met a nice young man, and had a family. We encouraged you, but you thwarted every attempt we made to help you."

"I had a GED. No decent college would have taken me."

"We've discussed that. There's always a way. Even now, Mallory Rose. You were headed back to school, but then the custody suit interfered. It didn't go the way any of us wanted, so you ran back here, away from family, away from school, and away from your husband."

The word *husband* unleashed a new wave of bitterness. "I told you, I don't have a husband."

Her dad sat up from his slouched position and drilled her with his eyes. "Therefore, what God has joined together, let no one separate."

"Really, Dad? You're going to start throwing Bible verses at me, after you taught me to lie? You and Mom left me little choice but to forge that birth certificate. Mom told me I would sign it. Period."

Silence stretched between them before he replied. "I'm not proud of that, Mallory Rose. I've spent years regretting that decision. My default has always been to protect your mother. I figured you were young and smart. You'd recover and move on. When it was done, I knew I made a mistake. I wish I had taken a different stand, but we can't change the roads we traveled. They brought us to where we are today. I don't want to see you make a mistake you'll regret. You're a married woman, and God wants to bless that."

"God and I have parted company."

One eyebrow arched. "So, who moved? You or God?"

Mallory tugged her blanket tighter. "I guess me. It's hard to face Him when you mess up so much. Same as it was hard to face all of you. Bottom line is, we're not exactly on speaking terms. He doesn't have much use for me anymore. His blessings have been a little too sparse."

"Sometimes we have to open our eyes a little wider to see the blessings."

She had no response, just stared at the breaking whitecaps, listening to their pounding rhythm.

Her dad looked at the sand, watching a sand crab scurry sideways past them. "You know, courts don't grant visitation to uncles." She heard his deep sigh.

"I've never kept Brady from seeing his nephew." While that was true, she hadn't made it easy for him. She stared beyond her dad to the restless ocean. Waves still crested and broke on the shore. When she looked back, she caught him searching her face.

"Did you know he came to see me?"

That caught her attention. "He did? Why?"

"He said he was in Raleigh for business. I wasn't convinced that was the reason."

She sighed away the momentary hope. Her dad had read too much into Brady's visit. "He has a major project in Raleigh—a new building in town. He always has some business there."

"He asked about you, checking to make sure you're okay."

"That doesn't surprise me. He's always been thoughtful. That's all."

Her dad's eyes narrowed as he stared her down. "It's more than that and you know it."

"No, Dad. I don't know it. I've told you about our marriage. It was never intended to be permanent."

"He's a broken man, Mallory Rose. I saw it in his eyes. I heard it in his voice."

"I know, Dad. He loves Samuel. You all do. I can't come back and face that every day."

"I'm not talking about Samuel. If you can give up martyrdom for a few minutes and take a hard look at your husband, you might be surprised what you see."

She shook her head. "You're wrong, Dad. Trust me. Brady's never expressed feelings for me. He's never even kissed me." That was enough to tell him. He could infer from there. Thickness lodged in her throat as she spoke. He may not have kissed her intimately or spoken words of love, but he clearly showed affection.

"Did you want him to?"

A cold gust of wind blew and she pulled the blanket tighter. "That's not exactly something you discuss with your dad."

"Everything about your marriage came in the wrong order. Did Brady give you reason to think he hoped it would grow? Maybe refraining from intimacy was an act of love."

Her immediate response was going to be no. But she remembered the words when he suggested they marry. *Maybe in time that will happen. That will be completely up to you.* She thought about their date night. He had said it was healthy for a marriage. So many casual touches. Had she ever reciprocated? She couldn't remember one single time when she reached for his hand. It was always him. Why hadn't she seen that? Had she been so self-absorbed that she missed the signs? He left it completely up to her, and she'd given him no reason to believe she cared.

"Mallory Rose, you've suffered loss. I know it's hard. I've suffered loss. I lost a daughter and son-in-law. I lost my wife, at least the wife and mother we've always known. I lost a grandson, relegated to seeing him when you and the courts allow. But I'm not running away. I get up every morning, make plans for the day, find projects around the house, visit your mother, and spend time with the grandkids. Yes, I'm still hurting, but I'm not giving up on life. Every day we give up is a day we can never have back."

They sat wordlessly, Mallory staring at the ocean, her dad staring at her. She let those words hang in her brain. *Every day we give up is a day we can never have back.* An ache the size of twelve lost years squeezed her.

He broke the silence. "Savannah Joy needs you."

She tilted her chin as one eyebrow rose. "Savannah Joy hates me."

He shook his head slowly. "She needs you. She has insecurities that run deep. A thin veil keeps them hidden. There're layers there that only a sister can reach."

There had been a slight breakthrough between them. Mallory told herself she needed to be Savannah's cornerman, the one to help her when she dipped into that dark place, as Jolene had once done. Then she ran away again, anticipating a return of Savannah's wrath when she lost Samuel. But had it returned? Mallory didn't stay long enough to find out. There was some truth in her father's words. She lived with a victim's mentality.

"I didn't mean to act like a martyr."

"I'm sorry if my words were harsh. You've given up too much in the last twelve years. Is this where you want to be a decade from now? Sitting here alone, facing another Christmas?"

The trickle of tears chilled her cheeks. "No."

"Then you better make a plan. A goal without a plan is just a daydream. I want so much more for you. Your mother and I both do. Your husband's waiting. And God's right where you left Him. Maybe you should give them both another chance." He rose and folded his chair. "I drove a long way to have my say. Now I need a hot cup of coffee."

Chapter 30

When her father left, Mallory recalled his words. But hadn't she made a plan when she took guardianship of Samuel? It wasn't the kind with a step-by-step outline. She planned to be the best mother she could be for the second half of Samuel's childhood. She'd stayed true to that, always putting his needs before hers. Yet everything she'd done had come to failure. Why should now be any different?

There it was. The victim mentality. It was her default and she'd have to work to overcome it, or as her dad had said, she'd find herself still sitting on a lonely beach years from now.

Every day we give up is a day we can't have back.

She needed a big dose of honesty, starting way back when she was sixteen years old and in love with Elliott Moore. No, it wasn't love. It was an attraction that she'd allowed to become an obsession. She had never truly loved him. She'd never known his character to the depth that she knew Brady's.

When she stepped outside to offer Elliott comfort after his argument with Andrea, she knew exactly why she went. There was no mistaking what would happen when they moved to the backseat of his car. She knew right from wrong and chose wrong, ignoring the possible ramifications. No one to blame for that but herself. Not even Elliott.

Yet for years, Mallory had nurtured bitterness toward her parents. Toward Jolene. Toward Elliott. It was a blame-shift. With someone else guilty, it allowed her to be a victim.

She missed Brady. She had resented marrying him the way she did. No romance. No white dress. No flowers, music, or dancing. Just signatures on a cold, flat piece of paper in the presence of two strangers. A ring for appearance sake. But who was to blame? Certainly not Brady. He sacrificed for her son, then tried to make the marriage work. As much as she allowed.

Mallory had loved the sense of family when the three of them were together. But she refused to embrace the ideal, certain that a time would come to end the façade. But what if it hadn't come? She couldn't deny Brady's efforts. He offered her hope, but she remained self-protective. Always the victim.

Could she allow herself to be vulnerable? *If you're sure that's what you want?* Brady's question as they stood staring at each other, the topic of divorce hanging heavy in their midst. Were they both too self-protective to break through that vulnerability? Too afraid to speak words of love?

All she knew was this—she missed Brady every day. She wanted a life with him, with or without Samuel. The only way to accomplish that was to face the fear of rejection and place her heart at risk of being broken.

****

Winter was anxious to come. Cloud cover brought a bleak, gray sky to the December day, adding to Mallory's apprehension. Brady's condo wasn't far from the neighborhood where Mallory grew up. She knew it well, and easily located the unit belonging to him. Each condo had a front-facing garage and a door tucked into a recessed entry. Mallory parked on the street near his house number. The windowless garage gave no clue to whether he was home or gone. It was the weekend so he shouldn't be traveling for work. She took the risk, hoping he'd be home. This was not a conversation for the telephone.

Her stomach knotted as she stepped from the car. *You don't want to live as a martyr.* She rang the doorbell. By the design, she knew it allowed him video, eliminating any element of surprise. After pressing the button, she waited with no answer. A cold breeze blew, causing Mallory to slide her hands into the pockets of her jacket. She resisted the urge to press the doorbell again. She waited another minute. Hope morphed into disappointment and she turned toward her car. Had he seen her and chosen not to answer?

She heard the click of the door before the sound of his voice. "Mallory?" Her head sprung around and she saw Brady standing in the doorway, his hand still on the knob.

Her breath caught in her throat. It had been so long since she'd seen his face. Today it wore no smile, just confusion.

"I didn't know you were in Charlotte."

Mallory retraced her steps back to the condo. Brady's form filled the doorway, so she stopped short of entering. No open-armed welcome. Only his look of uncertainty met her.

"Hi, Brady."

His eyes narrowed. "Is everything okay? Samuel? Your mom?"

Of course, he'd think that. She'd never given him reason to believe that she would come just to see him. "They're fine. I was hoping to talk to you."

He stepped backward and held the door. "Come in."

Mallory stepped in and saw the table in the dining area spread with architectural drawings and a laptop.

"You're working. Is this a bad time to interrupt you?"

"Not at all. I'm just filling time."

He motioned to a living area beyond the entry. The condo lacked any reminder that Christmas was a week away. She perched on the front edge of an upholstered chair questioning her decision. Was this a fool's errand? It felt too awkward.

He sat facing her. "I'm sorry. I haven't filed the papers yet if that's what you're wondering."

"No, I haven't thought much about that." A little ray of hope sprang from her knotted stomach. He hadn't been in a hurry to process the divorce. "Brady, I need to apologize to you. After the hearing, I … I guess I fell apart. I wasn't very nice to you. You didn't deserve that."

The pause spoke of his agreement. He didn't deny it, but he did offer some understanding. "It was a difficult time. There's no need to apologize. We both made mistakes."

Words swirled in her head. She didn't know which words to speak and which to leave alone. "I should have talked to you about changing Samuel's visit on Thanksgiving. It just seemed so logical to me."

Small nods accompanied his answer. "We should have talked about a lot of things."

The reply sounded cold. Maybe it was too late to restore whatever it was that they had. "There's another reason I came. Would you like to come to Raleigh when Samuel's there for Christmas? He'll stay until the twenty-seventh."

The relief was evident. "Thank you. I really want to see him."

"I know he misses you." Could she say what she came to say, to tell him how she missed him? Throw caution to the wind? She had never initiated anything that would show her feelings. She had to do it now. Mallory willed her eyes to look at him and not down at her lap. Her words came in not much more than a whisper. "I miss you too, Brady."

No response came. His gaze never left her face, but no words followed. His expression was impossible to read. When the quiet became unbearable, she rushed to find words to fill the awkward silence, to cover her foolishness. "So, let me know when you plan to join us." She started to stand.

"Mallory, wait."

She eased back to the seat, but stayed perched near the front.

Brady moved to the ottoman in front of her. His nearness sent her heart racing. "Let's go back to the part about missing me."

She lowered her eyes so she wouldn't feel so exposed.

"Mallory?" He waited for her to look at him. "Not a day passes that I don't think of you." She heard a catch in his voice, saw a slight tremble of his chin.

His words gave her strength to go on. Was it possible he meant what she hoped? She cared for Brady more than she ever dared to admit. Mallory had managed to bury those feelings deep, but it was time to open that door.

"You said I was running away again. You were right. I've spent all of my adult life running away, shielding myself against relationships. If you don't go deep, you don't get hurt. But Samuel changed all of that. I loved hard and hurt deep. When I lost him, it confirmed my fears about …" She wanted to say love, but it sounded far too intimate. "My fears about relationships."

His eyes were fastened on hers. "I didn't want to leave you, Mal. You were hurting, and I wanted to take care of you."

He wanted to take care of her. Her hope plummeted, landing like a boulder in her stomach. That's what it had always been. Pity. He didn't love her. It was always kindness. Tears threatened her eyes. She began re-erecting the protective wall. Why had she been foolish enough to open her heart? Her chin trembled as she fought tears. "I've taken care of myself for a long time. I don't need to be taken care of. And I don't need anyone's money." She should be thankful, but once again, it all came up short. "I think it's time for me to go."

She stood up and he rose, closing the distance between them before she could take a step. "Mallory, don't leave."

He stood close but didn't reach for her. His nearness rekindled an ounce of hope. Mallory had never taken the initiative for any casual touch. This would most likely be her only shot. Today they'd restore what little marriage they had, or they'd walk away from it.

She reached for his hand and curled hers inside of it. "I see why you think I need someone to lean on since I ran to you with my problems. I appreciate that you wanted to support me, but I want more than that, Brady."

He wrapped his fingers around her hand. "I regret so many things that happened—the way they happened. But I don't regret marrying you. There are words I wish I had said. Words I wanted to say. I wasn't sure you were ready to hear them."

She fought through the tears. "Try me."

He moved a step closer, caressing the hand he held. "I love you, Mallory. I loved you when I asked you to marry me. You were going through so much that I tried to allow things to happen in their own timing, watching for any sign of hope that you had feelings for me."

Mallory heard it in his words and saw it in his eyes. Brady loved her. She allowed those words to wash over her. She found his other hand, and they stood holding both hands between them. "My dad said I have a victim mentality, that I've chosen to live like a martyr. His words hit too close to the truth. It made me realize how much I lost over the years. And it made me realize that I don't want to lose you. I wasn't sure I had the right to come here after treating you badly."

Their eyes remained focused on each other for a long pause.

A sparkle lit Brady's eyes. "Will you sit for a moment?"

Mallory didn't want to sit. Didn't want to end his nearness. She was so close to being in his arms. But she allowed him to lead her back to her chair.

"I'll be right back." Brady disappeared into another room but returned quickly. He stooped before her, resting one knee on the floor, an open ring box in his extended arm. It was the same ring she had returned in a sealed envelope. "Mallory, this is what I should have said from the day I first asked you to marry me. I love you. I want to spend my life with you. To share your joy and sorrows, to grow old together. I want more than to be a father for Samuel. I want to be your husband and I want you for my wife. Will you do me the honor of marrying me?"

He loved her. Joy welled up and filled to overflowing. "Well, I guess I have a little dilemma." The start of a smile formed. "I'm already married. I have a husband that I love." She reached and stroked his cheek. "Even though he's never kissed me."

His dark eyes held hers, reminding her how many times she had looked away from their depth. "Well, he must be a foolish man." Brady's mouth curved slightly; his eyes filled with longing. "A very foolish man."

He slid the ring on her finger, stood and drew her upward. His hands cradled her face as he kissed her, warm and gentle, soft at first, but filled with longing. When their lips parted, he held her close, whispering against her face. "Oh, Mal."

After a moment, he pulled back and looked at her. "So, do you really love that husband of yours?"

She grinned. "Very much."

"Well, he's a lucky man."

****

Mallory woke to the gentle sound of Brady's breathing. She curled her arm under her head and watched him sleep. *My husband.* This was the first she'd ever thought of him that way. The marriage had always been uncertain. Temporary. Without a foundation. This morning it was none of those things. Today there was a foundation of love and, as Brady had suggested, a marriage designed by the Master Architect.

She stretched her fingers wide and admired the rings. At one time they were a symbol to signify a legal union. A sign to tell others they were married. The same rings now held new meaning. They changed, just as Mallory had. Today, they boldly proclaimed love.

He stirred, and his eyes fluttered open. The disheveled hair, scruffy face, and slight grin created a schoolboy look. "It must be Christmas."

"No, silly. That's still a week away."

"But I'm looking at the best gift of all."

Chapter 31

Mallory and Brady drove back to Raleigh a few days before Christmas. Over the past dozen years, Mallory never displayed more than a spattering of Christmas decorations. A sad little tabletop tree or a string of blinking lights on the apartment door, not that anyone ever trekked to the third floor of her Wilmington apartment. It didn't go unnoticed that Brady's condo lacked any sign of the approaching holiday as well.

Yet together, they transformed Jolene and Mark's home into a holiday postcard, something to bring Samuel joy on what was certain to be a difficult Christmas—the first without his parents. By Christmas Eve, everything was ready. They dressed for the candlelight service at her dad's church. His wide smile lit clear to his eyes when they walked in, Mallory's arm tucked lovingly in Brady's. She kissed her dad's cheek. A hard holiday for him as well. It was too much stress for her mom so they opted not to bring her to the service. She would join them tomorrow for a quiet Christmas at home.

On Christmas day, Andrea and Elliott drove Samuel to Raleigh by 1:00. The car had barely stopped when Samuel hopped out and dashed to the open front door where Brady waited. Brady caught him in a hug that transformed into a wrestling hold.

"I think you've grown a foot since I last saw you."

Samuel laughed. "Nah. I still only have two of them."

Elliott stood stoically at the car, the trunk up, revealing gifts and Samuel's suitcase. He had no intention of carrying them. Mallory stepped out as Brady and Samuel went to the car.

"I've got this, Mal."

Mallory watched as they lifted everything from the trunk, her gaze avoiding Elliott. He said a few words to Brady and handed him an envelope.

Samuel had no hug for Elliott and never looked back to the passenger seat where Andrea sat. He sprinted toward the door and dropped his packages in the entry. His arms flew upward in celebration. "I get to stay till New Years!"

"What?" Mallory looked at Brady. He lifted the envelope and nodded. Leaning in, he whispered. "We'll talk later."

The rest of Christmas held a flurry of activity. Exchanging gifts. Dinner at her dad's with Savannah's whole crew. Bringing her mom home for the day. During a few quiet minutes, Brady explained. "First of all, Elliott was pouting. He's upset that his Christmas was interrupted by making the trip to Raleigh."

Mallory raised her eyebrows and frowned. "They were already in Charlotte. I told him I'd pick Samuel up."

"I know. But he said they're heading back to DC. They need a little time for themselves, and they're coming back to Charlotte next week to spend New Year's Eve with friends. They want to pick Samuel up the following day on their way back to DC." He held the envelope up. "This is a formal request to alter this visitation."

Brady took the week off work so he could stay in Raleigh. Along with a few other gifts for Samuel, Mallory gave him one that contained two cardboard mailing tubes, concave and convex lenses, a tripod and directions to build a homemade telescope. Brady had asked her if she'd like to buy him a professional scope, but that's not what Mallory wanted. Maybe someday.

As the three of them worked together, cutting, painting, and fitting the pieces, Mallory stopped and turned away. She closed her eyes and breathed in the wonder of the moment. Her husband and her son. The room overflowing with love. She had imagined this moment back when she was certain it would never be. Maybe God hadn't forgotten her after all.

****

Mallory made Charlotte her home. She knew she would encounter old high school friends. She'd be the topic of whispered conversation, but she didn't care. She wasn't her mother. She and Brady spent time in Raleigh when they had Samuel with them and time in Washington DC when visitation ordered him to remain there.

"I forgot to tell you about my lunch with Savannah. She took the executor's fee. She still struggled with the idea of taking money from Samuel's estate, but dad helped to convince her. She said it's a huge burden lifted. She was able to pay off some medical bills."

"Good. It's what Mark and Jolene would have wanted."

"She knows that because Jolene had offered to pay her medical bills on more than one occasion. Richard was too proud to accept the gift."

"I can understand that. It's hard on a man's ego, but you have to do what's best for your family. She's earned the fee. It shouldn't feel like charity."

Mallory nodded her agreement. "I can't say everything's warm and fuzzy, but I think we reached a new understanding of each other. We're going to try to meet for lunch each time I'm in Raleigh."

"That's something we need to talk about. If you want to live in Raleigh, we can look for a place of our own. I commuted before. I can do it again."

"Actually, Savannah asked me … us, to move back in the house. She said there's no sense it sitting empty. It's always better to have someone living there than to have it vacant."

Brady's eyes quizzed her. "Would you like that?"

Mallory paused, thinking. "I don't think so. It doesn't make sense for us to leave Charlotte. There's no reason for you to commute. It was different when Samuel was with us."

****

Early February brought a snowstorm to the nation's capital. Mallory and Brady decided they'd better fly up for their visit.

They rented a car at the airport and braved the snow, arriving at Elliott's on time. At the sound of the doorbell, they heard Samuel's bounding footsteps. "I've got it." He opened the door carrying his overnight bag, and sprang out. "Let's go." He was tugging his coat on as he spoke.

Brady laughed. "Hold it, buddy. It's cold out here. And slippery. Is that all you're wearing?"

Elliott stood in the entry looking out at the gleeful reunion. Mallory ignored his hard jawline and folded arms. A tapping foot showed his impatience. "Samuel, please go upstairs. The adults need to talk. I'll call for you when it's time to go."

Samuel's eyes darted to Mallory in question, then back to Elliott whose authoritative tone allowed no dispute.

"And keep the noise down. Andrea's resting."

Samuel grunted a "Yes, sir," then shuffled toward the steps. His excitement ebbed into a sulk.

Elliott's stare followed him upstairs until he was out of their view. "Please come in here and have a seat." He motioned toward a small room to his left. An office with masculine furniture. Mallory wiped her snowy shoes on the mat and stepped inside. She wasn't sure what her offense may have been, but she would not allow him to bully her. She was grateful for Brady's presence. He had once threatened to deck Elliott, a sight that might bring her some amusement.

When they slipped their coats off and were seated, he closed a pocket door. He didn't sit, but instead, propped himself against a solid oak library table. "Samuel's a headstrong young man."

Mallory and Brady looked at each other, but neither responded.

"He's belligerent and won't acclimate to our home. It's been over three months, but he refuses to try."

Again, Mallory and Brady exchanged a glance before Brady replied, "What did you expect? You took him against his will. You and your wife were practically strangers, but welcomed him with rules and changes instead of trying to ease him through the transition. Relationships need some give and take. They're built on trust, and I haven't seen much of that happening."

Elliott's lips pressed together and Mallory saw a slight tic near the side. She suspected Elliott Moore was unaccustomed to being called down. He argued politics with the best of them, but didn't respond well to a personal attack. It was easier to talk about politicians' mistakes than to have someone expose his own.

"Nonetheless, he's old enough to know the meaning of respect. My wife tried every way possible, and he barely speaks to her."

Mallory had been in Andrea's shoes. She'd come into Samuel's life a stranger. It had taken time and patience on her part. She had overlooked minor offenses and treated him with respect. "Maybe she should have made him turtle brownies." It was an oversimplified statement but Elliott got her meaning.

"That's an insolent remark, Mallory Rose. You weren't here to see all that she's done."

"Maybe not, but here's what I have seen. Andrea was a stranger. In less than a year, Samuel has lost both of the only parents he ever knew. He found out I am his biological mother and you his biological father. Then against his wishes, you took him away to a new home, a new school, and two new parents, both complete strangers. What did you expect, Elliott? He's not a dog you can train to do tricks on demand."

Brady stood up. "Let's cut to the chase here."

Elliott nodded, sizing Brady up. "Andrea's pregnant."

Mallory's mouth opened mutely until she recovered from the surprise. "I guess congratulations are in order. I thought that couldn't happen."

"So did we." He shuffled. "We suspect that when she became distracted from trying so hard, something changed." He shifted uncomfortably. "This baby's too important to her ... to us. I can't allow Samuel to add this kind of stress."

Career and Andrea. Nothing had changed from high school. Samuel would never be first. Or second. When the new baby came, where would Samuel fit?

Brady's hands went to his hips. "Let's get to the point here. What are you suggesting?"

"My schedule's taxing. I'm on live TV every weeknight. I can't be here to intervene."

That wasn't an answer. Brady stared him down, waiting.

Elliott ran his hand through his signature blond hair. "Andrea and I want to relinquish custody. When you take Samuel this weekend, we'd like him to stay with you."

Mallory's hands sprang to her heart. Was she hearing this correctly? Would she get her son back? Brady confused her by shaking his head.

"Not so fast. You're talking about more than an altered visitation. We won't risk non-compliance with a court order. We need a signed statement with your desire to relinquish custody, asking us to keep him until legal action is taken. You'll need to contact your attorney immediately."

Elliott's hands moved to his hips as he and Brady vied for power. Finally, Elliott strutted to the table and pulled a piece of stationery from the only drawer. He wrote a few sentences, scribbled his signature, and pushed it toward Brady who now took charge of the conversation.

"With no one here to witness your signature, I'd like to record your request." Brady retrieved his phone.

Elliott challenged him. "Don't you think that's a little overboard?"

"Not at all. I'll not allow Samuel to be victim to your whims. You want him. You don't want him. We have no assurance that you won't change your mind again. This is a twelve-year-old boy we're talking about. Do you have any idea what that does to a kid?"

"Fine!"

"Before we tape this, let's be clear on some details. Do you intend to assume noncustodial visitation?"

It was a good thing Brady was here. She'd have taken Samuel and run, not thinking through the logistics. She would never have considered recording the request. She may not have even asked for a release in writing.

A hint of pink colored Elliott's cheeks. "I'm not sure."

Brady stood feet apart, arms crossed over his chest. "What exactly does that mean?"

He cleared his throat. "We don't want that lifestyle, the coming and going, explaining to our child how he or she has a half-brother. And there's still the issue of Samuel's disrespect."

Brady stared him down, echoing the words. "You don't want that kind of lifestyle." He shook his head, exchanging a look of disbelief with Mallory. It was all about them. They selfishly took him and they'd selfishly throw him away.

Elliott sat down for the first time since their meeting began. Brady followed suit, returning to his chair. He had established the upper hand and allowed his voice to become less challenging. "Under the circumstances, the right thing to do is to restore Samuel's name. That will occur if you'll terminate parental rights and allow me to legally adopt him."

Elliott slumped back, staring at the ceiling. "He *is* my son."

Mallory saw Elliott's struggle. She knew the root of it—Andrea. Would he disown his son for her sake?

Brady showed no tolerance for the indecision. "You can't have it both ways."

For a fleeting moment, Mallory saw the old Elliott, the high school boy struggling with advanced chemistry.

"If I do, can I still see him occasionally? I'd come to Raleigh, of course."

Brady crossed his arms over his chest. "Samuel's almost a teenager. That will be his decision." He made his point. The glaring difference between the two homes—she and Brady would listen to their son.

The deeply furrowed brow made Elliott look much older than his years. A perfectly planned out life. Except for thirty minutes in the backseat of his car. A thirty-minute swerve from his outline put a chink in the perfect picture. "Yes, I'll relinquish parental rights."

"We'll need to hear from your attorney no later than Monday."

"I'll call him as soon as you leave today."

Elliott stood, and Brady followed suit. Brady towered over Elliott, surpassing him in stature. Mallory saw beyond that. She saw who the man of character truly was.

He nodded to Mallory. "Anything else, Mal?"

"Do you plan to tell Samuel?"

Elliott shook his head. "I'll leave that to you. I'm sure he'll be happy."

"And his things?"

"I'll mail anything he leaves behind."

Brady pushed an icon on his phone and handed it to Elliott. With his face drawn and eyes downcast, he looked older than when they had arrived. He spoke clearly, the trained voice of a broadcaster, as he relinquished his parental rights.

Elliott stepped to an intercom on the wall and pushed a button. "Samuel, you may come down now. It's time for you to go."

Chapter 32

Crocuses, daffodils, and dogwood blossoms offered a splash of color as they ushered in an anxious spring. Inside the chapel, Savannah slid each tiny pearl button into the buttonhole on the back of Mallory's dress, then released the clip in her hair. "The white satin is a perfect backdrop for your thick waves of dark hair. It practically shimmers in the light."

Their mother watched them from a rocking chair in the small dressing room. She smiled on occasion. She didn't remember their names, but surely must know they were preparing for a wedding.

"Ready for the veil?"

Mallory looked in the gilded-framed mirror. "One minute." Her brush repaired a few errant strands of hair. She set the brush down and freshened her lipstick before she leaned her head toward her sister. "Okay. I'm ready."

Savannah adjusted the veil, then held up her index finger. "One more thing." She opened a jewelry box to reveal a delicate gold bracelet with sapphires interspersed. "This is Jolene's. I borrowed it from her jewelry box. She loved this and I think she'd like to see you wear it today."

The tiny oval sapphires glowed a brilliant blue. "It's beautiful, but I'm not sure how Samuel will feel about me wearing his mom's jewelry."

"Samuel knows. He helped me pick which one to bring."

"Then I'd be honored." Mallory held her arm out as Savannah hooked the clasp and hugged her. Mallory had never admitted how much her sister's approval meant. They had bonded in a way she never thought possible. Her eyes filled with grateful tears.

"Well, I already had something old and new. Now I have something borrowed and blue."

Music drifted to the dressing room from the small chapel at Wrightsville Beach. Mallory and Brady had both wanted a real wedding, one where they made promises to each other. Spring proved to be the perfect time. Considering that, and Mallory's mother's condition, a small gathering at an intimate venue felt right.

Savannah answered a knock at the door. Samuel stood there looking so grown up. He wore a boutonnière in the pocket of his dark suit.

"Grandpa said it's time for me to take Grandma to her seat." He walked to her chair and leaned forward. "Grandma, I'm Samuel. I'm going to take you to your seat now so you can watch the wedding." He held his bent arm for her to hold. Her gaze darted toward Mallory and Savannah who both nodded. Then she placed her hand on Samuel's arm and let him walk her down the short aisle. Her posture was as straight as it had ever been when they were little. Today was a good day. She showed no sign of fear.

The open door allowed them to see the small crowd gathered. Brady's parents and his grandmother. His sister Elise and her family. Richard and all five of their children. The only non-family members were Chloe, Liam, a pianist, and the pastor. Samuel reached the front row and seated his grandmother.

Her father appeared in the doorway. "Savannah Joy, you're next." He motioned for her to begin. Then, much like Samuel had done, he offered Mallory his arm. As Savannah reached the front of the chapel, Brady and Samuel stepped into place, facing the rear of the church where Mallory and her father waited.

What would Jolene and Mark think? Did a window from heaven allow them to see how the Carter and Donaldson families merged again? To see how perfectly Samuel fit? Why was it suddenly so easy to see God's provision? As soon as she relinquished her self-pity, she recognized the missed opportunities. The doors that God had opened while she stubbornly refused to walk through them. Yet He never gave her up, finally sending her Brady. God was the constant, the North Star, always there to show the way.

The pianist played Mendelssohn's "Wedding March" as Mallory began her slow steps, her arm hooked through her dad's, and her eyes focused on Brady. When they reached the front, Savannah lifted Mallory's veil and smoothed it back from her face, followed by a wink and a nod.

She looked back to her father as he spoke, his voice rich with emotion. "Be happy, little girl. I love you." He placed a kiss on her forehead and stepped away. Mallory slipped her hand through Brady's arm and they turned to the pastor.

"Friends and family, today we're here to celebrate the marriage of Brady and Mallory Donaldson. This is the first time I've officiated at a wedding for a married couple. I've seen married couples who want to renew their wedding vows, but for Brady and Mallory, they expressed their deep desire to share wedding vows for the first time, to profess their promises before God and loved ones."

There was scripture, music, and a message about marriage. Then came the time to share their vows. Brady began.

"Mallory Rose, I promise you my love and my faithfulness for all my life. I will always be honest with you, treat you with the honor and respect you deserve. I've learned from you what sacrificial love looks like. I will do my best to live up to that model. I give you my whole heart. I marry you without doubt or reservation. I look forward to sharing my life with you, through good times and bad, through hardship and plenty, through sickness and health for always. I love you."

Mallory closed her eyes and breathed in the joy of those words. Then she readied herself to speak her vows.

"Brady, I believe with all my heart that God brought us together. I feel safe when I'm with you. I love you, respect you, and want to be your best friend. I promise to be faithful and truthful. I believe in till death do us part. I will love you that long and beyond." She leaned close and whispered the last words. "And I promise I'll never run away again."

"I now pronounce you husband and wife. You may kiss the bride."

When they turned to begin the recessional, Brady reached toward Samuel and motioned for him to join them. Samuel centered slightly behind them and stretched one arm over Mallory's shoulder, the other behind Brady, like Alpha Centauri. Three stars in one cluster. A family.